Just One Kiss

CHRISTINA TETREAULT

Just One Kiss ©2026 by Christina Tetreault
Published by Christina Tetreault
Cover Designer: Amanda Walker
Editing: Hot Tree Editing
Proofreading: Hot Tree Editing

Digital ISBN: 979-8-9865744-6-2

Print ISBN: 979-8-9865744-7-9

One

"IS EVIE STILL MAD AT ME?" Matt asked as he brewed himself another coffee.

"She was never angry with you." His cousin Adam's voice came through the phone. "She was upset with the people on social media who can't mind their own business."

Matt could understand that. He didn't mind when fans posted photos of themselves with him. However, it annoyed the hell out of him when people took pictures of him doing everyday things, such as shopping, and then posted them on social media. The worst, though, was when people shared photos of him with women, sometimes ones who were friends or relatives, and then proceeded to speculate about their relationship. That was precisely what happened earlier this month when he joined Adam's girlfriend for breakfast before heading to the local high school where Adam was coaching. Unlike Evie, though, he'd opened himself up to that type of intrusion when he went into the music business.

"How are things going between you two?"

With anyone else, Matt wouldn't ask such a question. The way he saw it, if someone wanted to share, they would. However, Adam was more than a cousin. Matt considered him more like a brother. In many ways, Adam was more of a brother than Theo and Aiden.

"Couldn't be better. If the engagement ring I designed is ready, I'm going to propose when we go to visit my sister at the end of the month. She offered to babysit so that we can go out alone."

When he'd visited Adam, he'd briefly considered offering to watch Reagan, the almost seven-month-old little girl his cousin had recently become the guardian of. Well, maybe "briefly" wasn't the right word. The thought had zipped through his head faster than he could blink. He knew nothing about children. It would've been an utter disaster if he'd stayed alone with Reagan while Adam and his girlfriend went out.

"Not wasting any time, are you?"

Although he was happy for his cousin, Matt still found it almost impossible to believe that Evie was back in Adam's life. He'd heard of people reconnecting after not seeing each other for years, but never in such an unlikely way.

"I don't see any reason to wait," Adam answered.

Coffee in hand, Matt opened the glass door, stepped outside, and inhaled the ocean air. "How long are you staying in Boston?"

"Just for the long weekend."

While Adam, Evie, and Reagan could make the drive up to see him, it would mean a lot of time in the car and a short visit.

"Tory mentioned you stopped by to see her on your way to Maine."

His stops to visit first Adam in Virginia and then Tory in Boston had been just two of many he'd made during his drive from Florida to Maine.

"I knew she'd be jealous if I spent time with you on my way up and not her."

Dropping into a chair, he watched the waves down below. While he'd never pass on an opportunity to surf in Oahu or ski in Colorado, he preferred the rocky Maine coastline. Or more specifically, the coast of Maine and the town of Orchard Harbor. The restlessness that often plagued him disappeared when he was here, and if he was frustrated by something, the emotion subsided. He'd traveled the world, and no other place had the same effect on him. Orchard Harbor was his happy place. A spot he escaped to whenever he could. During the past year, though, he'd only managed one visit. However, for the foreseeable future, he planned to remain here. He was only leaving to visit friends and family members who called New England home.

"Tell yourself that if it makes you feel better," Adam replied with more than a hint of sarcasm.

Some statements didn't warrant a reply, so he ignored Adam's response. "It doesn't make sense for you to visit while you're up to see Tory. But this summer, the three of you should come and spend some time here."

He'd had only two visitors since he'd purchased the home. One was his friend Owen, and the other was his bandmate Jordan. But he'd enjoy a visit from his cousin and his girlfriend.

"Definitely. I'll talk to Evie, see when she wants to go, and get back to you. I'll let you go for now. I've got a meeting in ten minutes."

After the call ended, Matt sipped his coffee and enjoyed the peace and solitude—two things one could easily find in Orchard Harbor if they wanted. Located about twenty minutes from Acadia National Park, the town was about the same size but less well-known than its neighbor to the north, Bar Harbor. He most likely never would've heard of it if not for his college roommate at the University of Maine.

While Owen no longer lived there, he'd grown up in Orchard Harbor, and during their freshman year, he'd invited Matt to spend Thanksgiving with his family rather than alone at school, as he'd planned. The picturesque homes were so different from those he was used to, and its quaint Main Street, along with the Atlantic Ocean, had called to him like no other place he'd visited.

Throughout college and after graduation, he'd return, spending shorter visits at a hotel and longer ones at one of the many vacation homes available for rent. All the while, though, he'd kept an eye out for the perfect home. One had finally come on the market two years ago, although he had few opportunities to use it thanks to Eclipse's tour schedule and the most recent movie he'd made. But for the foreseeable future, he didn't need to be anywhere, and Matt intended to take full advantage of that.

There was no question about it: Performing in front of crowded stadiums had been his dream, and he loved it, but it wasn't the walk in the park most people thought it was.

Matt watched a seagull land on the beach below. Well, perhaps calling it a beach was generous, but the strip of land was sandy and along the ocean. It was also the farthest he'd ventured since his arrival five days ago, and the individual who delivered his grocery order last Saturday was the only human contact he'd had since going through a drive-thru for lunch somewhere between Wells and Orchard Harbor. The solitude had been just what he needed. Today, though, he planned to rejoin the land of the living.

His cell buzzed on the table, letting him know he'd received a text message. He wasn't surprised to see the name "Mom" on the screen when he picked up the device. Although Violet Sherbrooke's children were adults, she liked to check on them a couple of times a month, even when she knew he was touring with the band. The last time they had spoken was close to two weeks ago.

Mom: Are you free one day this week? Your dad and I are in Jupiter Island. We'd love to see you.

He'd been at his house in Palm Beach then, and he hadn't said anything about leaving. In fact, except for the handful of family members he'd visited on his way to Maine, no one, including his agent and bandmates, knew he was there. Although not a secret, he'd seen no pressing need to tell anyone either.

Matt: Wish I'd known you were coming. I would've waited to leave.

He wasn't lying. Unlike some of his cousins, he had a great relationship with his parents and honestly enjoyed spending time with them.

Matt: I'm in Maine right now.

A frown emoji appeared on the screen as he finished his coffee.

Mom: Will you be coming home soon?

Matt knew his mom was referring to California and not Florida. And while he had a house there, he hadn't considered California home in a long time. Actually, even though his driver's license claimed he was a resident of Florida, he didn't really consider any place home—a fact he didn't spend much time thinking about.

Matt: Not sure when I'll be out there.

Matt typed the word "but," then stopped to reconsider the offer he'd been about to make. The likelihood of his mom accepting his invitation to visit him in Maine was next to zero, so it seemed pointless to even make it.

Matt: I'll let you know.

Mom: Okay. Love you.

Returning the device to the table, he considered his plans for the day—or rather, his lack of plans. If it were late June or July, he'd go down for a swim, but while it might look inviting, he knew from experience that the water up here in May remained cold. A hike, something he hadn't gone on since the fall, would be a great way to spend the day. Unfortunately, he had an appointment at Atlantic Marina this afternoon at one o'clock. If he'd been smart, he would've made the appointment for earlier in the day. A day out on the water would be another perfect way to spend a few hours, but he didn't have a boat up here, hence his appointment with Atlantic Marina.

What options did that leave him with? Matt drummed his fingers against his thigh as he considered and dismissed ideas. A hike in Acadia might be out, but he could still drive to the top of Cadillac Mountain and enjoy the breathtaking view. Afterward, he could grab a late lunch and stop in the bookstore to see if they had Curt Hilton's newest release. No one outside his immediate family knew it, but Matt was, and had always been, a bookworm, and Hilton was one of his favorite contemporary authors.

* * *

Liv's eyes strayed away from the food Libby Horn had ordered for her sister's upcoming baby shower and once again looked at the clock mounted on the restaurant's wall.

How was it possible that only ten minutes had passed since

she last looked at it? Had someone hit a giant slow-motion button, grinding the movement of time to a slow crawl? Although not possible, it sure as heck felt that way this afternoon. And if only ten minutes had passed, then her grandfather and dad had just gone into their meeting with the Worm, aka Fredrick Waldman.

She'd never liked Fredrick—don't even think about calling him Fred, because he'd correct you before you could inhale. Although he didn't live in Orchard Harbor, he spent a month there with his grandparents, one of the nicest and most well-liked couples in town, every summer growing up. He'd also visited with his family during the holidays. Back then, he'd been a spoiled punk who always had to get his way. While he no longer spent weeks at a time in town, he came around often enough for Liv to know that although his looks had improved, his personality hadn't.

Oh, who was she kidding? Fredrick might have been an awkward-looking child and teenager, but he'd turned into a demigod. He could easily compete in the looks department with Hollywood's hottest actors. Unfortunately, Fredrick was a spoiled demigod who only cared about the person he saw in the mirror every morning. That was why she turned him down every time he asked her out—something he'd done at least four times now, but who was counting? And if the rumor were true, he would soon be throwing a wrench into not only her family's business but also her life.

It's just a rumor.

She'd told herself that more times than she could count over the past few days. She'd also reminded herself that rumors were a dime a dozen in Orchard Harbor, as her grandmother would say. Maybe if she kept telling herself both these things, they would prove true.

The sound of an oven timer, which happened to be her text message alert, pulled her out of her thoughts. Liv crossed her fingers and hoped the message was from her dad as she flipped the device over.

Unfortunately, it was her friend Emma and not her dad.

6

Emma: Can you talk?

At the moment, the restaurant was empty, and with the lunch rush over, she didn't expect business to pick up again until dinner, at least not this time of year. In another two weeks or so, when tourist season really got underway, it would be a different story.

Liv: Yep.

No sooner had she sent the message than "Loving You" by Eclipse erupted from her phone.

"Have you heard anything yet?" Emma asked.

"I would've called you if I had."

While it would affect Liv and her family significantly if the rumor that Fredrick planned to sell the building that housed the restaurant, her aunt's bookstore, and Liv's apartment proved true, Emma's livelihood might not go unscathed, considering who was rumored to be interested in the property. Liv had never formally met Rick Desmond, but the property developer had acquired numerous buildings up and down the East Coast for his company, which then promptly tore them down and built luxury condos, hotels, and spas. If Fredrick was selling and Rick was interested, she knew without question the same would happen here, and Orchard Harbor would never be the same again.

"What time was the meeting?" Emma asked.

Liv reached for her iced tea as she checked the clock again. It looked as though the silly hands hadn't moved. They must be stuck. Or maybe it needed new batteries. She couldn't remember the last time she'd replaced them.

"Three."

"Oh, I thought it was this morning," Emma said.

While they all would've preferred an earlier time, Fredrick had insisted he couldn't meet any earlier than three. Actually, they'd all gotten the impression he'd rather not meet at all, but after multiple messages with his executive assistant, he'd finally set something up.

"Do you think your dad will call you afterward or wait until he gets back?"

"I think it'll depend on the news."

"You'll call me as soon as you hear something, right?" Emma asked.

"Emma, you know I will."

Outside, a couple walking their dog stopped to read the menu by the restaurant's door. While they did that, the dog—Liv suspected it was a Great Dane—peered inside at her, and she smiled. As a lifelong dog lover, they always brightened her day, no matter what else was going on.

"How was dinner with Brian's parents last night?" Liv asked.

A conversation would help distract her, not to mention she was more than a little curious about her friend's first meeting with Brian's family.

"It was a little awkward at first."

Liv listened while she watched the cars outside. Right now, traffic wasn't too bad, but once Memorial Day, the unofficial start of summer, rolled around, the cars and bikes on the road would triple. While great for business, it made getting around town unpleasant, to say the least.

A gray Ferrari pulled up to the curb. Ferraris and other luxury vehicles like them weren't unusual once wealthy individuals descended on the town. Some owned vacation homes in the area, while others came to escape at the luxury spa that had opened two years earlier.

"By the time we finished our salads, it felt as though I'd known them forever."

That sounded promising to Liv.

"Well, at least his parents and brother. I'm not sure about Brian's sister and sister-in-law."

Liv didn't know Brian's sister, but her own brother, Owen, used to complain about her and their sister, Faith, being overly critical of his girlfriends. Who could blame them, though? Owen might drive them insane, but they had wanted the best for him. They'd also wanted to avoid a repeat of his first short-lived marriage after college. Thankfully, he'd met Jenny five years ago, and they'd all known she was the perfect person for him.

"I'm sure they'll come around. How could they not?" Emma

was one of the sweetest people Liv knew. "Do you have any plans this Saturday night?" Liv asked.

This Saturday night would be the first one she'd had off in a month. She'd like to do something besides clean her apartment or do laundry—two things she needed to tackle but would happily push to another day.

"I'm not sure yet. Brian mentioned camping this weekend if he can get Friday off."

Emma only used rest stop bathrooms as an absolute last resort. How would she ever manage to make it through the whole weekend without indoor plumbing?

"Camping? As in you sleeping outside in a tent?"

"Are you nuts? No, Brian has a camper."

Well, her friend's willingness to camp made a lot more sense now.

Across the dining room, the door opened, and Liv was glad her butt was safely planted in a chair. No one would disagree that the Worm was gorgeous, but the man who just walked in was pure male perfection—a full god she hadn't seen in about a year, at least not in person. Every other day, his face appeared on the internet or on a magazine cover, and she might have watched *One Last Heist* once or twice. But who could blame her? Anderson Brady and Matt Sherbrooke starred in it. She wasn't the only person on planet Earth who'd watched it multiple times because of them. Of course, it also helped that the plot was good.

"I'll let you know as soon as Brian finds out."

"Sounds good. A customer just came in. I'll talk to you later."

At one time, she'd waited tables three or four nights a week and every weekend. These days, though, she spent more time in the kitchen or meeting with clients who needed an event catered. But if Maggie, the waitress on right now, came out and saw who their newest customer was, she'd lose it. Matt might be used to fans bothering him, but if Liv could ensure he enjoyed his lunch in peace, she'd do it.

Liv switched her cell phone to vibrate and put it into her pocket as she opened the door to the kitchen. "I'll take care of the customer who just came in, Maggie."

"Okay, thanks," Maggie answered before she turned back toward Russ and resumed their conversation.

Lunch menus in hand, she crossed the dining room and ignored the butterflies that had taken up residence in her stomach. Seriously, she was too old to get butterflies just because she was around a handsome man.

"Hi, Matt. Just one today?"

Although she was a massive fan of his music, she'd known Matt too long to be starstruck around him. Unfortunately, his good looks still left her in need of a giant fan to cool herself off.

"Hey, Liv." His lips formed the sexiest smile she'd ever seen. Honestly, it should be illegal for a person to have a smile like that. "Yeah, I'm alone." Removing his baseball cap, he stuck it into the pocket of his jeans and raked his fingers through his dark hair.

She doubted he'd remain alone long. The man's name was linked with a different woman's every month. Actually, not long ago, pictures of him with a pretty brunette had been all over social media. In some, there had also been a baby. She didn't know if it was true, but some magazines were claiming the baby was Matt's secret love child. To her knowledge, he had neither confirmed nor denied the rumor, and she sure as hell wasn't going to ask him. Talk about invading someone's privacy.

"Do you want to eat in here or outside?"

After several days of rain, the weather gods had decided to gift Maine with a perfect late-spring day. If she were a customer at Ocean View Grill, she'd sit outside and soak up the sunshine.

"Inside today."

Somehow, she'd known he'd say that.

"Follow me."

Unlike some celebrities, Matt didn't intentionally call attention to himself. At least, he never did when he came to town.

"When did you get here?" Liv didn't need to look behind her to know he was following her toward the back corner booth. It provided the most privacy, especially at night when they lowered the overhead lights and lit candles on the tables.

"Saturday afternoon." Matt slid into the booth, and it didn't go unnoticed that he picked the side facing away from the dining room.

Liv handed him a menu and then removed the other place settings. "How long are you here for?"

Matt shrugged. "I'm not sure. Maybe for the summer. Definitely until July."

If he was going to be here that long, would the woman and baby he'd been seen with be joining him? Or were they already here but off doing something else? Then again, he may have already moved on to someone new. While she was curious, it wasn't any of her business. Moreover, although she considered him more than an acquaintance—he'd stayed at her parents' house while in college and had seen her wearing pj's—they weren't close friends either.

"Does Owen know you're here?"

Matt shook his head and opened his menu. "No. I almost stopped by to see him when I drove through Massachusetts, but I thought he'd be at work."

"He and Jenny will probably be up this weekend. They bought a house here over the winter, and they come up almost every weekend to work on it." The place was a total fixer-upper, but it had been in her brother and sister-in-law's price range, and neither minded doing the work.

"He told me they were thinking about doing that. I didn't know they found anything."

Liv's cell phone vibrated in her pocket. Maybe the text was from her dad, letting her know the rumor wasn't true. Unfortunately, she couldn't check while standing there.

"Can I get you something to drink while you look over the menu?"

"Just a seltzer water with lime for now."

With a nod, she turned and pulled out her phone.

Emma: I saw the driver of the Ferrari go inside.

Didn't her friend have flowers to cut and bouquets to arrange or something?

Emma: Is it anyone worth stopping in to see?

Emma was a great friend. She was also a flirt and a celebrity junkie. Whenever a well-known actor or musician visited the town, she went a little crazy. To date, she'd managed to take photos with Mia Troy, Anderson Brady, and Mark Walden. If Liv told Emma who was sitting in the corner booth now, she'd suddenly need a meal and close the flower shop so she could cross the street.

Liv hated to lie, but considering Matt had sat facing away from potential customers, he didn't want to draw attention his way. Besides, everyone deserved a chance to eat in peace, no matter what they did for a living or how famous they were.

Liv: I don't recognize him.

A frowning face popped up on the screen, followed by another text.

Emma: Any news from your dad?

Liv: Nope.

A second frowning face appeared. Liv shared her friend's sentiment.

When she returned to the table with Matt's drink and a basket of freshly baked rolls, the menu was still open, but he was focused on his phone rather than his meal choices.

He set the device aside, though, before she got the water glass off her tray.

"So, how have you been?" Matt had been friendly from day one, despite his wealth and family connections. And even though he'd since become a household name, that hadn't changed.

Overall, she'd been great. At the moment, she was an anxiety bundle on two legs. Until she got some answers from either her dad or grandfather, she didn't see that changing. However, Matt didn't need to know any of that. Not to mention, he'd asked to be polite, not because he really cared. In all fairness, she often asked people she ran into the same question simply to be polite.

"Fine. Yourself?"

She expected an immediate reply like hers. Instead, he seemed to consider the question before answering. "No complaints."

Something about his tone suggested that wasn't entirely true, but she accepted his answer and moved on to her reason for standing there. After all, her job was to serve him lunch, not provide him with counseling.

"Do you know what you'd like, or do you need more time?"

"I'm undecided. Is there anything you suggest?"

There wasn't an item on the menu she didn't like. They also had some tasty specials available today.

"Depends. Are you in the mood for a full meal or a sandwich?"

"A meal. I didn't have much for breakfast."

"If you like salmon, you should have the honey garlic glazed salmon. It's one of today's specials. You can order the dinner or the lunch portion."

Unless she hadn't eaten all day, the lunch portion was more than enough, especially if she ate the garden salad that came with it.

"That sounds really good. I'll go with the dinner portion. And I'll also have a cup of the lobster bisque."

She accepted the menu Matt held out to her. "What kind of dressing would you like on your salad?"

"The house dressing."

The house dressing, a recipe her grandfather had developed not long after opening the restaurant, was extremely popular. Countless times over the years, customers asked where they could buy it. She'd tried to convince her grandfather to see what they'd need to do to produce it in larger batches and bottle it so they could at least sell it in the restaurant. Unfortunately, while her dad was on board with the idea, her grandfather wasn't, and even though he'd turned much of the day-to-day operations over to her parents and her, he still played a role in what did or didn't happen.

Order memorized, Liv stepped back. "I'll be right back with your salad."

She was inputting Matt's order into the computer when the restaurant's door opened and a trio of women walked inside. So much for keeping Maggie out of the dining room and away from Matt. While she could serve the new customers too, it would be unfair to Maggie, who was saving most of what she made to pay for classes at the community college. However, Liv would seat them. With a bit of luck, they'd prefer to sit outside.

"Good afternoon. Would you like to eat inside or on the patio?" Liv asked as she grabbed three menus.

The taller of the trio looked at her companions and shrugged. "Up to you two. It doesn't matter to me."

"Outside gets my vote," the blonde replied.

Mine too.

"We'll sit outside," the oldest of the group, who Liv suspected was the mother of the other two, replied.

After showing them to a table with a great view of the water, Liv returned to the kitchen, where Maggie and Russ were still talking. Maggie had never said anything, but Liv suspected she had a thing for Russ. Based on the amount of time they spent talking when they worked together and the looks the grill chef sent Maggie, the attraction was mutual.

"You've got a party of three, Maggie. I seated them outside at table six."

Maggie nodded. "Thanks. I'll head out right now."

Message delivered. Liv got a small garden salad with a side of the house dressing and headed back into the dining room. She wasn't surprised to find Matt looking at his cell phone when she reached his table. After all, he didn't have anyone to talk to. But as she set the dish down, he put the device down and looked at her.

"When did you expand the restaurant?"

After more than eight months, she had grown so accustomed to the larger dining room that she no longer noticed it.

"Last summer. Dad had wanted to do it for a long time, and when Milly closed her art gallery and moved to Arizona, he took over the space."

Matt shifted so he could get a better view of the restaurant and then looked back at her. "Shouldn't the dining room be even larger than it is?"

She understood his confusion.

"We only used about half the space for the restaurant. The rest we turned into an office for the catering side of things."

She'd loved cooking from the time she knew what it was. And she'd always known her future would somehow be tied to the restaurant. A few years ago, she suggested they branch into catering—a service no other restaurant in town provided. It had taken a little time for them to convince her grandfather. When they finally had, they'd started small, catering events such as baby showers and office holiday parties. Last spring, when her dad took over, they'd decided the time was right to take on larger events. By taking over the adjacent space, they were able to expand both the kitchen and the dining room. They'd turned the remaining area into a formal space for her to meet with customers looking to hire them for an event. To date, the largest event they'd done was a fiftieth wedding anniversary party with one hundred guests. However, they had two large events booked for the summer. One was in July and the other in August.

"If I ever need anything catered, I'll know where to come."

The door opened again, and a group of four entered. With Maggie outside and the evening hostess not there yet, Liv needed to see to them.

"Your bisque should be ready. As soon as I seat this party, I'll bring it over to you."

* * *

Alone again, Matt picked up his phone and sent off a text to Owen. He hadn't seen his friend in close to a year and would enjoy catching up the next time Owen was in town.

From the corner of his eye, Matt spotted Liv heading toward the kitchen, and he mentally shook his head. Considering the number of people he'd met in his lifetime, he shouldn't remember the first time he met Liv, yet somehow, he did.

That semester, he'd planned to stay on campus rather than fly home to California for the Thanksgiving break. When his room-mate found out about his plans, Owen invited him to spend the holiday with his family. Despite all the traveling Matt had done over the years, the only parts of Maine he was familiar with were the towns near campus, so he'd agreed.

When they walked into the Middleton house that Tuesday afternoon, mouthwatering scents and Liv rolling out a pie crust while wearing an apron with the Swedish Chef on the front greeted them. After hugging Owen, she pulled out the apple cobbler she had made just for him because it was Owen's favorite. Then, as she worked on pumpkin pies, the two siblings caught up while Owen and Matt polished off the cobbler. At some point that day, he must have met Owen's parents and his other sister, Faith, but nothing from those introductions stood out. He didn't know why the encounter with Liv did. Maybe it had been the apple cobbler or the way she and Owen interacted. They'd teased each other mercilessly, but it had been clear they'd do anything for each other. Although Matt had two younger brothers with whom he got along well, they weren't as close as Owen and Liv obviously were.

Actually, although he was the oldest, he'd often felt like the odd man out growing up. As identical twins, Theo and Aiden did most things together. To make matters worse, he had little in common with either of them. Growing up, he often spent more time with his cousin Adam, who was the same age as him, rather than his brothers.

He never spent Thanksgiving with the Middletons again, but he'd made multiple trips back to visit with Owen while in college. Each time, Liv reminded him of the stereotypical girl next door. The one everyone in town liked. The one who always greeted you with a smile and asked how you were. And unlike her younger sister, Faith, she always seemed to be dressed for comfort. The most formal thing he'd seen her in was jeans and a sweater. If she had ever worn makeup, it hadn't been when he was around.

The phone on the table buzzed as Liv set down the lobster bisque.

"Do you need anything else right now?" she asked.

"What craft beers do you have on tap?"

"Keller, Beaverbrook, and Running Shoes."

"Someone named their beer company Running Shoes?"

Liv shrugged and smiled. "Maybe the names they wanted

were taken and they couldn't think of anything else. Of the three, it's my favorite."

"I'll try it, then."

His phone buzzed again, reminding him he had a text message. Once Liv was no longer within sight, he flipped the device over and read the message.

Owen: We'll be there Friday night. We bought a house over on Tall Oaks Drive.

Matt: Your sister told me.

Owen: Do you want to get together on Saturday?

Matt: Whatever works for you and Jenny.

Matt had no plans he needed to work around. He also had plenty of time on his hands for the foreseeable future.

Owen: Saturday is good for us. We usually leave on Sunday nights.

Matt: Your place or mine?

Most of the time, he didn't mind the attention he often got when he went out. Those he was with sometimes did.

Owen: We'll come to you. Time?

Liv said Owen and his wife came up almost every weekend to work on their house. Early evening should give them plenty of time to do that.

Matt: 5:00

Owen: See you then.

When alone, many people checked their favorite social media sites or the news. Matt preferred to avoid both, for obvious reasons. So after Owen's final text message, he opened the crossword puzzle he'd started yesterday and filled in the squares for thirteen down while he enjoyed his bisque. He didn't have lobster often. He found it too much work, but you couldn't come to Maine and not have some. Not to mention, Ocean View Grill's lobster bisque was the best he'd had anywhere in the state.

Matt lifted another spoonful toward his mouth and read the clue for seventeen down.

Who discovered the Titanic *wreck?*

Beats me.

He'd never cared about the history of the famous ship.

17

Honestly, he didn't understand why so many people remained fascinated by it. The vessel sank more than a hundred years ago, and no one who'd survived the disaster remained alive.

Right now, he only had two of the thirteen letters in the answer. Definitely not enough to even guess a name. Thanks to modern technology, he could find out before his meal even arrived. Hell, he could get that information as well as everything from a passenger list to what was served for dinner the night the ship sank. Instead of looking up the answer, he moved on to a new clue.

Who invented basketball?

This one he could answer. Even better, it gave him a letter in seventeen down.

"How's the bisque?"

At the sound of Liv's voice, he looked up. "Delicious. And you were right. Owen and Jenny are coming up this weekend."

"Thanks for the warning. Now I have time to come up with an excuse for why I can't help them. I've done enough sanding and painting in the past month to last me a lifetime."

He'd never lifted a paintbrush, but how hard could it be?

"Your meal should be out any minute. Do you want me to bring you some more water when I come back?"

"Please."

Maybe she knew the answer to seventeen down. "Hey, do you know who found the *Titanic*?" he asked, stopping her midturn.

"Yeah, it was...." Liv paused, and her eyebrows scrunched together. "Man, why can't I remember his name? I watched a special about underwater archaeology not that long ago, and they mentioned him. He also found some other well-known wreckages." She pulled her phone out, and he guessed she intended to look up the answer.

Before she did, though, she snapped her fingers. "Ballard. I don't remember his first name, but his last name is Ballard. He's a university professor somewhere."

It was more than he had now.

"Why do you want to know? It's kind of an odd question."

"It's a clue in a crossword puzzle."

"If you get stuck on any other ones, just ask. I'm usually good at them." Liv glanced at her phone and briefly closed her eyes. "I'll be right back with your meal." Phone still in hand, she turned and walked away.

Dismissing Liv from his thoughts, he focused on the crossword puzzle again. If he answered eleven across, he would have another letter in seventeen down.

A reddish-brown oxide formed by the reaction of iron and oxygen.

Matt reread the clue and thought back to high school science class. The answer only contained four letters, and the last one was a *T*. The answer had to be rust, which meant seventeen down started with an *R*. What were some male names that contained six letters and started with an *R*?

As he went through common male names, he grabbed the last roll. Both Richard and Raymond were too long. Ryan contained only four letters. Maybe Liv could help him when she returned.

Unfortunately, she wasn't the one who brought out his meal.

"Liv needed to make a phone call," the woman standing next to the table said as she placed his meal down.

"Thank you," he said, looking up from his phone. He didn't recognize her, but judging by her expression, she recognized him because her eyes doubled in size.

"Are you Matt Sherbrooke from Eclipse?"

Matt considered his options. He could lie and tell Maggie, according to her name tag, that he wished he were and that he got asked that all the time. Over the past few years, he'd done that whenever he wanted to be left alone, and oddly, people usually believed him. Or he could be honest and pose for any pictures she wanted.

This afternoon, he went with option number two and nodded.

"Oh my God!" Maggie's voice went up several octaves. "My sister is going to be so jealous when I tell her you were here. We're both huge fans. We saw your concert last year."

"I hope you enjoyed it." He'd had this same conversation countless times.

"We loved it. Next time you perform in the area, we'll be there."

Maggie and her sister might have to wait a long time for that.

"Would you mind if we took a picture together?" She pulled her phone out before she finished the question.

He'd known the request was coming. Regardless of his mood, he never said no when a fan asked for a photo. Without fans like Maggie and her sister, he wouldn't have a career.

"Sure thing."

Liv appeared at the table as Maggie took her second picture. "Maggie, your order for table 6 is ready."

"On it." Maggie stuffed the phone back into her pocket. "Thanks so much for the pictures. My sister is going to be super jealous when she sees them."

"Sorry about that." Liv gestured toward the other woman once she was out of hearing. "I needed to call my dad."

"Don't worry about it. Is everything okay?" He couldn't put his finger on it, but something about her tone was off.

"Oh, yeah, just some work stuff."

Matt didn't know Liv well, but he'd bet his Ferrari that she was lying. But if she didn't want to share, he wouldn't push the matter.

"Do you need anything else?" she asked.

"I'm all set for now."

"Then I'll let you enjoy your lunch. I'll be back to check on you in a little while."

Picking up his fork, he looked at the crossword puzzle still open and realized he'd forgotten to ask Liv if she knew any names that started with an *R* and contained six letters.

Several hours later, Matt stood in the same spot he'd started the day, only instead of holding a cup of coffee, he had a can of ginger ale in his hand. Although the sun was setting, there was enough daylight left to make out the cruise ship at sea. While he wouldn't want to be stuck on a ship with so many strangers, he was a little envious of the individuals out there tonight. It would be another two weeks before his new boat arrived and was ready for him to use.

Settling into a chair, Matt stretched his legs out and opened the paperback he'd picked up after lunch. Like most people, he owned an e-reader, but there was something about holding a paperback in his hands that he enjoyed. When he'd gone into the Book Nook after lunch, he'd browsed the shelves for a good half hour before purchasing the newest release from Curt Hilton, as well as books from two authors he was unfamiliar with.

He read the first page and stopped when the name "Liv" appeared. Immediately, an image of Liv from this afternoon popped up. Whether something was wrong or not shouldn't matter to him. She was someone he saw a few times a year, if that, when he went into the Ocean View Grill. That barely made them acquaintances. Regardless, he'd thought of her several times since he left the restaurant this afternoon. Something had happened to trigger the slight change in her. Whatever it had been, Liv's brother might know. But since they weren't friends, she might not appreciate him sticking his nose into her business. He sure as hell hated it when people did it to him. However, in his case, people often felt they were entitled to know everything about him because he'd picked a career that cast him in the spotlight. And while he gave them some leeway, it didn't mean he approved of the paparazzi trying to get onto his property or standing outside a restaurant, waiting for him to exit with his mom on her birthday.

Yeah, as curious as Matt was, he wouldn't text Owen and ask about Liv. However, he might stop by the restaurant again this weekend and see how she was. A man had to eat, after all, and Ocean View Grill was his favorite restaurant in town.

Two

FRIDAY AFTERNOON, Liv wasn't even fully seated when the door opened and a couple around her age walked inside.

Talk about good timing.

Standing, Liv walked out from behind her desk. She'd spent the earlier part of the day making phone calls and then ensuring that all the food would be ready for the retirement party Ocean View was catering later that day. Once done with that, she'd prepared for her afternoon meeting and then took care of a few errands—ones that shouldn't have taken her long. Unfortunately, thanks to some overtalkative acquaintances and traffic, she'd barely gotten back in time to unlock the door for her potential clients.

"Good afternoon. You must be Gina." Liv extended her hand toward the dark-haired woman.

Smiling, Gina shook her hand. "It's great to meet you finally. Once again, I'm sorry we had to reschedule so many times."

"I understand." As long as the couple booked Ocean View Catering, Liv didn't care how often they'd canceled their initial meeting.

"This is my fiancé, Blake." Gina gestured toward her companion, a well-dressed man who appeared to spend more time on his appearance in the morning than Liv did, which, in all honesty, wouldn't be that difficult.

"It's nice to meet you both. If you want to have a seat, we can get started." Liv gestured toward the small conference table. Although they could use her desk, she preferred the table because, at least to her, it made meetings like this feel more like a get-together with your friends rather than a business transaction.

Based on their previous conversations, Liv knew the couple was from Cambridge and that they'd decided to get married in Orchard Harbor after visiting a friend who had a home on the water. Although Liv wasn't sure "home" was the correct term for the ten-thousand-square-foot mansion Raymond Thatcher owned. Regardless, they'd fallen in love with the area and planned to get married at Raymond's estate. It just so happened that Ocean View catered the party Raymond and his wife hosted during Gina and Blake's visit. According to Gina, they'd enjoyed the food so much they'd asked Raymond's wife for the name of the catering company so they could hire them for the wedding reception. Of course, it helped that they were the only catering company in town.

She watched in awe as Blake pulled out a chair and waited for Gina to sit before doing the same. Granted, she'd seen men do that for women at the restaurant, but they were usually much older. She'd genuinely assumed only people from earlier generations still did it. Clearly, she'd been wrong, or Blake was simply a throwback to an earlier time. Either way, she wouldn't mind if a man did that for her every once in a while. Of course, she'd need to have a date first. Unfortunately, her dating life was almost nonexistent. But that was something she could think about later when she was alone.

"The last time we spoke, you had two possible dates in mind. Have you settled on one?"

Across the table, Gina retrieved her phone from her purse, and sunlight bounced off her engagement ring, all but blinding Liv. The thing had undoubtedly cost a small fortune, but she found it downright gaudy.

"We have. We're going with the twentieth."

As she spoke, Liv opened her calendar. Currently, they had nothing scheduled for September. Considering the news her dad and grandfather received earlier in the week, perhaps they shouldn't book anything, because the likelihood of them being able to buy the building was slim. However, even if Rick Desmond were to purchase the property, it would take time for the details to be finalized. And while she didn't know anything about real estate law, she hoped it prohibited Desmond from kicking them out the moment his company signed the purchase and sales agreement.

"That's a Thursday," Liv supplied. There was no rule stating people couldn't get married on a Thursday, but most people she knew preferred to do so on the weekend.

"No, it's a Friday," Gina answered, looking up from her phone.

Her father always said not to argue with a customer, but she had the calendar in front of her. And September 20 was a Thursday.

"Are you sure? On my calendar, the twentieth is a Thursday." Liv turned the calendar around and slid it closer to the couple.

Gina checked her phone and then the calendar on the table. "You're looking at the wrong month. We decided to get married in July instead of September."

Some people preferred short engagements. Her brother was an excellent example of that. Eight months and three days had passed between Owen proposing and when he and Jenny said "I do." What Gina was suggesting wasn't a short engagement but an almost nonexistent one. Even with eight months to plan, it hadn't been easy. Less than two months to prepare potentially tripled the difficulty.

"I realize it is rather short notice. But my uncle, who's conducting the ceremony, will be in Europe in September. I hope you're still available."

Liv flipped to the appropriate month. At the moment, they were catering a high school graduation party on July 1, the Garden Club Tea on the second Saturday of the month, and the Maine Writers' Guild retreat on July 28, but July 20 was open. "We can do the twentieth."

"Excellent." Smiling, Gina clapped her hands together.

They were there to discuss food options, not whether Gina and Blake had reserved the services of a photographer and florist. However, if the bride-to-be couldn't book those on such short notice, the couple might have to reschedule with Liv. With the sale of the building looming over her head, she'd rather not have that happen.

"Have you already found a florist?"

"Finding one is next on my list," Gina answered.

You're in luck, my friend.

While getting the catering side of the restaurant up and going had been her immediate goal, it wasn't Liv's ultimate one. She not only wanted Ocean View Catering to be successful, but she also wanted to develop a one-stop shopping event-planning business. A place where someone like Gina could come and hire everyone they needed to make sure their wedding or special event was perfect. She'd already approached Emma and Phoebe. Both were willing to jump on board when the time was right. Until then, they recommended each other to customers at times like this.

"I recommend you try Exquisite Flowers across the street. They do amazing work."

Hopefully, Emma could help the couple on such short notice.

"Let me see if I have any of their business cards left." Standing, Liv walked back to her desk. "What about a photographer?"

Even before she stood, Liv knew she had plenty of business cards for Exquisite Flowers on hand. After grabbing one, her hand lingered over the stack for Dalton Photography. Some people might not like it, but Liv saw nothing wrong with sending customers to her friends rather than their competition. They'd do the same for her if Ocean View Catering had any competition in the area.

"I'm waiting to hear back from one," Gina answered.

Liv pulled out one of Phoebe's business cards too. "If they don't get back to you or aren't available, try Dalton Photography. They're located nearby." She handed the other woman the two business cards as she sat down again.

"Have you already decided on a time?" Not that it mattered much. Ocean View wasn't yet large enough to handle two events on the same day, so Gina and Blake's wedding would be it for the day.

Gina nodded as she tucked the business cards into her purse. "The ceremony will be at four."

Why, Liv couldn't say, but she preferred evening weddings. While she'd never been married, she'd been a bridesmaid in several weddings and catered a few small ones. At least to her, there seemed to be less stress hovering over everyone when the event occurred at night. Maybe it was because people had more time to prepare. Or perhaps it was all in her head. Either way, she wanted an evening wedding if she were to get married.

"Four o'clock is a great time for a ceremony. Have you discussed whether you want a sit-down meal or a buffet?"

Once again, Liv had an opinion on the topic, and if this were her wedding, she'd want a buffet, so her guests had options. But many people considered sit-down meals more formal and turned their noses up at the idea of a buffet.

"Sit-down, but we do want a dessert buffet, similar to the one at Raymond's party, in addition to the cake."

After adding the answers to her notes, Liv passed Ocean View's updated catering menu across the table. "Our current dinner choices are in here. Any of the meal options can be modified. Each comes with either a soup or salad and your choice of bread for the table."

"We want to give our guests two or three options to pick from." Gina opened the menu binder. "We also have some guests with allergies, so they'll need special meals."

Gina and her fiancé were the ones who had to keep track of who wanted what, so Liv didn't care if they gave their guests twenty different options.

"That won't be a problem for us." Nowadays, restaurants and catering companies had to be prepared for food allergies if they hoped to remain in business. In fact, she hadn't catered an event yet that didn't require at least one special dish due to an allergy or special dietary requirement.

For the next few minutes, Gina and Blake discussed the meal options. Occasionally, they'd ask Liv what modifications could be made to a specific dish. Eventually, they—or, Liv should say, Gina —narrowed it down to six possibilities. Either Blake was the easiest-going person alive, or he'd decided beforehand that he was better off letting Gina make the wedding decisions—or at least the decisions about the meal.

"It's later than I realized. Do we have to decide today?" Gina asked after checking her watch. "We're supposed to meet Raymond and Scarlet at four. We're going sailing."

With the wedding in July, Liv would prefer to have all the details squared away sooner rather than later. But if Gina needed a few extra days, she could have them. "That's not a problem. Let me print out a contract so you can sign it, and then you can take the menu with you."

Nothing was permanently added to the catering schedule until she had a signed contract and a deposit in hand. People changed their minds all too often and sometimes at the last minute. Since they'd started catering events, it had happened three times. Thankfully, the initial deposits required helped offset the restaurant's losses.

"Do you want me to email you our meal choices?" Gina asked as she signed the contract and slid it toward Blake for his signature.

"That would be great." Liv preferred everything in writing. It helped solve any potential disagreements later.

"I'll get back to you by the end of next week."

She handed Gina back her credit card and stapled a receipt to a copy of the contract. "Sounds good. And if you have any questions—"

A sudden crash, followed by screeching tires, stopped Liv from finishing her sentence.

That can't be good.

Liv looked out the front window in time to see a large silver SUV hit a pole across the street. Unlike after the first crash, the SUV remained where it was.

"We parked on the street. I hope they didn't hit us," Gina said as she followed Blake to the door.

Damn it.

She'd parked the catering van on the street as well—something she rarely did, but she'd been running late, and it had saved her some time.

Liv crossed her fingers as she followed the couple to the door.

Several people stood on the sidewalk and across the street as they watched the driver of the SUV stumble from the vehicle. As if it were no big deal, he started to walk away, but a bystander stepped in his path before he could get far. While the driver looked unfamiliar, Liv recognized the passenger who exited the vehicle. Linda Burke had been a party girl in high school, and judging by the fact that she was swaying more than the leaves on the trees during hundred-mile-an-hour winds, that hadn't changed.

Neither the driver nor Linda was her immediate problem, though. Nope, the fact that the SUV had crashed into the catering van was.

This week just keeps getting better.

She didn't know much about cars, but the van didn't appear safe to drive. Even if it was drivable, she couldn't show up to an event with the van in that condition. If not for all the people around, Liv would sit down on the sidewalk and cry.

"At least no one was injured," Gina said to no one in particular.

Physically, no one was injured. Financially, it was another story. Sure, the insurance would help replace the catering van, and they could sue the SUV driver. But the insurance company wouldn't help them make their upcoming weekend deliveries.

While they'd recently purchased a second delivery vehicle, it was currently in the garage for maintenance. Liv had specifically chosen this week for it to be there, as none of the events they were catering were large enough to require two vans. Unfortunately, she'd never fit everything in her VW Bug, and she had no friends with a vehicle large enough to transport everything.

"Gina, we should go. Otherwise, we'll be late," Blake said.

"You're right." Gina turned toward Liv. "We'll be in touch soon with our menu choices."

"Sounds great." Liv forced a smile. What other option did she have? "Enjoy your afternoon."

As she watched the police deal with the SUV driver and his passenger, Liv ran through her list of acquaintances who might have a vehicle large enough and would be willing to help her for at least today. She'd deal with tomorrow then. Only one came to mind, but Joan and her husband were on a cruise. She'd told Liv all about its itinerary when they'd run into each other last week.

With borrowing a vehicle ruled out, Liv pulled out her phone. The closest car rental agency was thirty-five miles away. With a bit of luck, something she hadn't experienced this week, they'd have an SUV or a truck she could rent. If they didn't, Liv had no idea what she'd do. A failure to deliver the order would not only mean wasted food and a refund to the customer, but it would also ruin Irene Carr's retirement party—something she didn't want to do because, honestly, she really liked Irene.

A lifetime later, or at least it felt that way, Liv watched as Frank Stratford parked his tow truck near the van and hopped out as she rubbed the throbbing pain over her left eye and racked her brain for a solution. If Emma or Phoebe was available, perhaps they could help her transport everything in their cars.

Rather than get to work, Frank walked over to her as she scrolled through her contact list for Phoebe's number.

"What happened?" Frank's father owned the only garage in Orchard Harbor. Rumor had it that Frank Senior planned to retire within the year and hand the place over to his eldest son. Much like the Middletons, the Stratford family was a staple in town.

"The catering van had the audacity to move in front of the SUV that Joel is getting ready to tow." Liv gestured toward Frank's cousin across the street. "Then the utility pole did the same, and the drunk idiot driving hit it too."

She'd watched the police give Linda's friend a sobriety test— something she'd only ever seen done on television. If not for the damage the man caused, she would've found the sight funny.

"You weren't hurt, were you?" Frank asked as he examined the van's damage more closely.

Liv shook her head. "I was inside when it happened. And, thankfully, no one was across the street either." If there had been pedestrians on the sidewalk, the SUV might have hit them as well as the utility pole.

"Was the driver anyone we know?"

Much like her, Frank had spent his entire life in Orchard Harbor and seemed to know all the year-round residents and many of the individuals who'd owned summer homes in town for years.

"I don't think so. I've never seen him before, but Linda Burke was with him."

"He was probably the same guy I saw her with at the North-side Tavern last weekend. I heard Linda call him Doug. He could barely stand that night. There was another guy with them, and the two of them got into an argument about whether Doug could drive. Thankfully, Doug's friend won."

She'd never understood how people could be so irresponsible and get behind the wheel while drunk. "Too bad the friend wasn't around today." Maybe she wouldn't be searching her brain for a solution if he had been.

Across the street, Joel waved before getting into his truck and driving away. A moment later, Frank returned to work, and she selected Phoebe's number from her contact list.

When Phoebe's voicemail picked up, Liv left a brief message and disconnected the call. "Hey, Frank, do you know anyone with an SUV or a van they'd let me borrow so I can make today's delivery at least?"

"My sister-in-law drives a minivan, but she might be working. Her shift rotates. I can call her and check."

"That would be great."

Frank's sister-in-law wasn't originally from Orchard Harbor, and Liv knew very little about her, except that she worked as a nurse and was married to Frank's younger brother. But as her mom would say, beggars can't be picky. If she thought it would help, she'd cross her fingers and toes while Frank made his call.

She heard a car door close nearby as she waited for Frank's sister-in-law to answer, but she didn't turn around. If it was someone she knew, they'd stop to talk. Hopefully, though, it wasn't. She didn't feel like explaining what happened right now to someone else.

"Sorry, Liv. Dee's working," Frank said as he shoved his phone back into his pocket.

Based on everything else this week, she'd expected that answer. "Thanks anyway for trying, Frank."

Matt caught the tail end of Liv and the tow truck driver's conversation as he approached. He didn't know what Frank had been unsuccessful at doing, but he heard the disappointment in Liv's voice.

"We'll inspect the damage as soon as we can and call you. Your other van should be all set sometime on Monday for you to pick up."

"Sounds good, Frank. Enjoy your weekend," Liv said before the tow truck driver walked away.

"I'd ask you how your day was, but I can tell it's not going well," Matt said, stopping next to Liv once the other man climbed into his truck.

"You could say that."

"What happened?"

"Some idiot got behind the wheel drunk, and instead of using his brakes to slow down, he used the van. And now I don't know what the heck I'm going to do." Liv raked her hands down her face and took several steps away before turning back toward him. "We're catering a surprise retirement party tonight, and I have no way of getting the food there."

He'd attended catered events but never thought about how the food got there. Did it require a special vehicle capable of keeping food either hot or cold? Before he could ask, Liv continued.

"Everything won't fit in my car at once. It would probably

31

take me five or six trips to get everything from here to the VFW hall."

Well, that answered that question. No special vehicle was required.

"The car rental agency doesn't have anything available large enough, and the only person I know with an SUV is cruising around Bermuda right now." Liv's frustration became more pronounced with each word. "This couldn't have happened at a worse time."

On that, she was wrong. She knew someone with an SUV who wasn't cruising around an island. "I have an SUV."

"If this happened next week, I'd have the other van to use." Liv dropped her head back and looked at the sky as if she'd find an answer there. "Wait, what did you say?" she asked, looking at him.

"I have an SUV you can use." Matt had purchased the vehicle during a previous visit to the area, and to date, he'd only used it once for a camping trip he'd taken.

"Really?"

He wasn't sure if she was surprised that he owned such a vehicle or because he was offering to let her use it. Either way, it was sitting in his garage, and he didn't need it tonight.

Matt nodded. "We can head over to my house now, and you can get it."

Liv's eyes widened in surprise, and she threw her arms around him. "Matt, you're a lifesaver. I'll grab my things, and we can go."

An unexpected surge of energy sparked all his nerve endings. Women of all ages had hugged him, and he'd never experienced anything like it. "Not a problem. I'll wait for you by my car."

As if just realizing she was hugging him, Liv dropped her arms and moved away. "Sorry about that."

"No need to apologize." Rather than help, his response caused her face to go from resembling a cherry blossom to a strawberry.

"I just need to lock up, and then we can go." She took a few steps toward the building and then turned toward him. "Were you planning to get something to eat?"

It was a logical question since he'd parked so close to the restaurant. And while it had been part of his reason for being there, it wasn't the only one. He'd been unable to shake their last conversation and the sense that something was wrong, so his visit this afternoon had more to do with appeasing his curiosity and seeing her again than eating.

"Yeah, but I have food at home, or I can come back later and get something." Even though he'd offered her a solution to the immediate problem, she still appeared stressed. Not that he blamed her. The accident wasn't her fault, but she'd still have a lot to deal with because of it.

"Are you sure?"

"Positive." He wouldn't have offered if he didn't want her to use the vehicle.

For a second, he thought she would argue, but then she opened the door marked Ocean View Catering and walked inside.

When she returned, Matt opened the car door and waited for her to get inside. Instead, she looked at him as if he had grown a second head. He was used to getting a variety of looks from people, but this one was a first. "Is something wrong?"

"No, everything's fine. Why?"

"You look a little concerned." Although not accurate, it sounded better than "you're looking at me as if I've grown a second head."

Liv shook her head as she tucked some hair behind her ear. "Sorry, I just have a lot on my mind today."

If you say so.

They both remained silent as he pulled away from the curb and headed north.

"How many people are they expecting at the party tonight?" Matt asked when it became apparent that Liv wasn't going to start a conversation.

"They ordered food for twenty-five, but the guest list might be smaller. It's not unusual for clients to order a little extra just in case. Then they take any leftovers home."

It sounded like a small party, but then again, they were

talking about Orchard Harbor, not Portland or Boston. At least he assumed the party was for a resident of Orchard Harbor since it was being held at the VFW in town.

"Who's the party for?" Matt doubted he knew the guest of honor, but it seemed like an appropriate next question.

"Irene Carr. She's worked as the director of the parks and rec department for thirty years."

Not only didn't he recognize the name, but he'd never known the town had a parks and rec department.

"Her husband was a high school science teacher. I had him for chemistry and physics. He retired two or three years ago."

Maybe if he put some serious thought into it, he'd be able to recall the name of a teacher from high school, but he doubted it.

Matt turned left at the intersection and stopped so two middle-school-age kids could cross the road on their bikes.

"Is that the typical size event you cater?"

"So far, our largest event was a fiftieth wedding anniversary with one hundred guests. But we have two—actually, after this afternoon, three—events this summer with more than one hundred guests. Two are in July, and the other is in August."

"How many events do you typically do in a month?"

Liv considered his question before answering. "It varies. We were doing one or two events every weekend until about New Year's. Things slowed down in January and February. But since about the middle of March, things have picked back up again. I think we've only had one weekend in the past six weeks with only one event booked."

Ocean View Catering sounded busier than he'd expected, considering its location.

The sound of an oven timer erupted from Liv's purse, and she pulled out her phone. Matt glanced over in time to see her frown and then type a message.

"The events we do aren't always in town," Liv said, as if reading his mind. "The closest catering company is about forty miles away, so we get business from all the neighboring towns."

"Is tonight's party your only event this weekend?"

"No. We have another one tomorrow," Liv replied as the

sound of an oven timer once again filled the car. Something between a sigh and a groan soon followed.

"Is everything okay?" Matt asked as he turned and drove down the long driveway to his house.

"Bad news seems to be the theme of the week. Marissa was supposed to help me tonight. She just sent me a text letting me know she tested positive for strep this afternoon."

He had no plans for the evening. "I'm free to help."

"I appreciate the offer, Matt. Really, I do, but I don't think that's a good idea. I'll find someone to fill in for her."

Matt was prepared to argue his case but then reconsidered. She was probably right. If word got out that he was doing whatever Liv needed help with, fans might descend on the place and ruin the evening for the guest of honor.

"Well, if you change your mind, call me." He gave Liv his phone number, something few people had, as he opened the garage door. "Do you want to come in, or are you in a rush?"

He knew she needed to return to the restaurant to pick up the food before heading over to the party, but she hadn't shared her timeline.

"I don't have a lot of time. Lydia is expecting me at five."

He didn't bother asking who Lydia was because it didn't matter. If she needed to be there at five, Liv didn't have a lot of time to play with right now. "I'll run in and get the keys for you, then."

Less than five minutes later, Matt watched Liv drive away and realized he should've told her to keep the vehicle so she could use it for tomorrow's event. When she came back later, he'd rectify that. He'd also see if she'd open up and explain what she meant by "bad news seems to be the theme of the week."

Three

MATT STOOD in front of the fridge and considered his dinner options. Although he had plenty of food on hand, nothing appealed to him. While he could go pick something up, he didn't know when Liv would return, and he didn't want to keep her waiting for him. Unfortunately, while Matt had given her his phone number in case she needed it, he hadn't asked for hers, so calling or texting her to get an ETA was out of the question.

Grabbing a blueberry yogurt smoothie, he twisted off the lid. Before he could get the bottle to his mouth, though, his cell phone rang. When he saw the name "Theo" on the screen, he took a sip of his drink before answering because his brother could wait a minute.

"Hey, Theo. How's it going?"

Matt crossed the kitchen to the room's floor-to-ceiling windows. The weather app on his phone predicted the area would get one hell of a storm tonight. Already, a soft drizzle hit the windows, but the dark clouds filling the sky suggested that the rain would intensify soon. There was nothing quite like the ocean during a storm.

"I can't complain," Theo answered.

His brother's answer didn't surprise him. No matter how

grumpy or stressed Theo got, he rarely complained to anyone except his twin. Instead, he avoided people until he took care of whatever the problem was. Honestly, Matt didn't know how Theo managed to go through life like that. As far as he was concerned, sometimes it simply helped to find someone willing to listen while you got things off your chest.

"What about you? Mom told me you're hiding up in Maine."

No doubt their mom had used those exact words. While she enjoyed being near the water, she didn't like to be more than an hour's drive from a major city. His brothers were much the same way. Matt enjoyed visiting a city like Los Angeles from time to time, but not regularly.

"I wouldn't say hiding, but yeah, I'm in Maine. I got here last week."

As if an angry god controlled the weather, the sky opened. Heavy rain pelted the windows, making it almost impossible to see, and Matt was glad he wasn't driving. A car's windshield wipers would be of little use in a storm like this.

"How long are you going to be there?" Theo asked.

"I'm not sure. But at least until July. Why?"

"Brianna and I are heading to Maine in July. If you're going to be around, I thought we'd visit while we're in the area."

Theo rarely vacationed on the East Coast, and when he did, he spent his time in places like Miami or New York City. Matt couldn't recall his brother ever going to Maine.

"Brianna? What happened to Iris?"

Matt didn't keep tabs on his brothers' love lives, and Theo didn't share with him the names of everyone he dated. However, the last time he'd spent time with his brother, Theo and Iris had been attached at the hip. It'd been almost sickening to watch, actually.

"Iris received a promotion at work that she couldn't turn down. She moved to Seattle seven months ago." The annoyance in Theo's voice suggested there was more to the story. "We tried the long-distance thing, but it didn't work. We haven't spoken in about five months."

Had it really been more than six months since he saw his brother? It didn't seem possible. And if it had been that long since he saw Theo, it had been even longer since he saw Aiden. He'd have to do something about that soon.

"Brianna and I've been together for about three months. We met at a fundraiser."

Lightning flashed across the sky, and a loud crack soon followed, suggesting it had struck something. Matt's bet was on a tree.

"Why are you two coming this way?" If Brianna was anything like the women Theo usually dated, Maine wouldn't be on her list of places to visit.

"One of Brianna's sorority sisters is getting married."

His brother's trip to the East Coast made a lot more sense now. "I'll let you know if I'm still here. Do you know where the wedding is?" Maine wasn't the largest state in the US, but depending on where the wedding was, it could be a bit of a drive to Orchard Harbor.

The doorbell rang just as Matt finished asking the question.

"Brianna told me, but I don't remember. I'll ask her when I see her later today."

"Theo, can I call you back later? Liv's here." Matt was only expecting one person tonight, so it had to be her at the door.

"Yeah, sure, but before you go, is Liv the woman you were photographed with in Virginia?"

Matt exited the kitchen and walked down the hallway. "No. That was Evie. She's Adam's girlfriend, not mine."

"I didn't think you were involved with her. She's not your type."

He didn't think he had a type.

"I told Brianna I couldn't see you dating anyone with a child."

Whether a woman had a child or not wouldn't matter to him. If Theo thought it would, Matt wouldn't waste his time correcting him, especially since it was a moot point. He wasn't involved with Evie or anyone else, for that matter. He hadn't been in a relationship in months.

"Evie isn't Reagan's mom. Call Adam. He'll explain everything." Even if he had the time, it wasn't his place to share the recent developments in their cousin's life.

"Will do. Talk to you later."

Matt shoved his phone back into his pocket and opened the door just as another bolt of lightning streaked across the sky.

"Come on in." The overhang protected Liv from the full onslaught of the rain, but she was still getting wet.

"Sorry. I would've been here sooner, but the visibility is terrible tonight. I pulled over twice because I couldn't see anything." She handed him the car keys and the plastic bags she'd carried in with her. "After the party, I stopped at the restaurant and got you some dinner."

Judging by the size of the bags, she had gotten enough dinner for two or three people. "You didn't have to do that."

But I'm glad you did.

Now he didn't have to worry about either cooking or picking up takeout.

Liv shrugged as she pushed strands of damp hair off her forehead. "I felt bad that you didn't have a chance to eat earlier. Consider it payment for letting me use your car today."

"I appreciate it. It looks like you brought enough to last me tonight and tomorrow."

"I wasn't sure what you'd want, so I got an assortment of entrees."

He doubted she'd been able to eat while working, and he wouldn't mind some company. "Have you eaten yet?"

"It's on my to-do list when I get home."

"Why don't you share this with me, and maybe by the time we're done, the visibility will be better."

Liv raked her teeth across her bottom lip before she answered. "It's probably a good idea if you wait to drive me home."

Matt took that as a yes and locked the door. "The kitchen is this way."

"Do you want me to take my shoes off?"

Some people insisted you remove your shoes before stepping past the front door. He wasn't one of them. Life was too short to worry about such trivial things. "Whatever makes you comfortable."

After removing her sneakers, Liv left them and her purse by the door, then followed him down the hall to the kitchen.

"This afternoon, you mentioned you're catering an event tomorrow. You're welcome to use my car again if you need it. I would've called to tell you and saved you the drive here, but I didn't have your number."

"If you don't mind, that would be amazing."

He could tell by her tone that if he turned around, he'd find a surprised expression on her face.

"Use it for as long as you need to." Matt placed the bags on the table and gestured toward a chair. "Make yourself at home."

"It should be just tomorrow. I'll pick our other van up on Monday."

Grabbing two plates from the cabinet, he glanced in her direction. "What would you like to drink?"

"Whatever you're having is fine," she said as she opened a take-out container.

Lightning once again lit up the night sky. A loud boom soon followed it.

"Looks like Keith McCain was right for a change."

Liv said the name as if he should know who she referred to.

"The meteorologist on channel 10," she added, as if reading his thoughts. "This morning, he predicted we'd get a storm tonight."

He couldn't remember the last time he watched either the local or national news.

Liv opened the next container. "I'm not complaining. I love a good storm like this. But I don't enjoy driving when it's this bad."

"Me too." Many people complained when it rained or snowed. Not him. He didn't know many people who shared his views, though. "How do you feel about snowstorms?"

"As long as I don't have to go anywhere, I love them too. Especially if I have some hot chocolate on hand."

Matt added the plates and utensils to the table, then went back for the iced teas he'd poured. "Everything looks amazing." It was going to be difficult to decide what to eat first. "What do you suggest I start with?"

"If I were you, I'd go for the lobster mac and cheese. But if you're in the mood for beef, I suggest the meatloaf Wellington. It was one of today's specials."

Nothing in the containers on the table resembled meatloaf to him. "The lobster mac and cheese is a must tonight. Which one is the meatloaf?"

Liv pushed a container closer to him. "This one. I know it doesn't look like meatloaf. Dad wraps it in puff pastry and serves it with a mushroom demi-glace." She pointed to another container. "This is chili-glazed salmon. It was very popular in the fall as a special, so Dad decided to permanently add it to the menu."

He never would've thought to combine chili seasoning with salmon, but then again, his skills in the kitchen were limited. It might be the best thing he'd ever tasted.

"This is chicken piccata. If we didn't have the lobster mac and cheese, I'd probably have that tonight."

Matt cut the meatloaf into sections and added some to his plate before doing the same with the salmon. He didn't dislike chicken piccata, but tonight the other dishes sounded more appealing. "So, how did the retirement party go tonight?"

"Really well." Liv spooned food onto her plate and then lifted her glass toward her mouth, drawing his attention to her lips. "A few people asked for our business cards." She paused to sip her iced tea, and for half a heartbeat, he contemplated replacing the glass with his mouth.

"And Irene's daughter said she's going to reach out about catering a high school sports banquet in November. Hopefully, we'll be able to do it," Liv continued, breaking whatever spell he'd been under.

After seeing her yesterday, he'd been unable to shake the feeling that something was off with her. And her frown and tone now reminded him of her comment earlier about bad news being the theme of the week.

"Why wouldn't you be able to? Do you already have something booked for that day?" It was already May, so it was highly likely that customers had already booked events for the fall.

"We might. Lydia didn't mention a date, and I didn't have my calendar with me. But I'm not sure we'll be able to cater large events much longer."

Her response left him with more questions than answers. Based on everything she'd told him, Ocean View Catering was doing well, so why wouldn't they be able to work on large events?

"Are you short-staffed?"

The pool of potential employees in town was limited. In fact, he knew that some businesses only opened in the summer and employed people who liked to vacation there, so they opted to work in town for the season, or college students who would rather live and work there than return to their parents' homes.

With a mouthful of food, Liv shook her head. "I wish that was the reason why. Then I might be able to do something about it," she answered once she'd swallowed. "There's a good chance I'll be living at home again and preparing food in my parents' kitchen come fall, and there is no way I can cook food for a hundred-plus people there." Sighing, she stabbed a piece of lobster with more force than necessary. "We found out this week that the new owner of the building is selling it."

"That doesn't mean whoever buys it will force the current businesses out. Whoever bought it most recently didn't."

"Fredrick hasn't been the owner for long. His grandfather died suddenly three months ago. Fredrick was Mr. Waldman's only grandchild, and he left everything to him." Liv lifted the fork toward her mouth, but before it reached its destination, she put it down again. "Mr. Waldman bought the building not long before Gramps opened the restaurant. Over the years, they became good friends. They had a verbal agreement that if Mr. Waldman ever decided to sell, he'd give Gramps the opportunity to buy before putting it on the market. That way, Gramps wouldn't have to worry about competing with other potential buyers."

Matt didn't have a law degree, but he knew verbal agreements were useless.

"Fredrick won't honor the agreement?"

"The Worm only cares about dollar signs and his appearance."

He couldn't contain a smile. "The Worm? Is it safe to assume that isn't a name he uses himself?"

"No, but it fits him well."

"Can't your grandfather buy the building anyway?" Unless the owner had already accepted an offer, Matt saw no reason Mr. Middleton couldn't try to purchase it.

Liv used her fork to push the food around on her plate. "We're going to try. Dad and Gramps had an appointment at the bank today. But Rick Desmond is interested in the property."

Much like when she referred to the meteorologist, Liv said the name as if he should know who he is. "I've never heard of him."

"He's a property developer. His company is known for purchasing properties along the coast, demolishing existing structures, and then constructing luxury hotels and condos. Last fall, it bought all the beach cottages near Sandy Cove and built an upscale boutique hotel."

Matt hated when things like that happened. If someone tore down the building where the restaurant was located and built a hotel or condo complex, it wouldn't only force the bookstore and the restaurant to relocate, but it would also change the entire feel of the area.

"Has he already made an offer?"

"I'm not sure. Dad and Gramps met with the Worm yesterday, and he confirmed that he plans to sell and that Rick is interested. If they've talked numbers, he didn't say—not that it matters. Even with all of us as cosigners, we won't be able to offer the Worm more than Desmond's company."

The building's location was an ideal spot for a hotel or luxury condos, so he understood the property developer's interest in it.

And, unfortunately, since it was on the water, the price tag attached would be significantly higher than if the building were situated elsewhere in town.

"It's a long shot, but if Desmond does put in an offer, I'm hoping someone will counter with a higher amount and then keep the building as is."

Based on what she'd told him, it sounded unlikely but not impossible. "You never know. Is the building officially on the market?"

"The listing goes live Wednesday. Everyone in the building received a letter in the mail today letting us know."

He'd heard her comment about living at home again, but for some reason, it hadn't registered until now.

"Edith, my neighbor, knocked on my door crying when she opened hers. She's lived in the building for fifteen years. I didn't think to stop by yesterday and tell her." Standing, Liv picked up her dish. "It looks like the rain has let up."

It had been a while since the last rumble of thunder, and the heavy tapping from the rain pelting the windows had subsided.

"Where is the trash?"

"You can leave it. I'll take care of it." Matt gestured toward the table as he stood. "Let me walk you out."

She didn't speak again until they reached the front door, but she didn't have to. While she might be standing there with him, her thoughts were a thousand miles away.

"Thanks for dinner," she said as she tied her sneakers and then retrieved her purse.

"Isn't that my line?" He hoped a little teasing would at least temporarily remove the frown on her face.

"Well, thanks for sharing, then." Although not a full smile, the corners of her lips inched upward. It was better than nothing. "Are you sure you don't mind if I use the Suburban again tomorrow?"

"It's all yours." Matt handed her the keys. "Bring it back whenever you have time."

* * *

After parking in the small lot behind her building, Liv sprinted to the door. Although not as heavy as earlier, the rain continued, and if the forecast was to be trusted, it would persist throughout the evening. As long as she didn't have to drive in weather similar to earlier, she didn't care if it rained for the next several days. She couldn't remember the last time it had rained so hard. On the positive side, though, the thunder and lightning tonight had been spectacular.

At the memory of the storm, an image of Matt popped into her head. He'd always seemed like a nice person, and Owen, his ex-wife aside, had good taste in friends. Still, she'd been blind-sided when Matt offered her the use of his Suburban. Sure, they'd technically known each other for years, but they certainly weren't friends. And if he didn't stop into the restaurant whenever he came to town, she'd have zero contact with him. Yet, when she'd explained the situation, he offered her the use of his vehicle. She didn't think many people would do that for someone they barely knew. Then he'd remembered that she had another event tomorrow and unexpectedly extended his offer, solving at least one problem. Too bad someone couldn't help her solve the rest of them.

Before tonight, she'd discussed the situation with very few people. She hadn't even talked to her brother about the possibility that the building might be sold and the restaurant's future was uncertain. She certainly hadn't intended to tell Matt. To be fair, she hadn't expected to engage in such a lengthy conversation with him either. She'd picked up the food before coming as a way to say thank you, not to finagle a dinner date with him. And if the weather had been safe to drive in, she would've turned down his offer.

Liv tossed her top into the hamper and grabbed the first T-shirt she touched. Only after pulling it on did she realize it was one she'd purchased at the last Eclipse concert she'd attended.

Like I need another reminder of him.

Matt always looked gorgeous in photos and on television, but neither did him real justice, which was something she always forgot until she came face-to-face with him. The man was truly traffic-stopping. It was no wonder the *Star Report* had named him the sexiest man alive last year. The woman he'd been photographed with recently was one lucky girl, because not only was he worthy of god status, but judging by his actions today, he was also a super-sweet guy. Well, assuming she was his girlfriend. There hadn't been any more photos of them together, and if she'd traveled with him to town, she hadn't joined them tonight. There also hadn't been any evidence that there was a baby in the house, at least not in the portion she'd seen. However, the house was enormous, and for all she knew, he had rooms filled with baby toys and furniture.

Although a complete waste of time, Liv replayed their time together tonight as she enjoyed her tea. While it could've been an act—after all, Matt had successfully branched into Hollywood— he'd listened to her tonight. The last few men she'd had dinner with had either nodded at whatever she said or not given her a chance to speak. And after their dinners, Liv hadn't thought about any of them again. She didn't need someone to hang on her every word, but she at least wanted the person across the table to engage in an actual conversation.

Tonight, not only had Matt listened, but he'd genuinely seemed interested. Why couldn't she meet someone more like him? She'd tried Find The One, a popular dating app, for a few months last year. Phoebe met her boyfriend through it, and Liv suspected he would be her friend's fiancé before the end of the summer. Unfortunately, while it had brought Phoebe's perfect match into her life, it had only brought the opposite into hers. Following that failed experience, Emma had pestered Liv about meeting her cousin. Maybe pestered was putting it mildly. Whatever you wanted to call it, Liv had refused. Emma's cousin might be the nicest person on Earth, but he also lived ten hours away. When she was in a relationship, she didn't need to see the person every day, but being that far apart would make it difficult to see each other at all. Thankfully, Emma let the matter go when she found out Finn was in a relationship.

Liv sipped her tea and forced aside thoughts of her nonexistent love life as she picked up the remote control. Dwelling on her problems wouldn't solve any of them tonight or ever, for that matter. So at least for the next few hours, she'd pretend she didn't have a care in the world and lose herself in a few episodes of her favorite new television series. Then tomorrow, she'd make sure the food at Kay's baby shower was so good that everyone there would want to know who'd prepared it.

Four

WEDNESDAY AFTERNOON, Matt reached for his iced coffee as he read the script he'd received last night from his agent. When Ryan pitched the project to him, it hadn't sounded like one he'd be interested in doing. Still, he'd told Ryan to send him the script and he'd look it over. After all, the first role he'd played hadn't sounded right for him either. However, his agent had assured Matt he'd be perfect for the part, and the man had been right. Not only had Matt loved every minute of filming, but the role had also burst open the door to his acting career. Ryan might be correct about this project as well. And with his music career on pause, he certainly had the time to start on something new.

Unfortunately, he was about halfway through the script, and if someone asked him what the movie was about, he wouldn't have been able to tell them. No matter how hard he tried, his thoughts kept wandering. And for reasons he couldn't explain, they kept wandering in the same direction.

Matt hadn't seen Liv since Saturday. Around four o'clock, she'd shown up to return his SUV. She stepped inside long enough for him to put on his shoes so that he could give her a ride home. During the drive, they'd discussed some of the events the town had scheduled for the summer, including the big Fourth of July celebration. In all the years he'd been coming to Orchard Harbor, he'd somehow never been there on the Fourth.

Not once did anything personal come up in their conversation. Once he'd pulled up to the curb at her building, she'd thanked him again for his help, hopped out, and disappeared through the door marked Ocean View Catering. Despite the unexpected urge to follow her, he pulled back into traffic. He'd returned home not long before Owen and his wife arrived.

Although it wasn't his business, he'd brought up the news Liv had shared with him on Friday night. Owen had confirmed the details using his own choice words to describe Fredrick Waldman. And much like his sister, Owen didn't have much hope that the family would be able to purchase the building.

When Matt reached the bottom of the page, he stopped. According to the sentence he'd just read, he was having a conversation with a character named Daisy. Unfortunately, he didn't remember the character entering the scene. And hadn't Daisy died during the opening scene?

Matt flipped back to the beginning and scanned the pages. According to page six, Remington died, not Daisy. He didn't remember who the hell Remington was, and at the moment, he didn't care.

Tossing the script aside, he grabbed his cell phone and searched his contact list for Austin Windsor, the local agent who'd helped him buy his Orchard Harbor home.

"Good afternoon, Windsor Realty," a man's voice said after several rings.

"Hi, Austin. It's Matt Sherbrooke."

"It's nice to hear from you. What can I do for you?"

You're only asking. It doesn't hurt to ask.

"Can you find out if any offers have been made for the building on Main Street?"

"Are you referring to 5 Main Street or 26 Main Street?"

He hadn't known there were multiple buildings for sale on the street. "I'm not sure of the street number." He never paid attention to those when he drove through town. "But it's where the Ocean View Grill is located."

"That would be number 5. Yeah, I can call Dennis and find out. Are you interested in buying the property?"

The answer should be no. He was a musician with an emerging acting career. He knew nothing about being a landlord. Even if he did, he visited Orchard Harbor maybe once or twice a year and spent the rest of his time thousands of miles away. He had no business purchasing commercial property in town. But all that logic went out the window when he thought about what Liv had said and the look on her face Friday night.

He'd looked up Rick Desmond. According to his profile, Rick was a managing partner for Timberlane Development, a company founded by his father and responsible for acquisitions. And as Liv told him, Rick had helped the company acquire and develop multiple projects along the East Coast, with his most recent project being the one near Sandy Cove. Out of curiosity, he'd driven by the beach yesterday, and it looked nothing like the area he remembered. He didn't want the same thing to happen here. That was the only reason he was remotely interested in the property.

"Maybe." For now, he couldn't commit to anything more.

"I'll call Dennis as soon as I get a chance. I'm showing a couple some homes in the area this afternoon, and they should be here any minute. When I know something, I'll let you know. If he asks, do you want me to tell him you might be interested?"

Matt saw no harm in doing that. "Sure."

Two hours later, Matt turned onto Main Street and passed the small, stand-alone coffee shop, which had a For Sale sign out front. He remembered that there had been an antique store there last year, not a coffee shop. Either way, it must be the other property Austin referred to. Unlike where the restaurant was, though, he didn't see Rick Desmond being interested in the property. It wasn't large enough for the type of projects he was known for, not to mention it didn't have a waterfront view.

A car pulled away from the curb, leaving an empty spot just in time, and Matt snagged it before anyone else could. More than one person glanced at his car as they walked down the sidewalk. He didn't blame them. One of his newest toys, a Ferrari he'd purchased in December, it was a gorgeous vehicle and more fun than any car probably had a right to be, which was why he'd used it for the drive from Florida to Maine.

Matt checked his watch as he stepped onto the sidewalk. When he stopped by last week around this time, Liv had been at the restaurant. That didn't mean she was there every afternoon, though. For all he knew, she might only fill in when someone called in sick.

He was about to head toward the restaurant when the very person who'd occupied his thoughts far too often lately came into view. She had her cell phone next to her ear as she approached the small conference table in the unit next door.

Rather than enter, he stood outside and watched her. He didn't have many female friends. That wasn't to say he didn't know many females. However, he considered very few friends. The majority were either women he'd worked with on projects or dated. Although he wouldn't call Liv a close friend, he suspected she could be. While he had a multitude of friends, his list of true close friends outside of his family was short. And for reasons he couldn't explain, he wanted to add Liv to that list.

Or maybe he wanted more.

Liar.

Matt would prefer to ignore his annoying conscience, but he couldn't. There was no "maybe." His thoughts regarding Liv lately had fallen about as far out of the friend zone as possible.

A door chime announced his arrival. With her phone still attached to her ear, Liv looked up and waved, then gestured for him to sit.

He didn't hesitate to accept the offer. While she continued her conversation with someone who he assumed was a client based on what he heard, he took in his surroundings. The office designer had taken full advantage of the space. They'd also made it feel less like a cold work area and more like a homey spot to meet friends and discuss whatever came to mind. Newspaper articles praising Ocean View Catering hung on the far wall, and Matt wondered just how long the catering operation had been in business. Until the previous week, he hadn't even realized the restaurant had branched out, but if the framed articles were any indication, it wasn't a new development.

"Perfect. I think the menu options you selected will satisfy all your guests. I'll add the details to your account," Liv said, pulling Matt's attention away from his surroundings and to her. "If you think of any changes you'd like to make, just call or email me."

Liv nodded a few more times to whatever the client said before ending the call and closing her eyes as she put the device on the table.

He waited several seconds before speaking. "Difficult client?"

Slowly, Liv opened her eyes, revealing the most beautiful eyes he'd ever seen. They reminded him of the ocean during a storm. Somehow, they appeared both gray and blue at the same time. How had he not noticed them before today?

"I wouldn't call Gina difficult. More last minute. She's getting married in July and only signed a contract with me Friday afternoon."

"Seriously?" Even to him, who knew nothing about planning a wedding, it seemed to be cutting it close. Didn't most people spend months or years planning for their big day?

Liv pulled out the chair across from him and sat. "Yep. Gina and her fiancé were in here when the delivery van was hit. When she first called last month to set up an appointment, she gave me a few possible dates in September, but things changed." Frowning, she propped her chin on her palm. "Considering everything that's going on, it's probably a good thing they changed the date."

"Any updates on that front?" If Waldman had accepted the offer from the Middletons, Liv wouldn't be frowning.

"No. Dad and Grandpa met with Shirley over at Windsor Realty again earlier today, and she submitted our offer."

If Austin called back and told him one offer had been made, Matt now knew who'd made it. And he wouldn't submit one of his own, because at some point between his conversation with the realtor and walking in here, he'd made his decision. If it meant saving the building and the businesses that called it home, he'd make Waldman an offer he'd never refuse.

"Gramps is optimistic, but he doesn't know the Worm as well as I do. He's not going to accept it. He's going to either flat-out reject it or come back with a counteroffer that's out of our range. Either way, it's out of my control."

Matt assumed her comment meant she wanted to change the subject. He could respect that. "Where's the last-minute wedding being held?"

"One of the houses on Windy Bluff Lane. My clients and the owners are close friends."

Unless something had been recently constructed, there were only two homes on that road. He'd looked at one perhaps eight months before he purchased his home. Although beautiful, it hadn't felt right, so he'd passed on it.

"Are you headed to the restaurant?" Liv asked as the sound of an oven timer came from her phone, but she didn't reach for it.

"No. I wanted to see if you were busy tonight, but I don't have your phone number." A minor problem he intended to rectify today.

Liv's lips parted, drawing his attention to them, but no sound came out as the hand resting under her chin hit the table. "Uh, no, I'm not busy, but won't, uh.... Is that a good idea?"

Matt shrugged. "Why wouldn't it be?"

"In case you forgot, you're a world-famous musician. Oh yeah, and you've made a few mildly successful movies." Liv's voice continued with a hint of humor and sarcasm. "There's probably a 100 percent chance that people will ask for your autograph or to have their picture taken with you. Do you really feel like dealing with that tonight?"

Most people, especially women, wanted to be seen with him. It sounded like Liv wasn't one of them. "If it happens, it won't bother me. And you'd be surprised how often people assume I'm just a look-alike and leave me alone. But if you'd be more comfortable, we can get takeout and play pool or watch a movie at my house."

When he'd woken up this morning, he'd had no intention of spending time with Liv or anyone else tonight. But now it was precisely what he wanted, and it didn't matter to him if they hung out at his house or went somewhere in town.

"You had me at pool." Smiling, she rubbed her hands together.

"Why do I suddenly have the feeling I'm in big trouble?"

"I don't know what you're talking about." Liv's innocent expression didn't fool him.

"If you're ready, we can head to my house now."

"I have a few things I need to finish up here." Her phone received another text message. This time, she picked it up. Either it was an automated text or one that didn't require a response because she set it back on the table.

A glance at his watch told him it was only four thirty. "I don't mind waiting."

"If I get a ride from you, you'll have to drive me home later. It makes more sense for me to meet you at your house."

She made a good point. It did make more sense for her to drive herself, but that didn't mean he had to like it. "Come on by whenever you're ready."

"I'll probably be over in about an hour. Do you want me to bring dinner?"

"Nah. I'll order something and pick it up on my way home. How does pizza sound?"

"You must be a mind reader, because I was thinking about making pizza tonight. I'll eat anything on it except anchovies and buffalo chicken."

Both items, along with pineapple, had always seemed like odd toppings for pizza to him. Then again, he liked scallops on his, so maybe he wasn't the best person to decide what should or shouldn't be on a pizza. Standing, Matt pushed his chair closer to the table. "I'll see you in about an hour."

* * *

The door closed behind Matt, and Liv shook her head as she leaned back in her chair. Earlier, when she'd heard the door chimes, she'd expected to see Emma standing there because, unlike the other businesses along Main Street, customers didn't walk in off the sidewalk. Instead, they came when they had scheduled appointments, and she had none today. However, it wasn't uncommon for Emma to cross the street and visit.

To say she'd been surprised when she saw Matt standing there would be the understatement of the decade. She expected to see him in the restaurant when he was in town. The man had to eat, and in her opinion, the Ocean View Grill was the best place to go. But while she offered samples to clients if they asked, she didn't serve food, so Matt had no reason to come in here. Yet there he'd stood, looking far sexier than any man had a right to, and it had taken all her self-control not to immediately ask why he was there. Actually, she was rather proud of herself for waiting as long as she had before asking if he was headed to the restaurant. If he'd said yes, his unexpected visit would have made a little more sense. After all, it was easy to see inside her office from the sidewalk, so he would've known she was there. And although they weren't BFFs, she would've understood if he'd decided to say hello before going on about his day.

But that hadn't been the case. If she hadn't been sitting when he shared his reason for the visit, Liv would've found her butt on the floor. Somehow, she'd managed to keep her mouth shut and not share the first thought that came to mind, which had been "You must be either really bored or desperate." Even without sharing that statement, she'd sounded like an idiot when she answered him. In her defense, she'd been about to ask if his girlfriend would mind if they spent time together when she realized that wasn't any of her business, and she had to come up with another reason that it might not be a good idea if they hung out.

I wanted to see if you were busy tonight, but I don't have your phone number. Matt's words repeated in her head. He could've offered her the keys and title to his Ferrari outside, and she wouldn't have been any more surprised.

"He's being friendly because he's bored," Liv said to the empty chair across from her. It wasn't like Orchard Harbor was filled with nightclubs or whatever other type of places he spent his time at. "And it's not like he knows a lot of people in town."

Actually, other than her family, he might not know anyone else in town. Yep, boredom and a lack of friends in the area explained his invitation this afternoon.

With that argument settled, she retreated to her desk.

Before she did anything else, she needed to add Gina's meal selections to her file. While Liv waited for her computer to power on, she checked her cell phone. She'd received one text message while she'd been talking to Gina. She'd received two more during Matt's visit. The first was an automated one letting her know that her electric bill payment had been processed. The second and third messages were from Emma.

Emma: Phoebe and I are going to Northside Tavern for karaoke night. Do you want to come with us?

Every Wednesday night, the popular bar and grill down the street held karaoke night. For much of the year, only locals showed up. In another few weeks, though, the place would be packed with tourists or people with summer homes in town. While she enjoyed going with her friends, she preferred going in the offseason when every seat in the place wasn't occupied. So, if she didn't already have plans with Matt, she'd accept the invitation because this might be her last chance to go for several months.

She read the next message from Emma before responding.

Emma: Who's the new client?

Emma needed to spend less time looking out the store window and more time taking care of her plants.

Liv didn't want to lie. At the same time, if she said Matt wasn't a client, Emma would want to know why he'd been there.

Liv: Sorry, I can't tonight. I have plans. And Matt's not a client. He's a friend of Owen's, and he stopped in to say hi.

Liv reread her message before sending it. She wasn't lying; she'd just left out a few minor details, such as Matt's last name and the fact that Emma knew of him.

Rather than another message showing up, Liv's phone rang.

"Since when does your brother have friends who drive Ferraris?"

"When do you actually work?" Liv asked, avoiding the question.

"It's not my fault. I was redoing the window display when Owen's friend parked his car and went inside."

Emma had Liv there. She changed the front window display almost weekly, and if she'd been working on it, it would've been impossible to miss Matt's car outside.

"So I'll ask my question again. Since when does your brother have friends who are wealthy enough to purchase an Italian sports car?" Emma asked.

For half a second, she considered lying and telling Emma that Matt had rented the car. It wasn't unheard of for people to do that on vacation. Last winter, her parents had rented a Corvette when they'd visited wine country.

"Matt and Owen were roommates in college." Liv had never told anyone, not even Emma, that Owen's former roommate was not only the lead singer of Eclipse but also a member of the wealthy Sherbrooke family.

"Oh. I don't suppose he's single?"

At least she could answer that question honestly without leaving out details. "I don't know. But have you forgotten about Brian?"

"You know I'm only kidding."

She'd known that but hadn't been able to resist.

"What are you doing tonight?"

Not surprisingly, curiosity oozed from Emma's voice. Lately, except for the time she spent with her brother and sister-in-law on the weekends when they came up, all of Liv's plans were with Emma or Phoebe.

"Matt invited me over to play pool."

"As in Owen's friend Matt? The one who owns that beautiful sports car."

"Yeah, he has a house in town." It was more like a mansion, but the word "house" was close enough.

"Interesting."

She didn't care for Emma's tone.

"You two must know each other well if he's inviting you to

his house. How come you've never mentioned him to me before now?"

"We're not that close of friends. But other than me and my family, he doesn't know many people in town, and I think he's bored. Orchard Harbor isn't exactly an international hotspot."

"If you say so," Emma replied, sounding unconvinced. "But if your plans change or you and Matt want to join us, Phoebe and I are going to the Northside Tavern around seven."

"I'll keep that in mind," Liv promised, even though she already knew she'd never suggest that they meet her friends. The last place Matt Sherbrooke would ever want to go was the Northside Tavern for karaoke night.

After parking, Liv sat and admired the exterior of Matt's house, something she hadn't been able to do the last few times she was there. The home consisted of two floors. She couldn't see the back of the house from here, but there was no doubt that at least one deck was attached, providing Matt and his guests with a place to relax and enjoy the fantastic view. Unlike her parents' home, which until recently only had a one-car detached garage, his attached garage could house four vehicles. Clearly, someone took care of the grounds, because they were perfectly manicured and full of color.

She had no desire for a house as large as the one before her, but she wouldn't mind having a yard filled with flowers and a vegetable garden. While her apartment was convenient and within her price range, it made gardening impossible, and the only time she had flowers was when she splurged and bought some from Exquisite Flowers.

The front door opened moments after she rang the bell.

"Good timing," Matt said in greeting, gracing her with a who-turned-up-the-heat smile, and then stepped back so she could enter. "I only got home about ten minutes ago. It took Fireside forever to get our order done."

While the town was home to four pizza restaurants, only Fireside Pizzeria prepared theirs in a brick oven, making it one of the more popular establishments, and customers often had to wait longer than if they'd gone somewhere else. In her opinion, the wait was worth it.

"What's in the bag?" Matt asked with his eyes narrowed.

"Cue stick. What else?"

"I was hoping you were going to say your flute or clarinet."

"I've never touched either in my life. But if you want, I can go home and get my guitar. It won't take me long."

Matt closed and locked the door behind her. "No need. I've got two here. You can borrow one if you want. I knew Owen played, but I didn't know you did too."

Liv nodded. "Owen actually started lessons after me. I also play the piano. But I can't go home and get one of those."

She would also never ask to borrow one of his guitars because, while she played well, she'd never be able to perform for Matt, a man who played his guitar and sang for stadiums packed with people.

"Do you want to eat first or while we play?"

"Whatever is fine with me."

What she really wanted was a tour of the house. The little she'd seen of it so far was beautiful, and she wondered what the rest of it looked like. If Emma or Phoebe owned the home, she wouldn't think twice about asking, but not Matt. He might see the request as an invasion of his privacy, which, in a way, it was.

"Let me grab the pizzas from the kitchen, and then we can start a game."

After a quick stop in the kitchen, Matt led her down a hallway. Unlike at her apartment and her parents' home, there were no family photos on the walls. Instead, professional-looking photos of the ocean and various beaches provided the only decoration and left her longing for weather suitable for relaxing on the sand. The last one on the left captured her attention.

"Do you know where this is?" Liv pointed toward the photo.

"I took that one in St. Barts."

Thanks to the palm trees, she already knew the picture was taken in a tropical area, and it didn't surprise her that he'd visited there. She was surprised that he'd taken it, though, because it was as good as the ones Phoebe did, and she was a professional photographer.

"I took all these pictures," he explained, gesturing around him.

"They're great. I thought they were professionally done."

"Thanks. It's a hobby of mine. I took all the landscape photos hanging around the house. If you're interested, I can show you the others later."

Maybe she would get a tour of the house after all. "I'd like that."

At the end of the hall, he stopped at a door and gestured for her to enter. At least half the size of her entire apartment, he'd set the room up with entertainment in mind. A pool table, a bar complete with barstools, and two small high bar-style tables occupied the left side of the room. A flat-screen television hung on the opposite wall, accompanied by a large sofa and several comfortable-looking chairs, all positioned for perfect viewing. Although, if this were her house, she wouldn't come in here to watch television. No, she'd come in here for the view the floor-to-ceiling windows provided. Much like the hallway, this room didn't contain any family photos either.

"Would you like a glass of wine or a cocktail?"

Liv pulled her eyes away from the fantastic view outside to the one now standing near the bar. "Some red wine would be nice."

She watched as he poured each of them a glass of wine and searched her mind for a safe, unintrusive topic. "Did my brother tell you he was offered a promotion at work?" If anyone deserved it, Owen did. He regularly put in sixty-hour weeks.

"Owen mentioned he was one of the candidates," Matt answered, handing her a wineglass and an empty plate. "Help yourself."

Liv eyed the three pizzas he'd set on the bar. Either Matt was a mind reader, or they had similar tastes in pizza toppings.

"The company offered him the position on Monday." She added two slices of pizza to her plate and then took a sip of her drink.

"I'll have to call and congratulate him."

She should focus on her food or even assemble her cue stick. However, her eyes had ideas of their own and followed Matt as he walked toward the rack of pool cues on the wall. For the sake of the female population, the man should be forced to wear a shapeless potato sack. Though even that might not hide his broad shoulders and sexy arms. His T-shirt covered his chest and stomach, but judging by the way it clung to him, both would leave her drooling like a baby teething if she were ever within ten feet of him without a T-shirt on.

Before she could stop it, an image of Matt lounging on the beach materialized.

Don't go there.

She'd fallen headfirst in love with Matt the moment he walked into her parents' kitchen that Thanksgiving. Countless times, she'd stared at her bedroom ceiling and pictured them kissing or taking a walk along the beach at sunset—not that he'd noticed her. And why would he? He'd been a college freshman, and she'd been a high school student with braces and bad acne. While she'd never stopped finding him attractive, she no longer wasted her time daydreaming about him.

Liv mentally slapped the back of her head, dislodging the tantalizing image. Of course, when she got home, she might turn on *One Last Heist* and fast-forward to the scene where Matt exited the bathroom wearing nothing but a strategically placed towel.

"Owen's not sure he's going to accept it. He'd have to travel a lot." Yep, if she kept talking about her brother, maybe she wouldn't blurt out something inappropriate.

"Didn't he know that when he applied?"

"Owen didn't apply. His boss recommended him for this new position in the department. If not for the travel, he would've already accepted it."

"How much is a lot?"

She'd asked her brother the same question. "He said it would vary, but on average, he'd be gone ten to fifteen days every month. He doesn't want to be away from Jenny that much."

"I can understand that. Time apart can be hard on a relationship."

Was he speaking from experience? If the woman he'd been photographed with was his girlfriend, he hadn't mentioned her once.

Matt reached for his drink and gestured toward the pool table. "Why don't you break?"

Five

ALTHOUGH HE CONSIDERED himself a better-than-average player, Matt had suspected he was in trouble when Liv walked in carrying her own pool cue. After all, it wasn't a common item to own. Still, he hadn't expected to lose all the games they'd played—something that wouldn't have happened if he'd been facing off against his cousin Adam, who played just as well as Liv, because Matt wouldn't have been more focused on his opponent than the game.

He'd spent time around some of the sexiest women in the world and not been as distracted as he was tonight. He didn't know what it was about Liv, but he couldn't keep his eyes off her. It hadn't helped that each time she'd leaned over to take a shot, her T-shirt had dipped just enough to provide a tantalizing view of her cleavage. And don't get him started about what the position had done for her ass. All night, he'd fought the urge to place his hands on her perfectly shaped butt.

Liv made her final shot, once again winning the match, and leaned the cue stick against the table. "I think I'm done for the night."

"Tired of beating me already?"

"You said it, not me," she said, holding up her hands.

"Give me some time to practice, and we'll have a rematch."

"Just name the time and place, my friend."

Liv smiled, drawing his eyes to her lips, and once again, the need to feel them against his took hold of him. What would she do if he lowered his mouth to hers? Before he realized it, he took a step closer to her.

"I probably should've told you before we started that, until last year, I played in a pool league every Tuesday night," she continued.

"Perhaps I should hire you to give me some lessons before our rematch."

"I don't think people usually ask their competition for help. You might be better off asking my dad or brother. You can also try YouTube. It has some great videos about improving your game."

"Maybe I will."

He'd invited her over for pizza and pool. They'd finished both, so there was no reason for her to stay. But he wasn't ready for her to go either. Liv picked up the pool cue, but before she could take it apart, he removed it from her hands and set it aside again.

Except for outright asking her to stay longer, which she might find odd, he could think of only one way to get her to stick around. "Since we're done here for now, why don't I show you the other photos I've taken?" She'd seemed interested in seeing them when he'd offered earlier.

Nodding ever so slightly, she ran her tongue across her bottom lip, and he imagined himself doing the very same thing. "I, uh, forgot about those. Sure. I'd love to see them before I go."

Few people knew of his love for photography, and those who did had never shown any interest in seeing his work. Maybe Liv didn't have any genuine interest either and she was merely being polite. However, that didn't seem to be the case as he showed her the various photos he'd taken over the years. While she spent more time admiring some than others, usually the ones she lingered on were his favorites too. She had thoughtful comments about each one, and multiple times, she claimed they were as good as the work her friend, a professional photographer, did. While she might be exaggerating, he appreciated the praise.

Liv pointed at the framed photo on the wall. "This one might be my favorite so far."

They'd completed a tour of the first floor and much of the second and were standing outside his bedroom. Although he wouldn't label it his favorite, it was definitely among his top five. He'd taken it from the rooftop of the house at sunset. That night, the sky had been a canvas of colors, almost as if a painter had taken a paintbrush to it.

She looked away from the photo and at him. "The area looks familiar. Where did you take it?"

"I'll show you." Matt reached for her hand before his brain registered his intention.

As he started down the hall toward the staircase to the rooftop patio, he waited for her to pull her hand away or say something. Neither happened, so he kept walking.

"Now this is a view." Liv stepped through the doorway and paused as the scene opened before her.

He had to agree. In fact, he'd known this was the house he'd been searching for when he and his real estate agent stepped out here.

Now that they'd reached their destination, he felt a little silly standing there holding her hand. So, although not what he wanted, Matt released it as they crossed the patio to the spot where he'd stood while taking the photo.

"I took that picture from here the first week I owned the house."

"If this were my house, I'd be up here all the time. I might even sleep up here every once in a while," she said, turning toward him.

He'd never slept up there, but more than once he'd lain on the sofa and stared up at the stars while listening to the ocean. Right now, though, it wasn't the view or the sky that held his attention.

After tucking the strands of hair that had escaped her loose ponytail behind her ear, Matt trailed his fingers across her jaw and lowered his head toward hers. "I do spend a lot of time up here."

Liv's gaze briefly shifted away from his eyes to his mouth, and he knew the moment she realized his intent. When she didn't move away, he eliminated a little more of the space between his lips and their intended target.

"I'd love it if you spent some time with me out here."

Matt touched his lips to Liv's before she could reply. A tiny part of his brain insisted he should keep the kiss brief and urged him to back off. He ignored it, because now that he'd felt her lips against his, stopping was impossible. And when Liv's arms slipped over his shoulders and her fingertips brushed against his neck, he took it as a sign that she didn't want him to stop either.

Sooner than he'd liked, she ended the kiss and looked at him. Or perhaps it would be more accurate to say she studied him. He didn't need to read her mind; her expression and eyes told him it was working a mile a minute—on what precisely, he didn't know. He just hoped he liked whatever conclusion she reached.

She shoved the hands that had been caressing his neck moments before into her pockets and nodded toward the ocean. "I'd have to be crazy to pass up an opportunity to enjoy this view."

He was used to women throwing themselves at him. Women who didn't care how long their involvement might last as long as they could walk away saying they'd had sex with him. Not that he had a lot of one-night stands, but there were a few in his past. He was also familiar with women who used their association with him to further their careers. And don't get him started on the handful of women he'd gone out with, both in college and since his music career took off, because of the dollar amount in his bank account. Any of those types, he knew how to deal with.

Liv didn't fall into any of those categories, and he didn't know what to do about the uncertainty vibe she was giving off.

"This view was what sold me on this place. The one from the deck off the kitchen is almost as spectacular. Why don't we go check it out?"

He could practically hear the gears turning in her head as she looked at him, and he expected her to turn down the offer and leave.

"Sure." She brushed away the same piece of silky blonde hair he'd tucked behind her ear, and before Liv could put her hand back into her pocket, he reached for it.

Once they were in the kitchen, he paused. "Interested in some ice cream?"

He wasn't hungry, but dessert would keep her there longer. Not to mention, whether he was hungry or not, he was always up for some ice cream.

"Depends. What kind do you have?"

"Name a flavor and I probably have it." If he had one weakness, it was sweets, and ice cream was his favorite, no matter the flavor or the temperature outside.

"Coffee."

"Got it. Do you want one scoop or two?" he asked, opening the freezer.

"Wow, I don't think you have enough ice cream in there. Are you planning on opening a stand for the summer?"

She wasn't touching him, but he could sense her standing mere inches behind him. If he turned and took a step or two, he could wrap his arms around her and taste her lips—something he fully planned to do again tonight. But something, maybe the memory of her uncertainty upstairs, told him now wasn't the right time.

"Don't tell anyone, but I might be addicted to ice cream." Matt turned in time to see Liv grin.

"Your secret is safe with me, my friend. And I'll have two scoops, please."

Before his return to Orchard Harbor, he'd considered Liv something between an acquaintance and a friend. Now he wanted to be more than a friend, and he knew exactly when his feelings had started to change—the night she'd returned his car and brought him dinner.

"Coffee isn't a flavor most people buy. Is it your favorite too?"

Liv's question brought his thoughts back to the here and

now. "I'd say it's in my top five." Matt filled a bowl with coffee ice cream and added a spoon to it.

"I said two scoops, not enough ice cream for two people," she said, accepting the bowl he'd filled.

"Looks like two scoops to me."

Liv's smile seemed to fill the kitchen with warm sunshine as she shook her head. "You need a smaller ice cream scoop, then." Bowl in hand, she leaned her back against the counter. "If coffee isn't your favorite flavor, what is?"

"If I'm having a cone or a bowl like this, then my favorite is pistachio, followed closely by strawberry. When I get a sundae or banana split, it must be made with vanilla."

"Pistachio is okay. Strawberry, I'll only eat if it doesn't have pieces of frozen strawberries in it."

"Without the strawberries, it's not real strawberry ice cream." Since he already had the coffee out, he filled his bowl and then returned the container to the freezer. "Do you need anything else before we head outside?"

"Nope. I'm all set."

After grabbing a stack of napkins and his bowl, he led Liv outside.

Rather than dig into her dessert, Liv put the bowl down on a table and pulled out her cell phone. "I need a picture of this. The sky is gorgeous tonight."

He doubted anyone would argue with her. Various shades of pink painted the sky, much like in the photo she'd admired inside.

"Which do you think has a better view, the rooftop or here?" he asked while she snapped a few pictures. He dug into his overflowing bowl of ice cream as Liv considered his question.

She checked the photos she'd taken before setting the device down on the table. "I'm honestly not sure. They're both amazing."

He'd intentionally waited for her to sit, hoping she'd opt for the outdoor love seat rather than one of the comfortable chairs. Now, as she lifted the first spoonful of ice cream toward her lips, he watched as she considered her seating options. When she opted for the love seat, he took that as a sign they were on the same page tonight, and he sat next to her.

"Yeah, I know what you mean. There's something about the ocean that's mesmerizing."

* * *

Forget the ocean—she found *him* mesmerizing. Liv shoved an overflowing spoonful of ice cream into her mouth and tried not to read too much into the fact that not only had Matt kissed her upstairs, but he sat so close now. But damn, it wasn't easy. It didn't help that all her teenage dreams were pushing their way out of the little box she'd locked them in a long time ago.

"So, if you weren't here right now, what would you be doing?" Matt asked before eating another large spoonful of ice cream.

Heat from his body seemed to jump the space between them and invade her body, making it almost impossible to think. Either that or her internal thermometer was suddenly stuck at 105 degrees. Either way, she needed to focus on something other than their kiss or the fact that she wanted a repeat performance, so she was grateful he'd thought of a conversation topic.

"I probably would've met Emma and Phoebe at the North-side Tavern. Every Wednesday is karaoke night. Emma invited me right after you left my office this afternoon. She even suggested we join them when I told her I had plans with a friend. And if I didn't go there, I'd probably be at home watching television or reading." Or she'd be doing laundry, but there was no way she was sharing that with him.

He might find her response borderline pathetic, and Liv wished she could've come back with something more interesting. However, she wasn't going to lie to him either.

"Karaoke? I've never done that."

Big surprise.

"I would've gone with you tonight if you'd rather have done that."

Now that wasn't something she'd expected him to say.

69

"Maybe some other time." Although she made the statement, she didn't anticipate Matt joining her and her friends for karaoke anytime soon. She wasn't even sure she'd be spending time with him again, despite his comment and kiss upstairs.

"You said they do it every Wednesday, so how about next week?"

If she'd just swallowed anything more solid than ice cream, she would've choked. "The closer it gets to Memorial Day, the busier the place is. Going next week might not be a good idea."

She could just imagine the insanity if Matt Sherbrooke, lead singer for Eclipse, walked onto the stage to perform karaoke next week.

"I'm not sure I'll go again until the fall." No doubt by then, Matt would be long gone.

"Trust me, crowds don't bother me. But if you're not comfortable around them, I understand. I have a cousin who sometimes has panic attacks if there are too many people around."

If he wanted to believe that was the reason behind her reluctance, she wouldn't try to change his mind. She would, however, move the conversation away from herself.

"What about you? If you weren't here, what would you be doing?"

Matt ate another spoonful of ice cream before speaking. "Do you mean here in Orchard Harbor or here with you?"

Liv shrugged. She didn't care as long as the conversation remained away from her less-than-exciting life. "Either. Both."

"If I weren't in Orchard Harbor, I might still be in Florida."

When he'd been in college with Owen, California had been home for him. For some reason, she'd assumed that was still the case. But now that he'd mentioned Florida, she had noticed his Ferrari had Florida license plates.

"Is that home for you?"

"It's where I spend most of my time when the band isn't touring, so I guess it's home."

His response raised more questions than it answered, but she wasn't going to dig any deeper, because if she did, he might do the same.

"And if I weren't here with you, I'd most likely be sitting out here eating ice cream and reading." Matt placed his ice cream on the table and draped his arm across the back of the love seat.

Much like his earlier statement about them joining her friends for karaoke, his answer now surprised her. But maybe it shouldn't. Orchard Harbor was known for many things, but its exciting nightlife wasn't one of them—a fact that suited her fine, but she imagined it might grow old to Matt.

"What do you like to read?" She'd always been a fan of historical fiction and fantasy, although she did have one romance author who she really enjoyed reading. In fact, she owned every novel she'd written to date. Unfortunately, the author didn't release books often.

When his thumb brushed against her shoulder the first time, she assumed it was an accident. But then he did it again, and a ripple of excitement started in the center of her chest and spread. It'd been a long time since she'd experienced anything remotely close to what she felt now, and she hoped Matt didn't move his hand anytime soon. Then again, maybe it would be for the best if he did before she started to get any ideas that Matt Sherbrooke was interested in her, because while rock stars might fall for small-town girls in the movies, it didn't happen in real life, which didn't bother her in the least.

Yep, keep telling yourself that, and eventually you'll believe it.

"Mostly suspense. My favorite contemporary author is Curt Hilton. But occasionally I go for a fantasy novel like *The Lord of the Rings*."

She'd seen Curt Hilton's books in her aunt's bookstore but had never read one of them. As for *The Lord of the Rings*, she'd both read the books and seen the movies. While the movies were great in her opinion, she enjoyed the books more.

"I pegged you as more of a romance novel junkie." Liv managed to contain her smile.

"Seriously? Why would you think that?"

She'd only finished about half the ice cream that Matt had

given her, but there was no way she could eat another bite, so she put her bowl next to his. "I read somewhere you write a lot of the music for Eclipse, and you've got some seriously romantic ballads. I bet couples use them as their wedding dance song. Since you're so good at writing romantic songs, I thought maybe you enjoyed romance novels. Maybe even used them for inspiration."

Matt changed the angle of his body slightly and moved his hand from her shoulder to the back of her neck. "I've never touched one. But maybe I should. Are there any authors you suggest?"

"The only romance author I'll read is Lynn Kurland." Later, she'd regret this question, but she was going to ask anyway. "How do you come up with the lyrics, then?" She'd taken a creative writing class in high school because she needed another English credit, not because she enjoyed it or had a creative bone in her body, unless it involved creating a new recipe.

His fingertip skimmed across the skin on her neck, setting off internal fireworks to rival those the town set off on the Fourth of July.

"Jordan and I write about 50 percent of the lyrics together, including a lot of the songs you're thinking of. I know Jordan drew on some personal experiences for some. For a few, I did too, but sometimes I visualize a scene in my head, and it plays like a movie. Then I turn that into a song."

She couldn't picture Jordan Mead, the band's bass player, writing the lyrics to "Loving You" or "If I Had You." Then again, the old saying "don't judge a book by its cover" existed for a reason.

"You and Jordan wrote 'Loving You' together?"

Matt's lips slowly descended toward hers, allowing Liv plenty of time to move—not that she had any plans of doing that.

"No, I wrote that one." He brushed his lips against hers. "But we did work on 'If I Had You' together." Once again, he brushed his lips against hers, only this time they lingered slightly longer. "Jordan wrote 'Our Last Dance.'"

Matt touched his lips to hers again. Only this time, it was

anything but brief, and as he deepened the kiss, he teased her lips with his tongue until she opened for him.

And as if someone had snapped their fingers, the outside world disappeared. At that moment, the only thing she was aware of was the sweet taste of coffee ice cream that lingered on his lips and the feel of his hand buried in her hair.

The instrumental opening to "Loving You" echoed in the distance, and for half a second, Liv wondered where the music was coming from. When she realized it was her phone, she pulled away, unsure whether she should be thanking the device or cursing it.

She waited for him to comment on her ringtone. Instead, he skimmed his fingers over her shoulder and across her arm. "Do you need to answer that?"

"I'll call whoever it is back." After kissing Matt, her brain wasn't capable of carrying on an intelligent conversation with one of her friends.

Reaching for her hand, he laced their fingers together. "Do you have plans tomorrow?"

"I'm covering Maggie's lunch shift."

"What time are you done?"

With Matt sitting so close and holding her hand, thinking straight was impossible. Hell, she was lucky she could even breathe at the moment. But when she got home, she'd sit down and examine what had transpired tonight and what it might mean. In the meantime, she had to answer him. "About four at the restaurant, but I need to spend a little time at my office. We have two events this weekend. But I should be done by about five."

"Let's do something when you're done. Whatever you want."

If they went to a place like the Northside Tavern or Heavenly Ice Cream, Matt might be bombarded with fans. He might not mind that, but she'd rather not be dragged into it, especially since she didn't even know what was really going on between them yet. Of course, that was assuming anything *was* going on between them. Maybe Matt had kissed her because he was bored or lonely. Tomorrow he might get out of bed, pack his bags, and head back to Florida, and another year might pass before he stepped foot in town again.

"I've been playing with some new recipes. Why don't you come over, and I'll cook dinner for us?"

Friends could have dinner together. If he came over tomorrow and things remained strictly platonic, she'd know tonight had been a fluke. A once-in-a-lifetime chance to experience some of her teenage fantasies. Really, how many people got an opportunity like that?

"I'll bring dessert."

Six

LIV DROPPED her cell phone on the nightstand and fell back on her bed. During the ride home, she had focused on driving rather than what she really wanted to think about now— replaying the last several hours and maybe figuring out what it all meant, assuming it meant anything at all.

When Matt stopped by the office and suggested they spend time together tonight, a tiny part of her wished it was because he was interested in her. Who wouldn't want Matt Sherbrooke interested in them? As far as she could tell, the man was the total package. He was gorgeous, successful, talented, and genuinely a nice person. Regardless of her secret desire, she'd known he'd only asked because her brother wasn't around, and she was the only person in town, except her parents, that he knew.

Now, though, she wasn't as confident in her assessment.

Matt kissed me.

Correction: He kissed me multiple times.

If someone had told her this morning that Matt would kiss her, she would've either laughed in their face or told them to wake up from whatever dream they were having. But not only had they shared one kiss, they'd shared three.

Closing her eyes, she replayed those moments. The first kiss had been almost tentative, as if he was waiting for some sign from her. And when she put her arms around his neck, he turned the intensity up. There had been nothing tentative about their second, and she was glad she'd been sitting down for it. The final kiss he'd given her after walking her out to her car had fallen somewhere between the other two.

Thank God.

If he'd kissed her again like he had while sitting outside, she'd still be in Matt's driveway trying to remember how to drive.

But what did tonight mean?

Some people spent their evenings watching sports or exercising. Did Matt like to spend his evenings kissing whatever woman he brought home?

He was a rock star. They had a reputation for sleeping with a different woman in every city where they performed. And she had seen him photographed with countless women over the years, including the pretty brunette a couple of weeks ago. Although she didn't doubt that he'd dated a lot of women, she couldn't picture him hooking up with a groupie each time the band stopped to perform. She could picture the other members of Eclipse doing that, especially Travis Hart, the band's drummer, but not Matt. But he was also an actor. Maybe the Matt she knew wasn't the real him. Perhaps he lived the rock star lifestyle described in *Our Life on the Road*, a biography she'd read about her favorite rock band.

An image of Matt in bed with two beautiful women formed.

Don't go there.

Even though his lifestyle shouldn't matter to her, she hoped it wasn't anything like what she'd read.

But even if he wasn't into one-night stands and threesomes, that didn't mean boredom wasn't the driving force behind what happened between them tonight. Matt dated gorgeous actresses and supermodels. While Liv didn't consider herself ugly, she wasn't in the same league as the women he'd been linked to, so there was no way he'd ever be attracted to her. However, she was the only single female in town who he knew. But when she thought about it that way, though, it made it sound like Matt was using her.

The idea of him using her—or anyone, for that matter—

didn't feel right. Last weekend, he'd handed over the keys to his SUV without being asked or expecting anything in return. And tonight, before their first kiss, he'd given her plenty of time to move away if it hadn't been what she wanted. Afterward, he'd walked her outside, opened the car door for her, and waited until she drove away before going back inside the house.

Opening her eyes, Liv stared at the ceiling, the wheels in her brain spinning much the same way the blades on the ceiling fan were. Even without Matt sitting next to her, making it impossible to think straight, she couldn't figure out what tonight meant.

"Loving You" erupted from her cell phone, reminding Liv that someone had called her earlier. With her mind centered on Matt, she hadn't even thought to see if the caller had left a voicemail.

She wasn't surprised to see the name "Emma" on the screen, and after answering, she put the call on speaker so she could change into pj's and talk at the same time.

"We missed you tonight. It's not the same when you don't come with us."

Liv grabbed a pair of sleep shorts and an old New England Rebels T-shirt from the drawer. "If you guys are free this weekend, let's get together."

Between her catering schedule and Phoebe's busy schedule taking wedding photos, the three of them hadn't been able to get together in over a month.

"Brian and I have plans Sunday night. But I'm free Friday night and all day Saturday. Phoebe's working on Saturday, but it's a morning wedding, so she'll probably be free that night. I don't know if she has plans for Friday night or Sunday."

"I'll text her tomorrow." Spring and summer were Phoebe's busy season, and she spent almost every weekend taking photos for at least one wedding and outdoor family pictures.

"Sounds good, but that's not really why I called."

Liv expected Emma to ask about her night as she pulled on the Rebels T-shirt.

"You'll never guess who is in town again," Emma said instead.

"Superman?"

"He's better than Superman."

"Better than Superman, huh? I didn't think that was possible. So, who is the mystery person in town?"

"Matt Sherbrooke."

Emma and Phoebe loved the band's music too, and the three of them had attended the band's last two concerts in the area together.

Word was bound to get out that he was around. "How do you know?"

"Charlotte and Rob were at the Northside Tavern tonight. She was working when Matt stopped in to pick up pizzas."

Charlotte and her fiancé owned Fireside Pizzeria and spent a considerable amount of time there, ensuring everything ran the way they wanted—a habit Liv understood well.

"Well, he does own a house here, and the man does need to eat."

"I know, but I've only seen him in town once. Last spring, he was walking out of Hometown Brews, and I was stopped, waiting for some kids to cross the street."

She'd heard this story before and knew the only reason Emma hadn't parked and chased after him was because she'd been running late that day.

"I wish he'd stop in the flower shop."

"He probably doesn't have much need for flowers, Emma."

"Has he ever come to the restaurant?"

Surprisingly, Emma had never asked her that question.

"Uh, yeah. A few times." Emma asked *if* not *when*, so Liv saw no reason to add that he'd been in as recently as last week.

"And you never told me?"

After switching the fan to high and opening the second window in the bedroom, Liv pulled back the covers on the bed and sat. "Sorry. Just didn't think of it."

"Well, if he comes in again and you're there, call me."

"Emma, you've got some serious issues."

"I just want a photo with him. What's wrong with that?" Emma asked, sounding defensive. "The man knew what he was getting into when he pursued a music career, so he shouldn't mind when his fans ask for a picture or an autograph."

"Nothing, I guess." Emma had a good point, but that didn't mean he liked to get interrupted in the middle of dinner either.

"I didn't really call to talk about Matt Sherbrooke either. I wanted to know how your date went."

She almost laughed at her friend's statement. If Emma ever knew the man they'd been talking about was the very same man Liv had not only spent several hours with but had also kissed, she'd lose it.

"It wasn't a date." She didn't know what it had been, but she refused to label it a date.

"What would you call it, then?"

"Two people eating pizza and playing a few games of pool." Only torture would get her to admit they kissed or that she was cooking dinner for them tomorrow night.

"Sounds like a date to me, although maybe not the most exciting one."

Liv could picture Emma sitting in her favorite armchair, wearing an "I'm right and you know it" expression on her face.

"Like I told you this afternoon, Matt and Owen are friends, and other than me and my parents, he doesn't know anyone in town. He was bored and wanted someone to hang out with, and he asked me since Owen and Jenny won't be back until next weekend."

Dead silence followed her explanation, and Liv mentally slapped herself for mentioning Matt's name.

"Owen's friend Matt drives an Italian sports car that probably costs more than my house and doesn't know anyone in town but you and your family. And you spent the night playing pool and eating pizza," Emma said, putting all the puzzle pieces together. "No, it's not possible. It's just a coincidence. I mean, if you were hanging out with Matt Sherbrooke, you would've told me. I'm your best friend."

She hadn't lied earlier, but omitting some of the details was coming back to bite her in the ass.

"Liv, tell me I'm crazy. Tell me you ate pizza and played pool with a mega-wealthy CEO from Boston named Matt Johnson, not Matt Sherbrooke, the sexiest man on the damn planet," Emma said, her tone telling Liv that she already knew the truth but was having trouble accepting it.

Sighing, Liv rested her head against the headboard. She wasn't going to lie to her best friend, and even if she tried, Emma wouldn't believe her. "Emma, I wasn't with a wealthy CEO from Boston."

"Oh. My. God. How does Owen know Matt Sherbrooke?"

She thought she'd mentioned how they knew each other earlier, but she'd share it again. "They were roommates in college."

"Oh, right, you told me that this afternoon," Emma said. "I can't believe you never told me you know him. I would've told you in a heartbeat."

Yeah, that was probably true. Emma couldn't keep a secret if her life depended on it. "It didn't seem important. It's not like we're friends or anything. The only time I see him is when he's in town and comes to the restaurant to eat."

"Sounds like you're friends to me if he invited you over for pizza."

Emma would have a heart attack if she told her they kissed. "Okay, we're friendly. But we're not close like you and I."

"Uh-huh. When are you seeing him again?"

"Tomo—" Liv snapped her mouth shut. Usually, she thought before she spoke. Clearly, her brain hadn't fully recovered from kissing Matt.

Darn it.

"You're seeing him again tomorrow?" There was no missing the excitement in Emma's voice. If Liv could see through the phone, no doubt Emma would be bouncing up and down in her seat. "What time? And what are you doing?"

As her grandmother would say, the cat was out of the bag now. "I've been playing around with a couple of new recipes. Matt offered to come over and try one since he's not busy. You know I always like to get different opinions before we add anything to the menu."

Usually, she'd test any new recipes on her brother and his wife first. Then she'd cook the dishes for others. Most of the time, Emma and Phoebe were her next taste testers. But occasionally she'd ask someone else for their opinion.

"Sure. Whatever you say. Do you want me to come by and help you get ready before he gets there?"

"Emma, I'm cooking us a meal. We're not going on a date. I don't need help getting ready unless you want to stop by while I'm at work and make sure I have all the ingredients I need for dinner and pick up anything I'm missing."

"Just because you're not leaving your apartment doesn't mean you can't look nice."

"I appreciate the offer, but I'll be fine."

"Well, at least call the second he leaves. I want all the details."

* * *

Matt had stood outside until he could no longer see the taillights on Liv's car. Then, after pouring himself some whiskey, he'd headed back to the rooftop patio. He'd been sitting up there ever since, looking up at the stars and replaying the evening.

Other than female family members, he could only think of one woman other than Liv who he'd had a conversation with recently that had felt so easygoing and natural. Usually, he selected topics that weren't too personal, and he was always careful about his word choice. The last thing he needed was to offend the woman across the table from him or give her the impression that he wanted a relationship when he didn't. That hadn't been the case when he'd spent time with Evie, Adam's girl-friend, a few weeks ago. It hadn't been the case tonight either. Not once had he worried about sharing something that might get out to the media or saying something that might offend Liv. Instead, their conversation had flowed naturally, much like when he'd been with Evie.

Well, maybe not exactly. While he liked his cousin's girlfriend, he wasn't attracted to her. Liv, on the other hand, was a different story, and not only because she was beautiful.

He appreciated that Liv never made a big fuss over him. Whenever he came into the restaurant, she treated him like any other customer. All too often, that wasn't the case. But that wasn't why he'd stopped by her office this afternoon to ask her out.

Unlike a lot of people, she was real around him. Liv didn't hang on his every word as if what he said was the most fascinating thing in the world. Even before the band hit it big, women had done that after they found out he was a member of the Sherbrooke family. Some guys might like it. Not him.

When he talked to someone, he liked it to be a two-way conversation. Other people might have kept the problems her family was facing a secret, but Liv had been honest with him. And whereas a lot of people he'd met would've asked him to help them out financially so they could buy the building and save the restaurant and catering business, she hadn't.

Tonight, his attraction to her had grown. While playing pool, she teased him much the way he remembered her teasing her brother. When she wasn't doing that, she asked him personal but not intrusive questions, such as how he'd gotten into photography and what types of books he enjoyed reading.

Matt sipped his drink and thought about their conversation while eating ice cream. Books weren't something he discussed with many people. And when Liv said she pegged him as a romance novel junkie, he hadn't been sure at first if she was joking or not, which was why he'd asked if she was serious. This had led to Liv asking him something no one, not even his family, had ever asked him.

"How do you come up with the lyrics, then?"

Until she'd asked the question, he'd never realized how much it bothered him that no one had ever asked him anything about his music or his career other than when he'd be leaving on tour and when he'd be back.

Other than his grandfather, his family had never been against his decision to pursue a music career. But they'd never understood it either. Business and the corporate world were such an integral part of Graham and Violet Sherbrooke's life that they couldn't imagine someone thriving without it in theirs. His brothers were following in their parents' footsteps.

His thoughts drifted away from their conversation as he took another sip. The first person he'd ever kissed had been Leigh Vincent. They'd both been fourteen. She'd thrown a party to mark both the end of the summer and the fact that many of them were heading off to boarding school in a few weeks. Her parents had kept to themselves, only coming outside two or three times to make sure no one had drowned in the pool. Since then, he'd kissed a lot of women. But tonight had been different. When his lips touched Liv's, every neuron in his brain fired at once as the outside world slipped away.

His last relationship had ended almost a year ago. Since then, he'd spent time with women and physically desired them, but he hadn't enjoyed spending time with any of them enough to get serious. When he arrived in Orchard Harbor, Matt hadn't expected that to change.

Now he was hoping it might.

His phone chimed as he finished his drink. When he checked the device, he found a text message from Theo.

Theo: Brianna said the wedding is at a friend's estate in Orchard Harbor. Do you know where that is?

Someone had just booked a July wedding with Liv. Something told him it was the same one his brother and girlfriend were attending.

Matt: Yeah. It's where I am now.

Theo: Will you still be there in July?

Last week, he would've said "most likely," and maybe that should be his answer now. July was more than a month away. A lot could happen in a month. Hell, he could show up at Liv's place tomorrow night, and she might tell him to get lost.

Maybe it was the optimist in him, but he felt like he'd have a reason to stick around Orchard Harbor indefinitely.

Matt: Definitely. Why don't you and Brianna plan on staying with me?

Theo: Sounds good. See you then.

Seven

IT'S NOT *the end of the world.*

Liv had been repeating the same thing to herself since noon, when her dad shared the news that Fredrick had accepted someone else's offer on the building. Maybe if she repeated it to herself for another five hours, she'd believe it.

Shirley hadn't known whose offer had been accepted. All she'd known was that three parties had made offers. Her dad and grandfather were optimistic that someone other than Timberlane Development was purchasing the building and that they'd keep the status quo. She was trying to follow their lead, but she kept straying off the path. It was a known fact that Rick and Fredrick had been discussing the possibility of Timberlane Development purchasing the building before it even went on the market. Not to mention, she couldn't imagine many people who had the financial resources to compete with Timberlane Development and would want to leave the building as it was.

Despite her dad's optimism, she knew he was considering their options for the restaurant and catering business. And tomorrow she'd help him with that and start thinking about her living options. Both Mom and Dad had assured her that she could move back home if the worst happened. Even her grandparents had offered her their spare bedroom. She appreciated their offers, but staying with either would be a short-term solution. She'd moved out of her parents' house eleven years ago and had been living alone since Phoebe moved out four years ago. So tomorrow she'd start looking for an apartment.

Right now, though, she needed to focus on cooking; otherwise, dinner would be ruined, and she and Matt would be eating takeout tonight.

Liv lowered the heat under the saucepan and grabbed the meat thermometer so she could check the chicken. Why had she told him she was free tonight? If she'd told him she was busy, she'd be stressing about only her future right now instead of that *and* the fact that he would be there soon. Unfortunately, with him sitting so close and her lips still tingling from his kiss last night, it had been hard to think about anything but seeing him again.

There was a knock on her door as the thermometer registered the necessary temperature.

Before opening the door, she scanned the apartment and once again wished she hadn't invited him over for dinner. Her apartment was neat, and she'd spent a lot of time decorating it. However, compared to his house, it was a tiny hole-in-the-wall.

Too late now.

Matt wasn't the first man she'd had over at her apartment. He was the first, though, to show up with roses.

"Come on in."

"Whatever you're making smells delicious."

Matt handed her the champagne pink roses and kissed her cheek. "I wasn't sure what your favorite flowers were."

"They're beautiful. Thank you. I'm assuming you got them at Exquisite Flowers?"

"I did. Why?"

"Then you probably met my friend Emma. She works there."

Matt followed her across the living room and into the kitchen. "The woman who helped me was probably in her mid-sixties with light brown hair and glasses."

Well, that explained why Emma hadn't called to tell her she'd finally met Matt Sherbrooke. "Sounds like you met either Emma's mom or her aunt."

Boy, was Emma going to be disappointed when she found out Matt finally went into the flower shop when she wasn't there. On second thought, maybe Liv wouldn't tell her. Heaven knew what Emma might read into the fact that Matt showed up with flowers. Yep, keeping her mouth shut was the smarter option.

"I didn't know what you were making, so I brought a bottle of chardonnay and a merlot." He set a reusable wine bag and a bakery box on the counter.

"I made my version of chicken chasseur."

"Well, as I said, it smells delicious."

If it came out as well as she'd hoped, she had planned to have Dad add it as a special at the restaurant and include it as an option on the catering menu. Now it might not matter how it tasted.

"Well, we'll soon find out." Opening the top drawer on her left, she pulled out the bottle opener. "Do you mind pouring the wine while I plate our meals?"

Not only did she have Matt all to herself, but he'd brought her a dozen roses. Most women would do anything to be in her shoes right now. Liv should be walking around on cloud nine, not wishing she could drown her sorrows in a container of ice cream.

"No problem." Accepting the opener, he put it down next to the bakery box and moved closer to her. "What's wrong? You don't seem like yourself," he said, tucking the piece of hair that had escaped her braid earlier and had been driving her crazy ever since behind her ear.

Regardless of whether she was happy, sad, or somewhere in between, she'd never been good at hiding her emotions, which was just one reason she never played poker.

"Dad heard back from Shirley earlier today. Fredrick accepted someone else's offer on the building."

Don't cry.

After taking a deep breath, she slowly exhaled and reminded herself it wasn't the end of the world. It was also something to focus on later when she was alone and could cry all she wanted while eating ice cream from the container.

"I know."

News spread fast in town, but that was a record even for Orchard Harbor. "Who told you? Owen?" She knew her dad planned to let her brother know, but she assumed he would've waited until later tonight. Owen would just be leaving work now.

Matt's forehead creased in confusion. "Liv, Fredrick accepted *my* offer."

"Your offer?"

She was dreaming. That was the only explanation for the past twenty-four hours. Yep, and all the signs were around her, starting with the fact that not only was Matt Sherbrooke standing in her kitchen, but she knew exactly what his lips felt like against hers. It also explained why he'd just told her the Worm had accepted his offer on the building.

"Yeah. I made it yesterday before you came over."

"You made an offer on the building?" That made no sense. Matt had no stake in the businesses that called the building home.

He nodded. "I called Austin at Windsor Realty yesterday. He helped me find my house. And I had him write up an offer. I remember you saying Shirley worked at Windsor too." Matt shrugged. "I assumed she'd known since she works in the same office as Austin."

"You're buying this building?" Complex math aside, she didn't usually struggle to comprehend things. Right now, though, she couldn't wrap her head around what Matt was telling her.

He put his hands on her waist and kissed her forehead. "I should've called you as soon as I knew. I'm sorry. I honestly thought she would've told your dad."

"But why?"

"I saw what Timberlane Development did to Sandy Cove and didn't want to see it happen here." He pulled her closer and brushed what barely constituted as a kiss across her lips. "My favorite restaurant in town is also in this building, and I didn't want to see it go out of business." Matt kissed her again. This time, he let his lips linger almost long enough for her to enjoy it.

"I'm also interested in someone who calls this building home and who's worked her butt off to make her catering business a success."

She was about to correct him about it being her catering business, but he silenced her with another kiss.

"Don't deny it. Owen told me Ocean View Catering is your baby. And I read all the glowing reviews on Yelp."

"You're really buying the building?" Maybe if he told her yes one more time, it would finally sink in.

Matt gave her the same who-turned-up-the-heat smile he'd given her last night, and she wished her apartment had air-conditioning. "Don't worry. I won't increase your rent."

He was serious. As crazy as it might seem, Matt was buying the building, not some property developer. She didn't need to find a new apartment or worry that the restaurant, Ocean View Catering, and her aunt's bookstore would go out of business.

Matt's lips were almost on hers when she realized her dad didn't know.

"I need to call Dad and tell him." She stepped around him and headed for the end table where she'd left her cell phone.

"While you do that, I'll open the wine."

Thankfully, it took her dad a little less time than it had her to wrap his head around the fact that Matt was buying the building and not Timberlane Development or a company like it.

"I take it your dad was okay with the news?" Matt handed her a glass of wine when she joined him near the counter again.

"It's possible he's celebrating and opening the merlot he's been saving for a special occasion." Liv took a sip of what was possibly the best wine she'd ever tasted and then set her glass down. "There's a salad in the fridge. If you can grab that, I'll finally plate our dinner. I'm anxious to hear what you think."

"I can handle that, but there is something I need to do first." After placing his wineglass next to hers, he pulled her in closer.

Firm lips covered hers, and Liv closed her eyes as the heat inside her built.

Matt slipped a hand under her braid and changed the angle of his mouth over hers. She didn't wait for him to make the next move. Instead, she put her arms over his shoulders and stepped closer, not stopping until her breasts pressed against his chest.

Matt moved the hand resting on her waist to the small of her back as he teased her lips apart and sent any rational thought straight out of her head.

Then, sooner than she would've liked, he pulled his lips away.

"Now, I'll get the salad or do anything else you want."

Holy. Wow. He knows how to kiss.

Liv refused to think about why that was the case. "Just, uh, the salad. I, uh, can handle everything else."

At least in terms of looks, the two plates she placed on the table were five-star-restaurant worthy. She hoped they tasted as good as they looked—and not only because she wanted to impress Matt. She'd spent a lot of time experimenting with this recipe, and she'd hate to find out it had been a waste.

"Okay, I want your honest opinion. Don't just tell me it's good because you don't want to hurt my feelings."

Her brother and Phoebe were always brutally honest when it came to new dishes. Emma and her sister-in-law were honest too, but they always took a gentler approach when they didn't like something she made. If Matt didn't like it, she didn't care which approach he took as long as it was the truth.

"You'll get it. Promise."

For the next several minutes, she spent more time watching Matt than eating. Sure, he'd said he'd give her his honest opinion, but he might have just been saying that. And while a person could lie when they were done and tell you it was delicious, their facial expression usually gave them away when they ate something they hated.

"This is amazing," Matt said as he cut another piece of chicken. "What's in it?"

"Chicken thighs, dry white wine, and vegetables served over creamy polenta."

"Well, I'm not sure I've ever had this before, but it is delicious."

"Do you think we should make it a special at the restaurant and add it to the catering menu?"

"Liv, I'd make it a permanent addition to both menus."

* * *

When they finished eating, he'd offered to help with the dishes, but she'd insisted he was a guest as she cleared the table. Now Matt watched Liv add their salad bowls to the dishwasher.

"I know you already said I should add the chicken chasseur to the menus, but do you think I need to change it at all?"

Despite the success he'd had with the band, occasionally he worried fans wouldn't like a song he'd written. And no matter what anyone said, his doubt lingered until the fans responded to the song, so he knew that no matter what he said now, she wouldn't be entirely convinced. But that wouldn't stop him from trying.

"Trust me. If you put it on the menus, customers are going to love it."

Liv closed the dishwasher and then washed her hands. "I'll talk to Dad about it tomorrow. Are you ready for dessert, or do you want to wait?"

He was ready for dessert, just not what was inside the bakery box. The kiss they'd shared last night had turned his world upside down. But it was nothing compared to what he'd experienced when he'd kissed her in the kitchen with her body pressed tightly against his and her fingers caressing his neck.

"Let's wait."

"That's fine. I can't eat anything right now anyway."

She drummed her fingertips against the countertop, and Matt wondered if she even realized she was doing it.

"Do you want to watch a movie?" she asked.

What he wanted was to find the closest bed, because based on his body's reaction to just kissing her, making love to her would be like nothing he'd ever experienced. But now wasn't the right time. Liv was far more relaxed with him tonight, but there was still a trace of that uncertainty vibe he'd noticed last night. He wanted her 100 percent comfortable around him before they had sex. And it wasn't a question of if but when in his mind.

"Sure. Do you have one in mind?"

She grabbed his hand on her way from the kitchen to the sofa. "I was thinking *The Fellowship of the Ring*, but we can look through what I have and see if anything sounds better." She switched on the television and then sat next to him.

"Tell me if you see anything you like." She glanced at him before scrolling through her movie collection.

The first several movies were classic Bogart films. He enjoyed most of them, but tonight he wasn't in the mood. Next were several movies based on Jane Austen novels, which were immediate noes for him. He'd been twelve when his mom had rotator cuff surgery, which forced her to take things easy for weeks. To cheer her up, he'd sit with her after school. Sometimes they'd play board games, other times they'd watch movies. One of her favorites was an adaptation of *Pride and Prejudice*, a movie so boring that no twelve-year-old boy should be forced to sit through it. More than once, he had fallen asleep while watching it.

He almost commented when he spotted the icon for *One Last Heist*, the movie he'd done with Anderson Brady, sandwiched between another movie starring Anderson and one starring his cousin's husband, JT Williamson. Not that he wanted to watch it, but he would like to know what she thought of it. Matt kept his mouth shut, though. She liked it at least enough to own it.

"Wait, stop. You've got the original Star Trek movies?" His brothers were die-hard Star Wars fans, but not him. He was a card-carrying Trekkie.

"I've got all the Star Trek movies that have been made. I also have the episodes from all the television series made, except the most recent one."

"Where have you been all my life?"

A splash of pink appeared on Liv's cheeks. "Orchard Harbor, Maine," she said before looking back at the television and taking a sip of her wine. "So you're a Star Trek fan too. I knew there was a reason I liked you. Do you know my brother prefers Star Wars to Star Trek?"

"Believe me, I know." He'd had more than one heated argument with Owen over which was the better movie universe.

"I once refused to talk to him for an entire month until he finally agreed that a Federation phaser was far superior to a Jedi lightsaber," Liv said.

"How old were you?" He hadn't subjected his friend to the silent treatment, but they'd had a similar argument not long after they first met.

"Ten. And it drove Owen crazy. You know how much he loves to talk. I wouldn't even acknowledge him at dinner when he asked me to pass him the salad."

Laughing at the image her statement created, he reached for her hand and lifted it toward his lips. "Before we go any further, I want you to know, I agree 100 percent with you." Matt kissed her knuckles. "Hands down, Star Trek technology is better than anything in the Star Wars universe." Turning her hand over, he pressed his lips against her palm. He couldn't stop his smile when Liv's hand trembled ever so slightly in his.

"I'm glad we're on the same page, because if we weren't, I'd have to ask you to leave."

"You'd really do that?" He trailed his fingertips up her arm and to the back of her neck.

She fought to control a smile as she nodded.

"Then I'm glad we agree."

Adrenaline and need shot through him the second his lips touched hers. And when her tongue traced his bottom lip, he changed the angle of his head and deepened the kiss as an intense urge to find her bedroom, remove her clothes, and look at her overwhelmed him. He'd desired plenty of women before, yet somehow this time it was different, more intense and overwhelming.

Matt allowed himself one more pass over her lips before digging into his self-restraint, pulling his mouth away from Liv's, and resting his forehead against hers.

Several seconds passed in silence; the only sound in the room came from the dishwasher in the kitchen.

"Should we start with the first movie starring the original cast or the first movie with the cast of *The Next Generation*?" he finally asked, because it was either do that or kiss her again. He wasn't sure his body could handle just kissing right now.

"It's not my favorite, but let's start with the first one the original cast made."

Matt didn't believe in soulmates, but if he did, Liv might be his. "Yeah, I don't love it either, but let's watch it and get it out of the way."

Eight

MONDAY AFTERNOON, Liv heard the door chimes and checked the clock on her computer screen. She had an appointment with Misty and Evan Walker, who wanted their twin daughters' graduation party catered. Even though their appointment wasn't for another fifteen minutes, she expected to see them when she turned around. After all, some people simply preferred to arrive early.

Instead, she found Emma standing there holding an enormous arrangement of flowers.

"Hey, stranger," Emma greeted her, placing the vase smack-dab in the center of the conference table.

Although they'd discussed getting together over the weekend, it hadn't happened.

"I have a special delivery for you." Emma pulled out a chair and made herself comfortable.

"For me?"

"Unless you know another Liv Middleton who works at Ocean View Catering."

She could only think of one person who could've sent them. *This is going to be fun.*

Coming around the desk, Liv prepared herself for the interrogation she was about to get.

Why couldn't they have more than one florist in town?

"Mom took the order this morning."

Liv opened the card nestled among the flowers.

I wanted you to know I'm thinking about you. Matt

"Are they from who I think they are?" Emma asked, leaning forward.

There was no point in lying. Emma knew the only person who ever sent her flowers was Owen on her birthday. He sent flowers to their mom and their sister as well. But today wasn't Liv's birthday.

"Yes, they're from Matt."

"I knew it. I knew he wasn't hanging out with you because he didn't know anyone else in town." Emma bounced in her seat as she rubbed her hands together. "Details. I want details. All. The details. Don't leave anything out."

Liv shrugged and checked her watch. Why couldn't clients arrive early when you needed them to? "We've just been spending time together, Emma. There isn't anything to tell."

"Come on, Liv. You can share more than that. It's not like I'm asking you to tell me if he's good in bed. Although, with a body like that, he must be," Emma said, picking up a folder and fanning herself with it. "I could watch that scene in *One Last Heist* when he gets out of the shower all day long."

You and me both.

"Emma, we—"

The door chimed, and the Walkers entered.

Saved by the bell.

Emma stood and pushed in her chair before turning to the couple. "I can't believe Shea and Tatum graduated this year. I remember babysitting them."

Emma's parents lived next door to the Walkers, and from about the age of sixteen, she'd spent almost every Friday night watching the two girls until she graduated from high school.

"Trust me. Neither can we," Misty replied.

"Liv, I'll stop back later," Emma said before heading out the door.

She'd known this appointment would only be a short respite from sharing enough with Emma to satisfy her curiosity.

Liv moved the vase to her desk and grabbed her notebook and laptop.

"Those are gorgeous. Whoever sent them has great taste." Misty gestured toward the flowers.

She heard the unasked question in her former high school history teacher's voice. Misty wanted to know who'd sent them, because it wasn't a secret that Liv was single and had been for a long time. A downside of living in a small town was that everyone usually knew everyone else's business.

"I agree." Liv liked Misty but wasn't going to share anything personal with her. "When you called, you said you were thinking of having sandwich platters and an assortment of salads for the party. Is that still the plan?"

Misty nodded. "We also want a dessert buffet."

She handed Misty the binder that listed all the sandwich and salad options they offered. "I'll grab the dessert information for you."

Forty minutes later, Liv had a signed contract, deposit, and completed menu in hand. "If you think of anything you want to add or change, call me."

"What is the latest we can make changes?" Misty asked.

The party was scheduled for the last Friday in July. Since they would only be responsible for delivering the food, she didn't need to schedule her usual serving crew. "The sooner the better, but no later than July 15."

Misty wrote the date on her copy of the contract and then added it to the folder Liv had given her, which contained copies of all the details they'd agreed upon. "Sounds great. Thank you."

Liv watched the couple leave and then gathered up her things. She didn't make it back to her desk before the door opened again.

When she glanced over her shoulder, she wasn't surprised to see Emma walking inside. "Were you watching for them to leave?"

"No, but I was adjusting the window display and looked up just as they walked out."

"Convenient."

Emma tried to maintain a neutral expression but failed. "What can I say? I'm curious. A superhot rock star slash actor who, according to the media, is also a super-nice guy, is sending my best friend flowers and inviting her over to his house for pizza."

When she put it that way, she'd be curious too if the tables were reversed. Plus, maybe talking with Emma would help her sort out what was going on between her and Matt. All the signs pointed to a developing relationship. If he'd been someone she'd met through a dating app or someone who'd lived in town year-round, she wouldn't question it. But this was Matt Sherbrooke.

The man had fans around the world. He'd dated women like Jasmine Locke, his love interest in *One Last Heist*, and Milan Novak, one of the most sought-after runway models in the world. Why would he be interested in a woman who ran a catering business and occasionally waited tables at her family's restaurant?

And even if he was, a relationship between them couldn't last. Her life was in Orchard Harbor, a place he visited once or twice a year.

"So, what's up between the two of you? Most men don't send flowers to a woman because they're bored."

"This is actually the second time he's given me flowers. Thursday night, when I cooked for him, he brought me some too."

"And you didn't tell me?"

At least this was an easy question to answer. "I knew you'd be disappointed if you found out he went into the shop when you weren't there."

"Somehow I doubt that's the only reason you didn't tell me." Emma took a sip from the iced coffee she'd brought with her. "But back to my original question. What's up between you two? Are you and Matt officially a couple?"

Liv retrieved her water bottle from her desk and then sat. "You make it sound like we're in middle school."

"Come on, you know what I mean, Liv."

Yeah, she did, but giving Emma a hard time was too much fun. "Honestly, I'm not sure."

"How can you not be sure?"

"It's not like we're in sixth grade and he passed me a note asking me to be his girlfriend."

"Fair enough. But there are usually signs. I'd say that right there is one." Emma gestured toward the flowers. "Have you seen him since Thursday night?"

"Just Friday night. He spent the weekend with a cousin in Providence. He planned to come back today."

"You saw him three days in a row. Sounds promising. Did you hear from him while he was in Providence?"

"I covered Maggie's shift Saturday night, and he called about ten minutes before it started, so we didn't talk for long. Yesterday we exchanged some text messages, but they weren't earth-shattering."

"Liv, how can you possibly wonder if he's interested in being more than a friend? Three months ago, if I'd told you Brian and I had gotten together three nights in a row, that he'd called while visiting his family, and then sent me flowers, what would you tell me if I told you I wasn't sure what was going on between us?"

Liv shrugged. "That the two of you were in a relationship, or at least headed in that direction."

"Exactly, so why are you wondering about the status of you and Matt? It's obvious to me, and if you ask Phoebe, she'll agree."

"Brian also lives twenty minutes away and spends his days writing computer code. Matt has fans around the world and dates supermodels. Not to mention, he lives more than a thousand miles away and only comes to town once or twice a year."

"Just because he's dated supermodels doesn't mean he can't be interested in you. As for him living so far away, he's here now. Maybe he'll decide to stay."

"I guess." He owned a beautiful home in town, so he obviously liked Orchard Harbor. But that didn't mean he liked the area enough to call it home. "Speaking of Brian, how are you two doing?" At least for now, she was done talking about her and Matt.

"Great. Sunday, I went with him to his aunt and uncle's fortieth wedding anniversary. I think I met just about his entire family. And his sister and sister-in-law were much friendlier this time."

She was glad to hear things were going so well. Emma's last boyfriend had turned out to be a two-timing jerk, and it had taken Emma a long time before she started dating again.

"And you'll never guess who was at the party."

Maybe it was because they'd spent so much time talking about Matt, but Eclipse's bassist was the first person to come to mind. "Jordan Mead?"

"I wish. No, Fredrick."

"As in Fredrick Waldman?"

Emma nodded. "Yep. He's dating Brian's cousin." She made air quotes when she said "dating." "Considering I saw him hitting on another woman at the party, I don't know how long it will last."

"Why am I not surprised he did that?" The man was more of a creep than she'd thought. "That reminds me, I didn't tell you. I found out who's buying the building."

She'd shared that her family's offer hadn't been accepted right after she found out. However, she'd never told Emma they didn't have to worry that Timberlane Development or another company like it would tear down the building and replace it with a hotel or condos.

"Matt."

Emma's eyebrows disappeared under her bangs, and her chin nearly hit the table. "That's crazy. I mean, it's great, but he's the last person I would've expected to buy the building."

"Trust me, I was shocked when he told me too." She'd had four days to digest the news, and she still half expected to wake up and find out she'd dreamed the entire conversation with him.

"Did he tell you why?"

Liv replayed their conversation Thursday night. "He said he'd seen what Timberlane Development did to Sandy Cove and didn't want to see it happen here. And that his favorite restaurant in town is in the building, and he didn't want to see it go out of business." She intentionally skipped the third reason he'd given for buying the property because she didn't want Emma to insist once again that Matt was interested in a long-term relationship.

"Sounds like he'll be in town a lot more. Maybe he's even thinking about living here year-round."

* * *

Matt finished the page he was reading and reached for his drink. He'd been sitting outside for the last hour, enjoying the sunshine, ocean breeze, and the book he'd started last week but hadn't touched since before the night Liv came over to play pool. Not that he was complaining, but he'd prefer to be sitting there with her rather than reading now.

Instead of starting the next chapter, he set the book down and stared out at the ocean as his mind wandered.

He'd come to Maine because it was his favorite place to be. Today, though, that wasn't the only reason he was glad to be back from his weekend away in Providence. As much as he'd enjoyed visiting with Trent and his family, he'd missed Liv. He couldn't remember the last time he'd truly missed someone the way he'd missed her. He'd considered stopping by her office when he'd gotten back into town but decided against it. While he had nothing but time on his hands, she had a business to run and didn't need him dropping by and interrupting her day. Matt had sent her a text, though, when he got home, letting her know he was back and that she could come over whenever tonight, as they had planned.

The cell phone on the table chimed as he raised his glass to his mouth for another drink. Turning the device over, he found a message from Liv.

Liv: Leaving work in a couple of minutes. Do you need me to bring anything?

Matt: Pool cue.

They might not get around to it, but he wouldn't mind a chance to redeem himself.

Liv: Will do. See you soon.

Before he put the phone back on the table, it rang, and the

name "Jordan" appeared on the screen. At one time, he wouldn't have hesitated to answer. Now he did, because he had a feeling he already knew the reason behind the call from his long-time friend and bandmate, and he didn't feel like talking about it. If he didn't answer now, though, Jordan would call again, so ignoring him was only a temporary solution.

"Hey, are you still in Virginia?" Jordan asked after greeting him.

It sounded like Jordan had seen the same pictures as Theo's girlfriend.

"Nope."

"Where are you, then? I stopped by your house last week."

Other than his parents, Jordan was the only person he knew who'd show up without either being invited or calling first. "Maine."

"I should've known."

Unlike Matt, Jordan had grown up in Maine, but even before his parents moved out of the state, he'd rarely visited. Now that he had no family there, the only time he came back was when Portland was a stop on Eclipse's tour.

"When are you coming back?" Jordan asked.

"I have no idea."

"Dude, we need to start working on some new material."

It had been almost two years since they released a new album and nearly eight months since he'd written anything new.

"If you really don't know, I can fly up there so we can get started."

"You're welcome to visit, but nothing has changed. I'm done until Carter gets his shit together."

"Not that again. Come on. Just let it go. Even McKenna moved past it. And if you do, Travis will."

While it pissed him off that Carter had cheated on his wife of less than a year, it wasn't the reason he could no longer work with the band's keyboardist. He'd already explained that to Jordan and the others.

"You know there's more to it, Jordan."

The app on his phone beeped, letting him know someone

was approaching the door, and he headed inside as Jordan once again tried to change his mind. He could say one thing about the guy: Jordan was persistent.

Opening the door, he gestured for Liv to come in.

"Sorry, not happening. But if you want to come up for a visit, you're welcome to. But listen, I have company, so I'm going to have to talk to you later." Ending the call, Matt stuck the device into his back pocket and dismissed his conversation with Jordan from his mind.

"You didn't have to cut your call short."

Matt wrapped his arms around her, then brushed his lips against hers. "Jordan and I were done. How was your day?"

"Busy, but good. And thank you for the flowers. They're beautiful."

"Glad you liked them."

He wouldn't want flowers, but he knew many people, including his mom, loved to receive them. In fact, even though they'd been married for close to forty years, his dad either sent his mom an arrangement or brought home a bouquet once a month.

"What do you feel like doing tonight?"

"You told me to bring my pool cue, so I was looking forward to kicking your butt again tonight. But if you've changed your mind and want more time to practice, I won't complain."

"I don't want you to be disappointed, so we can start with that."

After a quick pit stop in the kitchen for snacks, he led her down to the entertainment room.

"How was your weekend in Providence?"

While he knew she liked Eclipse's music, he wasn't sure what else she enjoyed, so he selected a playlist from his phone that contained a mix of genres. "Nice. The last time I saw Trent and his wife was when Eclipse did a show in Providence last year, and I'd never met their second child. Trent's brother and sister-in-law live in the same building, so they stopped by Saturday night."

"I tried to get tickets to that show, but it sold out too fast. I saw you two years ago in Boston. Do you know when you might go on tour again?"

"We've got nothing planned, and it's possible we won't do another tour or album."

He'd shared that information with only a handful of people. He didn't know about the others, but since nothing had appeared in the media, he assumed they hadn't shared the news with many either.

Liv froze, half her pool cue in each hand. "Seriously? You're not going to release another album? I haven't read anything about you guys breaking up."

Matt almost laughed because she made it sound like they were in some weird multi-person romantic relationship. "Officially, nothing has been announced. But Travis and I are done with the group right now."

"Why?" Before he answered, Liv shook her head and went back to putting her pool cue together. "Never mind. That's none of my business."

He appreciated the fact that she was willing to let the matter go, especially since many people wouldn't, but he trusted that whatever he told her would stay between them. "For the lack of a better description, Carter's always been the wild child of the group, and we've all tolerated his behavior."

It was no secret that Carter lived the stereotypical rock star lifestyle. And even if she weren't a fan of the band, Liv would've seen stories about his behavior in the media.

"But after his most recent incident, Travis and I decided we've had enough, and until he gets his crap together, we're done."

"Are you talking about the rumor that he was found passed out in a hotel room with a naked woman?"

How their publicist and manager had managed to keep all the details from coming out was a mystery to him.

"It wasn't a rumor, and the woman he was found with had turned eighteen the day before. She'd gone to the concert to celebrate her birthday and then came backstage, which is how she met Carter. And he brought her back to his room, where they spent their time having sex, getting high, and drinking." Matt clenched his teeth as he remembered the scene he'd walked in on that morning. It hadn't been the first time he'd found his band member in a similar situation. "Cheating on his wife was bad enough, but he had no business being with someone that young."

"I agree."

"Eric and Jordan want to act like it never happened. But Travis and I can't do that, and Carter refuses to admit he has a problem, so the band is in limbo."

Which also meant his music career was in limbo unless he took his agent's advice and started a solo career.

Matt removed the rack from the table. "Ladies first."

"Are Carter and his wife still together? I remember reading about them getting married, but I haven't seen anything about them since," Liv asked before hitting the cue ball and sending it across the table.

He watched the balls scatter in different directions, but none reached a pocket. "Yeah, she forgave him. Why, I don't know."

Matt could understand McKenna forgiving Carter if he'd forgotten her birthday or if he'd promised to call every day while they were on the road and hadn't. But he couldn't wrap his head around her forgiving him after what he'd done.

"I wouldn't be able to." Liv gestured toward the table. "Your turn."

"You didn't leave me many options." He considered his possible shots before settling on the solid blue two ball.

"Sorry. I'll try harder next time to make sure I leave you with an easy shot."

As he hoped, the ball moved across the table and dropped into the corner pocket. "I have a good feeling about this game tonight." Stepping back, he wrapped his arms around her and pulled her close before kissing her.

He intended it to be a quick kiss. Unfortunately, the moment his lips touched hers, everything went hot and tingly from his scalp to his toes. Pulling his mouth away from hers was impossible.

Liv's fingers touched his neck half a second before the sound of something hitting the floor reached his ears, breaking the spell. A glance to the left revealed the source of the noise, and he reached down to pick it up. "You might need this. It's your turn."

"Why do I get the feeling you kissed me, hoping it would distract me enough so that you have a chance of winning tonight?"

"The thought never entered my mind." Matt took her hand and kissed it before handing her the pool cue. "But now that you mentioned it, it's not a bad idea."

Nine

"BRIAN'S UNCLE IS RETIRING, and they're throwing him a party. I'm going shopping for a new outfit. Do you want to come?" Emma asked early Saturday afternoon.

Liv enjoyed a day out shopping almost as much as she loved cooking. And if Emma had called a day or two earlier, she would've accepted in a heartbeat. She couldn't remember the last time she'd spent a day out with a friend shopping. Not to mention, her summer wardrobe could use a little work.

"Wish you had asked sooner. I have plans with Matt today."

"I had a feeling you'd have plans with him today, but I thought I'd ask anyway. You two have been spending a lot of time together. Is it fair to assume things are going well?"

They'd spent time together ten out of the last fourteen days. Sometimes he came to her place, and she'd cook dinner for them. Then afterward, they'd watch a movie or a baseball game. Over the last two weeks, she'd learned that Matt was almost as big a baseball fan as she was. Other nights she visited him. To date, though, the closest they'd come to going somewhere public together was the afternoon he stopped in the restaurant before he headed out of town to visit his cousin in Boston.

"Maybe." Liv flopped back on her bed and watched the blades of the ceiling fan. "I don't know. It's not like a relationship between us will ever last." As much as she enjoyed spending time with Matt, she reminded herself of that fact regularly.

"Why not? If he wasn't interested, why would he be spending so much time with you?"

"He's here on vacation. Before the summer ends, he'll go back to Florida." She assumed that was where he'd go, anyway, although he most likely had homes in multiple states.

"Did he tell you that?"

He doesn't have to.

"No, but come on, let's be realistic, Emma. He isn't going to move here permanently to be with me. And I'm not interested in a long-distance relationship. Been there, done that."

"You never know. He's been visiting town at least once a year for how long now? He might be willing to relocate. And it's not like he has a desk job to worry about in Florida. Actors and musicians live anywhere they want and travel when they need to be somewhere."

"Emma, let it go. Neither of us has declared our undying love, and I don't see it happening. But I'm okay with that."

More or less.

Was her heart trying to get invested in whatever was between them? Yes. Her brain, though, wisely reminded her that this relationship had an expiration date, much like a gallon of milk, and that she should just enjoy the time they spent together.

"Fine, you win *for now*," Emma answered, emphasizing the end of her sentence. "What are the two of you doing today?"

"I wish I knew. Last night, he just said he had a surprise for me today."

Some people loved surprises, while others hated them. She tended to be a middle-of-the-road kind of person.

"Any idea what it might be?"

She'd spent a lot of time last night when she got home, and then again this morning, trying to guess what Matt's surprise might be. So far, she hadn't come up with any good possibilities.

A knock reached Liv in the bedroom before she answered. "Nope, but I think I'm about to find out. Matt's here." She wasn't expecting anyone else today.

"Call me tomorrow and let me know what you guys end up doing."

"Will do," Liv said as she crossed into the living room. And if she didn't, Emma would be calling to find out.

No matter how many times she opened her apartment door and found Matt on the other side, the sight of him standing there left her mentally shaking her head and wondering if she was dreaming. The Matt Sherbrookes of the world didn't spend time with people like her. No, they took gorgeous movie stars and models to charity events and music award ceremonies. They didn't eat home-cooked meals and then spend the night watching the Red Sox on a 32-inch television. And if they did watch a baseball game with a woman, it was while sitting in luxury seats at a ballpark.

"How's my girl?" Matt asked, wrapping his arms around her waist and pulling her close.

The feel of his body against hers sent a wave of heat through her, and despite her brain's constant reminder that this wouldn't last, her heart got a little more invested every time he held her close.

"Curious."

It was a far better answer than telling him the truth—that what she really wanted to know was what she should read into his greeting.

"If you're ready, we can go."

"Just need some shoes. But how about a clue? It's hard to pick the right footwear when you don't know what you're doing."

"Wear something you'll be comfortable walking in."

"That's not much of a clue."

Matt kissed her cheek, then released her. "It's all you're getting for now."

There was a lot she didn't know about Matt, but she knew him well enough to know she wasn't getting anything else from him, at least not until he was ready to share.

Downstairs, the door opened before Liv touched the handle,

revealing perhaps the last person she would've expected to see standing there.

"Sebastian?"

I'm dreaming.

If she were wide awake, Matt Sherbrooke wouldn't have greeted her by calling her "his girl," and her ex-boyfriend wouldn't be standing in front of her.

"Sebastian," Liv repeated. "I, uh, it's nice to see you."

It wasn't, but it seemed like the appropriate thing to say.

"I stopped by the restaurant to pick up takeout. Maggie told me you weren't working today, so I thought maybe you were home."

Liv glanced down at the plastic bags he held. Sebastian was free to get lunch from anywhere, but that didn't explain why he'd been about to climb the stairs to her apartment.

She sensed Matt behind her even before his arm brushed against hers.

"Sorry, it looks like you have plans," Sebastian said, his eyes darting toward Matt before settling on her face again.

"Sebastian, this is, um, my friend Matt." Calling him a friend seemed a safe way to introduce him. "Matt, Sebastian used to live in town." Unless Matt asked, she wasn't sharing any other details today.

"You look familiar. Have we met before?" Sebastian asked, extending his hand.

If she weren't so confused about her ex's sudden appearance, she would've laughed at Sebastian's question.

Shaking his head, Matt took Sebastian's hand. "No, but I get that a lot."

Liv barely contained a smile at the humor in Matt's voice. Sebastian wasn't a fan of Eclipse, but they'd gone to see them in concert once when they were together. Even if they hadn't, Matt regularly appeared on magazine covers and on the internet. She doubted there were many people in the United States who hadn't seen his face at least once.

"Are you visiting your sister?" she asked him. It wouldn't

explain why he'd decided to visit her, but it would explain why he was back in town.

"I'm staying with her for the weekend, but I'm moving back to town soon. I closed on a house yesterday. I'm having some renovations done on it before I move in."

The surprises just kept on coming.

"Congratulations. I'm sure your sister is happy you'll be close again."

"Since you have plans, I won't keep you. But let's get together and catch up soon," Sebastian said, pushing the door open again and allowing in bright sunshine.

"Um, sure." Although he was her ex, she had no real hard feelings toward him, and they had known each other a long time.

Neither she nor Matt spoke as they walked outside to his car. Parked between her VW Bug and Edith's late-model Corolla, Matt's car stood out like a rose in a vase full of carnations, and Liv shook her head when he opened the door for her. Ferraris and those who drove them were far removed from her day-to-day life, and if she knew what was good for her, she'd remember that.

"Since you seemed so surprised to see him, I'm guessing Sebastian isn't someone you talk to often," Matt said as he fastened his seat belt and started the engine.

"No, at least not anymore. We went to school together, but today was the first time I've talked to him in almost two years. I see his sister occasionally. She still lives in town, but usually she goes to visit him."

"But he was stopping by to see you?"

Is he jealous?

Almost as soon as the thought popped into her head, she dismissed it. This was Matt Sherbrooke. He had no reason to be jealous of another man.

"Sebastian and I were together for about a year, but that was a long time ago. Before today, I can't remember the last time I saw him."

Well, she could, because it was the day they'd officially ended their relationship after trying to do the long-distance thing, but Matt didn't need that particular detail.

* * *

Back at Liv's apartment, when Sebastian said he'd asked about her whereabouts at the restaurant and then decided to see if she was home, an unfamiliar emotion had overcome Matt. Liv's announcement that they had been a couple not only reinforced the feeling but allowed him to give it a name: jealousy. While he recognized it as irrational, he hated the idea of an ex-boyfriend showing up at Liv's place out of the blue.

Who was he kidding? He hated the idea of one visiting her period. But if he knew what was good for him, he'd keep his big trap shut. While Liv clearly enjoyed spending time with him, Matt wasn't sure how invested she was in their relationship yet. And the last thing he wanted was to send her running in the opposite direction because she thought he was a jealous asshole who tried to control who his girlfriend spent time with. And, yes, although he hadn't come to town looking for a relationship, he thought of Liv in those terms. Most of the time, he sensed his feelings were reciprocated. Every once in a while, though, Liv sent him some confusing messages. If that continued to happen, he'd address it with her, but for now, he was going to enjoy spending time with her and getting to know her better.

He'd passed by the recreational complex located about twenty minutes outside of town several times, but he'd never been. But during a conversation earlier in the week, Liv mentioned how much she enjoyed mini golf, and a visit to Smugglers' Cove seemed like a great start to their day. In addition to mini golf, the complex also offered guests batting cages, boats that could be rented for a relaxing trip around the lake, go-carts, and a ropes course. While he'd only planned for them to play mini golf, if Liv wanted to hit some baseballs or complete the ropes course before moving on to his second surprise of the day, he wouldn't object.

"Smugglers' Cove," Liv said when he turned into the parking lot. "How did you know I like it here?"

"The other night you said you loved mini golf."

"I did?"

"We were talking about things we loved to do when it's nice outside. And based on the reviews, this place has the best course in the state."

"The reviews are not wrong. When I was younger, I used to come all the time with my friends. It's been well over a year since I was here."

Matt navigated his way through the crowded parking lot. It appeared as though they weren't the only ones taking advantage of the gorgeous weather.

"Are we just playing mini golf while we're here?"

"I'll leave that up to you, but I do have plans for us later this evening, so we can't spend all day here." He took her hand as they moved away from his car.

"They sell Heavenly Ice Cream here, which is out of this world. And since I know your little secret, I think we should get some."

"You had me at ice cream. Consider it done."

Based on the complex's website, the facility actually consisted of three separate courses. The one labeled bronze was a basic, family-friendly nine-hole course with silly, cartoonlike animals placed throughout it. The second one, labeled the silver course, consisted of eighteen holes, and according to the website, the shots were more challenging yet not impossible.

The gold course sounded the best to him, however, and it was the one he'd opt for today if left up to him. The website's description said the course's twenty-four holes were spread out through a maze of trees and flowers. In the pictures, a small stream flowed past several of the holes and sometimes even through many of the greens. He imagined more than one player had their ball land in the water instead of where they'd intended.

A teenager chewing gum and wearing far too much makeup looked up from her cell phone, a look of pure annoyance on her face when Matt greeted her. "Bronze, silver...." The teen's voice trailed off, and as her eyes doubled in size, he knew what was coming next before she continued.

"Oh. My. God. I know you!" The teen hopped to her feet and

covered her mouth with her hands. "You're Matt Sherbrooke, the lead singer of Eclipse."

He'd never been so happy that no one was around. Today was the first time they'd ventured out in public together. While he'd suggested outings before, Liv always insisted she'd rather either stay at her house or his. He didn't want their first outing in public to turn into a spectacle. But if the teen didn't turn the volume down a few notches, people were going to get curious.

"I love your music. I've seen you in concert three times. Is the band going to release any new songs soon?"

Matt glanced at the teen's name tag. "I don't know, Kirsten."

"Can I get your autograph and a picture? My friends are never going to believe you were here." Even before he answered, the teen slapped a piece of paper and a pen in front of him.

Nodding, he pasted on a smile. The sooner he gave the fan what she wanted, the sooner they could be on their way. "Sure."

Four pictures and an autograph later, Kirsten remembered she was there to work, not fawn over customers. "Do you want tickets for the bronze, silver, or gold course?"

"What do you think, Liv?" he asked as several more people got in line behind them.

"The gold course is my favorite."

"Gold it is, then." He handed over his credit card.

Kirsten gave Matt a scorecard as she ran the credit card. "The balls and clubs are behind you. Return them here when you're done." Smiling, the teen handed him back his credit card and then grabbed her buzzing cell phone.

At the equipment rack, Matt reached for the red ball, and his fingertips landed on it just as Liv's did.

"If you want this one, I'll take another color," she said, moving away.

He didn't much care what color he used. They all did the same job. "Doesn't matter to me. I just thought you'd go for the pink or yellow one."

Liv selected a purple one instead before removing a red ball and handing it to him. "Purple and red are my favorite colors. They always have been. Certain shades of blue and green, I like.

Yellow, I hate, and pink ranks down near the bottom, unless we're talking about nail polish."

Matt made a mental note of the details. A guy never knew when it might be useful to know his girlfriend's favorite colors.

Somehow, they managed to make it through the whole course without losing a ball in the water. After, they both attempted the final extra shot of the course. The shot was beyond difficult, and if a customer made it, they received a gift card for five free visits. He'd watched the group ahead of them try the shot, and they'd all missed. He'd assumed the same would be the case for him and Liv.

It wasn't.

While his ball missed the hole as he'd expected, Liv's didn't.

Instead, she hit the ball, sending it up the ramp and through the narrow opening. Then it landed in the hole instead of the gap surrounding it, which was where most players' balls ended up—his included.

"I'm shocked that you made that last hole," he commented as they waited in line for ice cream. "Are you a mini-golf pro or something?"

Not only had Liv made the impossible shot at the end, but she had made all but three holes under par. Kirsten, the employee at the customer service booth, told them Liv's score was the second-best ever for the course and added their scorecard to the Wall of Stars.

"Is that even a thing?"

In his peripheral vision, he saw the trio of young women walking toward them and somehow knew they weren't coming over to get in line for ice cream.

"I have no idea." Matt momentarily considered getting out of line and heading in the opposite direction, but he dismissed the idea almost immediately. The group had seen him, and if they were determined to talk to him, they wouldn't care if he got out of line. Instead, they would follow them, possibly creating an even bigger scene than if he stayed where he was and talked to them.

"I knew it was you," the tallest of the group said when they reached him. "Nadine said I was crazy and that you'd never be here, but I knew she was wrong." The twentysomething nodded toward the dark-haired woman standing next to her.

"Sara didn't believe you either," Nadine replied.

"We're, like, your biggest fans, Mr. Sherbrooke," the first woman said.

As he'd expected, thanks to the trio, other people were turning their attention toward him and Liv.

"Lyndsey is right. We even flew to Oregon once to see you because your concerts in Boston and Portland were sold out," Sara said. "Can we get your autograph and some pictures with you?"

What he wanted was to get some ice cream and then enjoy it while taking a walk with Liv along the path they'd passed on their way over here. Any other day, he would've agreed without blinking an eye. He wasn't alone, though.

"I can get our orders while you do that," Liv said before he could ask if she minded.

"Are you sure?"

Most of the women he'd dated didn't like it when random fans interrupted them while they were out.

"Yeah, just tell me what you want."

"Surprise me. You know what I like." Matt kissed her cheek before stepping out of line.

As often happened, once people saw him with other fans, they decided to approach him too. Not only did he take photos with the trio who'd first spoken to him, but he also posed with ten other fans.

Before anyone else decided ice cream was a good idea and recognized him, he headed for the picnic table where Liv was waiting for him.

Matt kissed her cheek before sitting next to her. "Sorry about that."

"It's not your fault, and I don't really blame them. Last

summer, if I'd been about to get in line for ice cream and I saw you standing there, I would've done the same thing."

Something between a laugh and a snort escaped him. He'd gone into the restaurant more times than he could count in the past, and she'd never asked him for anything more than his lunch order. "No, you wouldn't have."

Liv raised a spoonful of ice cream toward her mouth. "Yeah, you're right. I wouldn't have done that to you. But if it were Jordan Mead or Travis Hart, I would've been just like your fans earlier. I am, like, their biggest fan," she said, altering her tone to match the young woman's.

"And all this time I thought I was the member of Eclipse you liked the best." Sighing, Matt shook his head. "I can't do it today, but I promise I'll introduce you to Jordan or Travis so you can get their autographs and some pictures."

Although he knew Liv was being silly, he did want her to meet his friends and his family, which was something that rarely happened with the women he dated. In fact, the last girlfriend he'd introduced to his family had been Juniper Stanley. Seven years ago, she'd been an up-and-coming actress with a recurring role on a popular sitcom. Thanks to her acting ability and the attention she garnered from being with him, she was now a household name with four blockbusters under her belt and another being released this fall. Before her rise to movie dominance, he'd thought she might be the one. After her first film catapulted her to the top, however, she'd changed—and not for the better. Now, he occasionally saw her at charity events and awards shows, but otherwise, he had no contact with her.

"I can't wait." Liv pushed his bowl toward him before taking another spoonful of her own. "I almost got you a banana split, but the ice cream here is so good it should be against the law to put toppings on it."

Matt scooped up a large spoonful of pistachio ice cream. "The jury is out on that. I happen to be a connoisseur of ice cream."

"I've heard of wine connoisseurs, but ice cream? I think you're making that up."

A few of the people in the line for ice cream kept looking in his direction and then talking to each other before glancing his way again. Before they came over, interrupting his time with Liv again, maybe they should take the walk they originally intended.

Standing, Matt reached for her hand. "If we're going to get in that walk before we leave, we should go now."

Liv didn't argue, and with their ice cream in hand, they headed toward the path that started to their right.

Thankfully, the path that took them through wooded areas and around the lake was empty, but it also led them past the entrances to the go-carts and the ropes course. Today, both were crowded with people of all ages.

"The last time I was here, they were still working on that area." Liv pointed to the ropes course. "But I wouldn't mind trying it sometime."

"I've done a few. We'll have to come back and do it."

"You snowboard, ski, surf, and do things like that." Liv pointed toward the course. "Sounds like you're a bit of an adrenaline junkie."

She wouldn't be the first person to accuse him of that. "Did I forget to tell you that I enjoy skydiving?"

"Uh, yeah. Why would anyone be willing to jump out of a perfectly good plane?"

"Funny, my mom has asked me the same thing."

"Seriously, do you have something against sitting still?"

"No, but while I love getting lost in a good book, life's too short to spend all your time cooped up inside. Honestly, I can't think of an activity I won't try at least once."

"I think you'd get along well with my cousin Andrew. If it's labeled dangerous or, in some cases, stupid, he'll do it without batting an eye."

So far, Matt had only made one emergency room visit in his life. "The worst injury I've ever had was a broken ankle, and I got that running track in high school."

The path rounded a corner, leading them past the north entrance of the mini golf course and then back into the woods.

"So, Mr. Connoisseur of Ice Cream, what's your verdict on

Heavenly's pistachio?" Liv pointed at the remaining ice cream in his bowl.

Rather than answer immediately, he ate the last spoonful. "It's really good," he admitted. "But I've had better."

"Where?"

"Two places immediately come to mind. Pirate's Cove in Newport, Rhode Island, and Vanilla Moon in Healdsburg, California."

"I've never been to Newport or Healdsburg, and I don't see myself getting there anytime soon, so I'll settle for ice cream from Heavenly."

"California might be out for a long weekend trip, but Newport's only about a five-and-a-half-hour drive from here. If we fly, we'd be there even quicker. Just name the week and I'll make us reservations." He had cousins in the area, but she might be more comfortable at a hotel.

"I'll get back to you. We have a lot of weekend events we're catering this summer."

Ten

SHE'D INTENTIONALLY AVOIDED GOING out in
public with Matt for three reasons. The first was that she wasn't
sure how she'd feel about random people interrupting them.
While she hadn't appreciated the fans today, it hadn't been as
annoying as she'd feared, at least not for her. Despite Matt's
friendly smile and willingness to pose for photos, she'd sensed his
annoyance. Her second and third reasons were tied together.
She'd been seeing pictures of Matt with women for at least a
decade. More often than not, including the photos this spring
with the dark-haired woman, the headlines claimed the two were
in a romantic relationship. Liv wasn't used to the spotlight, and
the idea of her picture appearing on the *Star Insider*'s website or
a popular social media site made her cringe. However, what she
feared even more than the pictures circulating was seeing some of
the comments people would make, which would no doubt leave
her in tears. Keyboard warriors thought nothing of posting mean
and spiteful comments. And Liv could only imagine what some
people might say about her, especially if they compared her to
some of the other women Matt had been linked to over the years.
At least there hadn't been any paparazzi hanging around today.
Even she would have noticed some random person walking
around with a state-of-the-art camera and snapping pictures. As
for photos that fans had taken, they'd been too obsessed with

getting pictures of themselves with Matt to snap any of her with him. The longer he stayed in Orchard Harbor, though, the more likely it would get out that he was in town. In turn, that might send professional photographers with their fancy cameras to town. But at least for the moment, she didn't have to worry about that.

"You're awfully quiet over there," Matt said as he turned into his driveway. "I don't think you've said anything since we left Smugglers' Cove."

"Sorry. I've been trying to guess what else you have planned for us today." So far, he hadn't dropped a single clue. "But since we're back at your house, does it involve me beating you in a game of pool again?"

They'd played multiple times, and while he'd done better against her, he'd yet to win a game.

"Nope, not tonight." He waited for the garage door to open and then drove inside. "But soon I want a rematch."

"Name the date and time, and I'll be there." She waited for him to come around and open the car door. She found it unnecessary, but he insisted. Since it seemed to be important to him, she didn't fight him on it.

"Pool is out. So, are you going to give me a private concert while I eat grapes and cheese on the roof?"

"Hey, that's not a bad idea. I'll keep it in mind for another night. Do you prefer green grapes or red ones?"

Taking her by the hand, he led her past the other vehicles in the garage and into the house.

"Red, but I'll eat either. Just make sure they're seedless."

"Noted."

Matt grabbed the basket on the counter as he made his way to the refrigerator. "I just need to pack up a few things, and then we'll be ready to go."

She watched as he added what were clearly take-out containers to the basket before selecting two bottles from the wine fridge and adding them as well.

"Are we going on a picnic?" The last time she remembered doing that, she'd been in middle school.

"Not exactly." With the basket in one hand, he reached for her left hand. "Follow me."

After crossing the kitchen, they exited the door that led out onto the back deck. Matt didn't stop there, though. Instead, he led her down the stairs and across the lawn to the dock.

She noticed the yacht moored there. She couldn't think of the vehicle at Matt's house as merely a boat. Despite growing up near the ocean, she didn't know a lot about boats. She'd never been interested enough to spend any time learning about them. However, even she recognized that the only thing the boat Matt owned and the one her aunt and uncle had at their lake house in New Hampshire had in common was that they could both be used on water.

He escorted her up to the upper deck and gestured toward the sofa that looked nicer than the one in her living room. "Make yourself comfortable."

It didn't take long before they were pulling away from the dock, and Liv watched as Matt's house grew smaller and smaller in the distance.

"I never would've guessed this was what you planned for tonight." Although he'd told her to make herself comfortable, she'd opted for the seat next to his rather than the sofa behind him.

Reaching over her, he kissed her cheek. "There's more, just wait. Once we get far enough out, I'll drop anchor, and we can enjoy the rest."

It had been a long time since she'd been out on the open water, and while Matt concentrated on operating the yacht, she soaked up the ocean air. Eventually, though, they reached the spot Matt had intended, and he took care of whatever he needed to ensure the boat stayed relatively in one place.

"Follow me." After grabbing the basket he'd left on the table, he reached for her hand.

"Before we do anything else, how about a tour?"

He'd told her to make herself at home, but much like at his house, it had seemed inappropriate to explore the other levels without him.

"Sure. I'll follow you," Matt said, gesturing toward the stairs that led to the main deck.

As with the upper deck, there was ample seating for passengers, a table, a complete entertainment system, and a small galley. While the majority of the deck was enclosed by glass, the backmost portion, which she vaguely remembered was called the stern, had a well-placed door that allowed the owner to keep the elements from ruining their day.

A third set of stairs brought them to the lower deck. She'd expected the yacht to have sleeping accommodations, as well as some kind of bathroom similar to the one in the camper her parents used these days. Although the Class C motorhome they'd upgraded to was far nicer than the camper the family used when she was growing up, it still wasn't anything like what the yacht's lower deck contained.

There were three bedrooms. The largest contained what looked like a king-sized bed. There was a full-sized bed in the second, while the third had two twin beds. There were also two bathrooms. The larger of the two could only be accessed from the main cabin, while the slightly smaller one was obviously intended for whatever guests were on board. Despite the slight size difference, both had decent-sized showers.

Once they'd finished the tour, they returned to the main deck. But rather than sit down near the table, Matt grabbed the basket and walked toward the front of the boat. From the one cruise she'd taken, she remembered it was actually called the bow, although she didn't understand why boats had to have special names for the different sections. Front and back seemed sufficient to her.

The designer had completed the area with a small table featuring seating in the shape of a semicircle, ensuring that no matter where you sat, you'd have a great view.

"You could spend weeks out on the water." Her first thought was that the yacht was nicer than her apartment. But that would only remind him of their vastly different backgrounds.

"That's kind of what I have in mind." Coming up behind

her, Matt wrapped his arms around her waist. "I'm hoping you'll come with me."

Before Liv could process his words, he kissed her neck. "I know your weekends are pretty booked through July, but maybe we can get away in August. It doesn't have to be for weeks. We could go for five or six days and then plan on something longer when Ocean View isn't as busy. What do you think?"

She thought she was dreaming, and at any minute she'd wake up, because it sounded as though Matt wasn't thinking of their time together as a distraction until he got bored with town and left. But that couldn't be. Someone like Matt would never be happy living in Orchard Harbor year-round. Eventually, he would get bored. Maybe he'd make it until August. Although she doubted it, he might even stick around until the winter. Fall in this area of the country was breathtaking with its vibrant colors. But year-round, never.

"Yeah, I think we have at least one event every weekend between now and the end of July." While some events were small and didn't require her attention, Ocean View wasn't hurting for business right now.

"August it is. We can head down to Sanborn Island or Martha's Vineyard."

She'd never visited either of the places he mentioned and wouldn't mind a short vacation. The farthest she'd traveled in the past year was to see her brother in Boston.

"Or if we don't get there before then, we could go to Newport."

Liv considered her words before speaking. "Do you think you'll still be here in August?"

"Why wouldn't I be? Do you know something I don't?"

He brushed his lips against the other side of her neck, setting fairies loose in her stomach. And before she changed her mind about the conversation she was about to start, she stepped out of his embrace and turned to face him.

"Orchard Harbor isn't exactly home for you, Matt. You told me that Florida was." His exact answer had been less straightforward, but it didn't change the fact that Orchard Harbor was just one of many places where he owned a home and spent time.

"No, I said it was where I spent most of my time, so I guessed it was home. I like it there, but it's never really felt like home. If that makes any sense?"

Liv shrugged. "A little." Except for when she'd attended college, she'd never lived anywhere else.

"I've been visiting here for sixteen years. Do you know why?"

Matt brushed his fingers across her cheek and then settled on the skin below her ponytail, sending a jolt of energy across her skin.

Honestly, she had no clue why he'd been visiting town for so long. As she'd pointed out to Emma recently, Orchard Harbor wasn't an international hotspot. "Your favorite restaurant is here?" The answer made about as much sense as any other she could come up with.

A slow smile spread across his face. "Ocean View Grill is one of my favorite restaurants." He lifted her hand toward his lips. "But no, that isn't why I bought a house here."

Matt kissed her knuckles, sending her heart even further out of the friend zone than it already was. Oh, who was she kidding? Her heart had left the friend zone weeks ago.

"Orchard Harbor is, for lack of a better word, my happy place. Whenever I'm here, I feel—" He paused, and she could almost see the wheels turning in his head as he searched for the right word. "—like I'm where I belong. I love Florida and parts of California, but I'm restless when I'm there. Eager to go somewhere else. That doesn't happen when I'm here." Releasing her hand, Matt stepped closer. "And now, I have even more of a reason to stay."

Liv didn't know how to respond. Thankfully, it didn't matter because he pressed his lips against hers, leaving her unable to do anything but close her eyes and focus on his kiss. At the same time, her heart tap-danced against her rib cage, an experience she couldn't recall ever happening while being kissed. Then again, she knew for a fact that she had never been kissed by anyone with a mouth as talented as Matt's either. And she sure as hell didn't want to think about how it had gotten that way.

Gradually, he brought their kiss to an end and rested his forehead against hers. "If we're not on the same page, tell me now."

She knew what he was asking. Although she still had a difficult time wrapping her head around it, her heart already knew the answer. "I'm pretty sure we're on the same page."

"Good. Now, do you think you can schedule me in for a little vacation away in August, or should I start planning a kidnapping now?"

"I'll see what I can do. I don't want you to get in trouble for breaking the law. It wouldn't be good for your image."

Matt's lips formed the same who-turned-up-the-heat smile he was known for, and Liv briefly wondered how many women had been on the receiving end of that smile and simply handed over their phone numbers.

I don't want to know.

There was one thing, though, that she did want to know but had avoided asking. Now seemed like a good time to bring it up.

"Matt, I need to ask you something."

"You can ask me anything."

"Last month, a bunch of the magazines had pictures of you with a woman and a little girl." She didn't want him to think she wasted her time reading magazines like the *Star Insider*. "All the captions claimed the two of you were romantically involved. One even claimed the little girl was your daughter."

"Yeah, I know the ones you're talking about. Evie and I were never together. She's my cousin's fiancée. The little girl's name is Reagan, and she's not my daughter. Her parents passed away recently, and Adam is her guardian."

Something similar to relief washed over her. Until this moment, she hadn't realized how much the photos and the possibility that Matt had gone from being in a relationship with someone to spending time with her had bothered her.

"They're going to visit sometime this summer, so you'll meet them. And you'll also meet my brother in July. He and his girlfriend are attending a wedding in town."

"Your brother and his girlfriend are going to a wedding in Orchard Harbor?" Who could either of them possibly know in her corner of the world? "Do you know whose it is?"

Matt shook his head. "I only know the bride was one of Brianna's sorority sisters and that the wedding is taking place at an estate owned by friends of the bride and groom."

It really was a small world. "I think I've met the bride and groom. We're catering a wedding in July that's being held at an estate on Windy Bluff Lane. Blake and Gina are friends with the owners, Raymond and Erin Thatcher."

"Is this the one for the clients who booked you at the last minute?"

Wow, he had a good memory. "Yep."

* * *

Overall, the day had gone as Matt planned. The fans at Smugglers' Cove had been a bit of an annoyance, but Liv hadn't complained about the interruption. Her questions about their relationship, though, had blindsided him. Since the beginning, he'd assumed they'd been on the same page and that she realized he considered her more than just a summer fling while he was in town. In hindsight, he should've known better. He'd never told anyone how he felt about Orchard Harbor, and sometimes several months separated his visits. It'd been only natural for Liv to assume he didn't plan to stick around for long. Hopefully, they'd gotten that cleared up, because even if he didn't feel at home in town, since Liv was here, he wouldn't be leaving anytime soon. He'd been wrong before, but his intuition kept telling Matt that their relationship was special and not like the ones he'd had in the past. He didn't want to risk it by returning to Florida or anywhere else.

After securing the boat for the night, Matt climbed back up to the upper deck where he'd left Liv stargazing.

Scooping her up, he sat her on his lap. "See anything good?"

"I found the Little Dipper, but that's it."

"That's better than I usually do. I've never been good at

finding constellations." Matt trailed his fingertips across her cheek and then down her neck, his eyes never leaving hers.

"It helps if you look in the right direction."

"I'm looking at exactly what I want."

"Oh, that was smooth, my friend."

"Doesn't mean I'm not being honest." Right now, tasting her was the only thing he could focus on.

"That could be true." Liv pressed her palm against his cheek before sliding it around to the back of his neck, sending a ripple of need through his body.

Matt had desired women before, but he'd never wanted to kiss one the way he did now.

Before he made the first move, Liv covered his mouth just as the final rope holding him back snapped.

She brushed her lips back and forth against his, each pass sending his pulse higher.

As he'd imagined doing to her earlier, she traced the seam between his lips with her tongue. He didn't need any additional encouragement. When Matt's tongue touched hers, the outside world disappeared.

Liv tasted like red wine and something unique to her. And he couldn't get enough.

The blood pounded in his ears as every cell in his body urged him to take things to the next level. To remove her clothes and see how accurate the image in his dream last night had been.

At some point in the future, he planned to do it. He just wasn't sure if it would be tonight. He'd leave that entirely up to her.

Unable to simply end the kiss, he gradually turned down the intensity. And after brushing his lips against hers a final time, he pressed his forehead to hers.

"Stay here tonight."

Liv pulled away and searched his face, making him wonder if he should've kept his mouth shut.

"Nothing has to happen that you're not ready for, but I want to fall asleep holding you." It'd be absolute torture to do nothing but hold her as they slept, but he'd never forced a woman before, and he sure as hell wouldn't start now.

Matt knew the moment she made her decision. "By here, do you mean on the boat or back at your house?"

"Either. Whatever you want. But if we stay out here, I can't serve you breakfast in bed." He hadn't been thinking about spending the night on the boat, but if that was what she wanted, he was okay with it.

Standing, Liv reached for his hand. "Breakfast in bed. You should've led with that. Let's head back up to the house."

Eleven

MATT GRABBED his ringing cell phone after he flipped the omelet in the pan. There weren't many things he cooked well, but he made a damn good omelet.

"Hey, Adam," he greeted after putting the device on speaker so he could finish preparing breakfast. "What's up?"

"Other than avoiding calls from my mother, not much."

He didn't blame his cousin. Although he'd always known his aunt and uncle weren't the warmest people in the world, he still couldn't believe how they'd reacted when they found out Evie and Adam were engaged.

"Have you and Evie decided on a wedding date yet?"

When Adam asked Matt to be his best man, he shared that they planned to get married sometime in July, but he hadn't been sure of the exact date or location.

"That's one of the reasons I'm calling. The last Saturday in July. We decided to get married on the beach."

Assuming she wasn't working that weekend, it sounded like he and Liv would be going away sooner rather than later.

"I'll be there."

"Should we add a plus-one to your invitation?"

"Let me check with Liv, and I'll get back to you."

"I'm assuming that's the woman you were photographed eating ice cream with yesterday."

Not again. People needed to learn to mind their own damn business.

"Yeah. I did some pictures with fans, but I didn't realize anyone took any of Liv and me."

Except for a few brief times, such as when they'd gotten ice cream, they'd been alone much of their time at Smugglers' Cove. He'd hoped that meant no one snapped any photos of them together like the day he'd spent with Evie. While he knew it was bound to happen eventually, he wanted to keep their relationship off the radar for as long as possible. Exposure on social media added stress to any relationship, but it could be devastating to a new one.

"Where did you see the pictures?" Not that it mattered, but Matt was curious.

"Evie saw them. They're trending on CHAT."

Social media was both the greatest and worst invention.

"Thanks for the heads-up." At least Liv was still asleep, and he could break the news to her before she found them herself. Although, he wasn't looking forward to the conversation.

Matt wasn't stupid. Even though she hadn't said it, he knew she'd been reluctant to go anywhere in public with him because she was worried about pictures of them on social media. He'd hoped that if they started going places together where large crowds were unlikely, she'd see that while it might happen, it wasn't an everyday occurrence. It was just bad luck that it happened during their outing yesterday.

"How did you meet her? Aren't you in Maine?"

"I am." Matt grabbed the toast and added two slices to each plate. "Actually, we've known each other for years. Her brother was my college roommate and the reason I first came to Orchard Harbor."

"Interesting."

There was no mistaking the curiosity in Adam's voice, and Matt understood the reason for it. The last time he'd dated a woman who wasn't either a model or an actress had been in college.

"How does her brother feel about you two being together?"

"I'm not sure he knows." At least, Matt hadn't told him. As far as he was concerned, it wasn't any of Owen's business. And if Liv had told her brother, she hadn't mentioned it to him.

"Well, if he didn't before, he probably will soon. Assuming you two are still friends, you might want to call him before he finds out thanks to CHAT," Adam replied. "If any of my friends were involved with Tory, I would've wanted to find out from them, not a picture on social media. And depending on the friend, I would've had an issue with them being together."

"I've met some of your friends, and I would've had an issue if they dated Tory too," he said as he put the dirty pan in the dishwasher. His cousin Tory was more like a sister.

"I wouldn't talk. Your friends aren't all saints either. Since we're on the topic, have you talked to Carter?"

Besides Liv, Adam and his fiancée were the only people he'd discussed the band's issues with.

"No, but Jordan called me a couple of weeks ago." He expected another call from the guy soon. Ever since Matt told them he was done, Jordan called him every few weeks and pleaded his case. Before now, he'd never realized just how stubborn Jordan could be. "Do you mind if I call you back later? I just finished cooking breakfast for us, and I'd like to eat it before it gets cold."

After promising to call Adam back once he knew if Liv was coming with him to the wedding, Matt added two coffees to the tray and headed upstairs.

Usually, the first thing he did in the morning was open the curtains. Today, he'd left them closed when he left the room. The floor-to-ceiling windows provided a breathtaking view and filled the room with natural light. This morning, though, he'd wanted to keep the light from waking up the sleeping woman so that he could surprise her with breakfast. It had been a while since he'd woken up with a woman in his bed. And while their relationship might be new, the sight of Liv there felt right, as if it was where she'd always belonged.

After setting the tray down on a table, he sat on the edge of the bed and brushed his fingertips across her cheek. When she remained asleep, he repeated the action, only this time using his lips. In response, she rolled over onto her back and opened her eyes. Judging by her expression, it took her a moment to remember where she was.

"Morning," Liv said as she moved into a sitting position and tucked her hair behind her ears. "Have you been up long?"

"Long enough to make breakfast. I hope you're hungry."

"You cooked us breakfast?"

"Last night I promised you breakfast in bed. Did you think I wouldn't deliver?" Matt stood and retrieved the tray he'd carried up.

"I just thought it would be a bagel or a muffin with some fruit. Not this." She gestured toward the tray he put on the bed. "You even remembered to put milk in my coffee."

He'd seen her drink coffee enough to know she liked extra milk and two spoons of sugar, unless she was drinking iced coffee. If that was the case, she added four.

"And two sugars," he said, handing her the cup.

"I'm impressed." She took a sip before picking up a fork and cutting into her omelet.

Following her lead, Matt reached for his coffee first. He'd enjoyed a cup while cooking, but one was never enough in the morning.

"My cousin called this morning. He's getting married the last weekend in July. If you're not working, I'd love it if you'd come with me."

An emotion he couldn't identify crossed her face before she glanced down at her plate and cleared her throat. "I, uh, don't know if we have something booked that weekend. If I had my phone, I could check."

"Tell me where you left it, and I'll go grab it." He hadn't paid attention to where she'd put her things when they came inside last night.

"It's on the counter in the kitchen."

Leaning forward, he kissed her before heading downstairs.

The sound of an oven timer and the instrumental opening to

"Loving You" came from the device the moment he handed over the phone.

"Someone's popular this morning," Matt said, grabbing a slice of toast.

"It's my brother. He's probably coming up this weekend and wondering if I'm around to paint," Liv said before answering the call.

Damn. He should've told her about the pictures circulating on social media as soon as he came upstairs.

While it could be a coincidence that Owen was calling now, Matt's gut told him Liv's brother had seen the photos and was calling with questions.

* * *

"Hey, Owen. What's up?"

"You tell me."

Okay, that wasn't the response she'd expected.

"How long have you and Matt been together?"

Liv choked on the coffee she'd just swallowed, and across from her, Matt cringed.

"For a few weeks," she said once she could speak again.

"And when did you plan on telling me?"

It wasn't that she didn't want Owen to know, but since she'd assumed Matt viewed their relationship as a temporary diversion while in town, she'd seen no reason to tell her brother or anyone else.

Usually, she could gauge Owen's mood. Right now, she couldn't tell if he was angry or annoyed. Liv momentarily considered making something up. But if he was furious, saying she'd planned to tell him the next time he visited wouldn't help.

"I don't know. Maybe...." Liv paused as she fully processed her brother's question. The only person she'd told about Matt was Emma. And while Emma and Owen were more than acquaintances, they didn't speak unless they happened to run into each other. Even if they did communicate regularly, Emma never would've told Owen that Liv was involved with someone.

"Hold on a minute. How do you know about us?" she asked.

Across from her, Matt raked a hand through his hair and frowned.

"You're really asking me that? Half the world knows, Liv. Pictures of you together are trending on CHAT."

Closing her eyes, Liv rested her head against the headboard.

"There are pictures of us on CHAT?" Her brother wouldn't lie, but wouldn't she have noticed if someone had been taking pictures of them yesterday?

"Yeah, someone posted three. I don't know if there are any on other sites."

Crap. She'd known this would likely happen if they went somewhere together. However, she hadn't expected it to happen the first time they went somewhere public. Although she didn't know why. From a logical standpoint, it wouldn't matter if it was their first time out in public or their one hundred and first.

Her phone alerted her to another text message, reminding her she'd received one right before she answered the phone.

"Can I call you back later?"

"Yeah, of course."

She knew before she even checked that at least one of her recent messages was from Emma. She wouldn't be surprised if she also had some from Phoebe.

Liv found five missed text messages. As she'd expected, she had one from Emma and two from Phoebe. The last two were from college friends.

Since it was the oldest, she started with Emma's message.

Emma: In case you didn't know, the cat's out of the bag.

Liv: I know. Just talked to Owen.

After sending her reply, she moved on to the next message.

"Owen called because of the pictures?" Matt asked.

Nodding, she read the next text.

Phoebe: When were you going to tell me you were seeing Matt Sherbrooke?

Liv: Soon.

"You know about the photos on CHAT?" she asked.

"Yeah, my cousin told me. I was going to tell you, but Owen called before I got the chance."

"Have you seen them?"

Matt shook his head.

Before she second-guessed her decision, Liv opened the app on her phone. Sure enough, pictures of her and Matt popped up on the screen.

They weren't kidding.

Her brother and her friends had told her photos were trending on the site, but still, she hadn't been 100 percent prepared to see them.

"Why would someone take a picture of us eating ice cream?" Didn't people have better things to do?

"People do weird things."

Even as she scrolled down to the comments, she recognized it was probably a bad idea.

"I've had people take pictures of me leaving the grocery store," Matt said.

Although she'd expected some less-than-kind comments, she didn't find any—at least not yet. Instead, the comments consisted of people wondering who she was and commenting on Matt's looks.

"I know you avoided going out in public with me because you were worried this would happen." Matt's statement pulled her attention away from the comments.

She'd never told him that because she thought he'd find it a silly concern.

"Why didn't you say anything?"

Reaching over, he took her hand. "I don't know. But I hoped no one would notice us yesterday, and when you saw people wouldn't bother us everywhere we went, you'd get more comfortable going places with me."

Her phone alerted her to another text message, and she groaned.

"Unfortunately, things didn't go as I planned."

Liv didn't blame him. "It's not your fault."

"Are you okay with this?" His eyes reflected the worry and

concern in his voice. "It doesn't happen every time I leave the house," he continued before she could answer. "I know it might seem that way, but photos of us won't show up on social media every day."

She'd never thought much about it, but Matt's statement made sense. "I know."

He squeezed her hand. "That doesn't answer my question, Liv. Are you okay with this? Because it will happen again."

Before last night, she would've said no. A short summer fling wasn't worth public scrutiny. Now, though, she knew he wasn't spending time with her as a way to pass the time while in town. While there was no guarantee that they wouldn't eventually go their separate ways, she was willing to face the keyboard warriors on social media to see where things between her and Matt went.

Leaning closer, she pressed her palm against his cheek and smiled. "I'm not thrilled about it. But for you, I'm willing to deal with it."

Twelve

THE BUZZING CELL phone on the table alerted him to someone at the door. Even without looking, Matt knew it was his brother and his girlfriend. Theo had texted him about an hour ago with their ETA.

Closing the book he was reading, Matt stepped back into the house. Like every day this week, the weather was picture perfect. The kind of day you didn't waste sitting inside, so while he waited for Theo, he'd taken the newest novel he'd picked up and headed outside.

"Couldn't find a town farther away from civilization?" Theo asked by way of greeting.

"Hey, I tried, but this was the best I could do. If you think you'll survive, come on in."

Theo cracked a smile and hugged him. "It's good to see you. And from what I saw on the drive in Orchard Harbor, it's a cute little town."

Matt slapped his brother on the back. "I'm glad you're here."

"Matt, this is Brianna." Theo gestured toward the fashionably dressed woman next to him.

Weeks ago, his brother accused him of having a type—something Matt disagreed with. However, if anyone had a type, it was Theo. Every woman he remembered his brother dating shared the same physical characteristics. Hell, the woman standing in front of him even resembled Iris, Theo's last girlfriend. He hoped Brianna's personality wasn't similar to her as well.

"It's nice to meet you."

"Thanks for letting us stay with you." Brianna's subtle Southern accent told him she might live in California now, but she'd grown up somewhere else.

"Liv won't be here for at least an hour. So if you want, I'll show you up to your room so you can unpack, and then we can have a drink outside while we wait for her."

"Sounds good to me," Theo said.

Fifteen minutes after Matt left his brother and Brianna upstairs, Theo joined him in the kitchen.

"I still don't understand why you like it here so much, but I can see why you selected this house. The view is incredible," Theo said.

Matt set the charcuterie board Liv had put together on the table. "Give the town a chance. It might grow on you."

His brother falling in love with Orchard Harbor was about as likely as it snowing tomorrow. That didn't mean he couldn't warm up to it.

"Yeah, I don't see that happening."

"Did Brianna decide she's had enough of your company for the day?"

Theo picked up a plate. "She's on the phone with Gina. What are we drinking?"

"I was thinking wine, but I can make you just about anything." In his opinion, wine complemented the assortment of cheeses and meats. But if Theo wanted a beer or a cocktail, that was fine too.

"Wine sounds good," Theo replied as he added an assortment of food to a plate. "Is Liv the woman you've been photographed with recently?"

He'd held his breath when new photos appeared on CHAT. While Liv claimed she was willing to deal with it after the first time, he'd worried she'd rethink her decision when more showed up five days later.

Thankfully, she hadn't—at least not yet.

"Yeah." After selecting a wine, he carried it and three glasses back to the island.

"Is she a native or another confused part-time resident like you?"

"Native? We are talking about a person, not a species of birds. But to answer your question, Liv's always lived here."

In case Brianna wanted something else, Matt only filled two wineglasses before following his brother's lead and making himself a plate.

"Where did you meet, the library?"

A sudden urge to wipe the smile off his brother's face struck him, but instead of doing it, he frowned and reached for a glass. "You're not funny. Well, maybe you're funny looking."

"Lighten up. It's a fair question. I didn't see any clubs when I drove through, and Orchard Harbor doesn't seem like the kind of place where organizations would hold large events."

Theo's comments were understandable, and he wasn't wrong. Still, they annoyed him.

"Her brother and I have been friends since college." As far as he could remember, he'd never told Theo about how he'd come to know of Orchard Harbor.

"I didn't realize you had friends in town."

"Owen lives in Boston now, but his parents and younger sister still live here."

Across from him, Theo drummed his fingertips against the granite, a signal that he was thinking. "Was he your college room-mate one year?"

Matt nodded as he chewed. "Freshman year. He invited me to have Thanksgiving with his family that year."

"I wondered how you found this place."

"Sorry, that took longer than I expected," Brianna said, entering the room. "Gina gets talkative when she's excited."

Before Matt could offer her a drink, she pointed toward the wine bottle. "Can I have a glass?"

Nodding, he filled a glass and handed it to her. "How long are you staying?" His brother had given him an arrival date, but he'd never shared how long they planned to be in town. Since it didn't matter to him, he hadn't asked until now.

"Unless you need us gone by a specific date, we thought we'd play it by ear. We both have the week off and don't need to be anywhere until Adam's wedding next weekend."

If Theo and Brianna stayed past Monday, he'd be shocked, but even if they left Sunday morning, it would give him a chance to catch up with his younger brother.

Across from him, Theo rechecked his watch and shook his head.

"Got a hot date or something?" Matt asked.

"Just wanted to know what time it was."

Matt wasn't buying it, but if Theo didn't want to share, he wouldn't push the issue. Instead, he switched on the baseball game. "What do you think of the Dodgers so far this year?"

"I think they have a good chance of making it to the World Series this season," Theo answered.

"Yeah, if they can keep Williams and Perry healthy and not repeat last season. Have you made it to many games this year?"

Much like him, Theo was a big baseball fan, and for years, he had had season tickets.

Frowning, Theo shook his head. "Brianna's not into baseball."

"Doesn't mean you can't go."

"I've been working a lot and would rather spend the weekends with her."

"Fair enough." Matt raised his glass to his mouth, but before he took a drink, his cell buzzed, letting him know someone was at the door. "Liv must be here. Do you want anything while I'm inside?"

Since they'd have more space, they'd taken their drinks and snacks up to the rooftop earlier.

"Some more wine would be good."

He could hear Brianna's voice as he passed by the guest room. Less than fifteen minutes after they'd gone outside, she received a phone call and came back inside. That had been at least forty minutes ago. Matt couldn't imagine talking to someone on the phone for so long.

Downstairs, Matt opened the door and once again reminded himself to get Liv a key so she could come and go.

"I would've been here sooner, but I stopped home to change," Liv said as she stepped into the house.

He didn't need her to tell him that. He could tell. While she didn't have a uniform in the traditional sense, she always dressed in black pants and a white top when working at the restaurant or catering an event.

"Don't worry about it. Theo and I have just been catching up." Slipping his arms around her, Matt pulled her in close and kissed her. "I'm glad you're back. You're staying here tonight, right?"

Before Liv answered him, he pressed his mouth against hers again. Unlike his first kiss, which had been a brief "Hello," he took his time caressing her lips until she opened for him. The moment his tongue touched hers, the outside world disappeared. Liv tasted like iced coffee and something unique to her. And he couldn't get enough.

Blood pounded in his ears, blocking out everything around them as every cell in his body urged him to take things further. To lead her upstairs, remove her clothes, and pick up where they'd left off that morning before she headed into work.

Thankfully, one of them was still grounded in reality, and Liv pulled away before he could act on the fantasy running through his head.

"Now might be a good time to stop." Judging by her voice, the kiss had affected her just as much as him.

Matt touched his forehead to hers and took in a deep breath. "Yeah, we should probably go outside before I change my mind and we go to my room."

"Your brother just got here. It would be rude to do that."

"He'd understand," Matt said as he ran his fingers through her hair.

"What about his girlfriend?"

"She's been in their room on her phone almost the entire

time she's been here. I doubt she would even notice." Theo hadn't said it, but Matt knew he was annoyed that Brianna had spent so much time in their room since they arrived.

Liv stepped out of his embrace and took his hand. "C'mon, let's go."

"Before we head up, I need to grab another bottle of wine." Matt allowed her to lead him toward the kitchen. "You never answered me. You are staying here tonight, right?"

She'd spent the night with him six out of the last ten days. When she wasn't there, his bed felt empty in a way it never had in the past, and his mornings lacked something he couldn't identify.

"Are you sure you want me to? You have guests."

"So what? It's just my brother." Even if his parents were the ones visiting, he'd want her to stay.

"As long as you're sure, I'll stay."

He wanted more than for her to just stay the night. Matt wanted Liv to move in with him, which was something he'd never considered asking any of his girlfriends to do. But he wasn't sure she was ready for that. Until he felt more confident of her answer, he'd wait to ask.

Theo was shaking his head at something Brianna had just said when Matt and Liv joined them.

"But —"

His brother nodded in their direction. "Let's talk about it later, okay?"

Crossing her arms, Brianna huffed. "Fine."

He didn't need a crystal ball to know that later, Theo would get an earful and possibly find himself sleeping on the floor.

As he made introductions, Matt poured Liv a glass of wine and refilled his brother's.

"We have dinner reservations at Rosso Linea for six." This time of year, if you didn't make reservations on a Friday night, you weren't getting a table. And while the Ocean View Grill was perhaps his favorite restaurant in town, he assumed that after spending the day working there, Liv would prefer something else.

"That sounds lovely, but I'm meeting up with Gina in a little while."

The look Theo shot in Brianna's direction required no explanation. He wasn't happy with his girlfriend's plans.

"We haven't seen each other in ages," she continued.

Matt didn't care if she joined them or not. Clearly, his brother did, though. "I get it. We can go out some other night while you're here."

Brianna glanced at Theo before looking at him and smiling. "Thanks for understanding."

"It's up to you, but I'd rather stay here and get takeout," Theo said.

Matt was happy to stay home and have something delivered, and he wasn't all that surprised that Theo wanted to stay in. His brother hated when they went out together and fans approached him, which seemed to happen more often than not when Matt and Theo were together.

"Liv?" Matt asked, although he already knew the answer.

"Takeout works for me."

* * *

Liv couldn't remember the last time she'd seen siblings look so similar. While Theo's hair color was a shade or two lighter, he and Matt could've passed for twins. Even their voices were identical. In fact, if Liv closed her eyes and listened, she'd have had a hard time determining who was speaking. She wondered if Theo had a great singing voice too. However, unlike Matt, she could picture Theo wearing a suit and sitting behind a desk all day. Even if she didn't know Matt was an actor and popular musician, she couldn't see him working in an office setting.

"When we had dinner with Mom last week, she asked me to remind you that you haven't visited in six months," Theo said when he rejoined them from walking Brianna out to their rental car.

"Sometime in the fall, when Liv can take some time off, we'll visit her and Dad."

They'd talked in general terms about her meeting his family, but this was the first she'd heard about them visiting his parents in California.

"You might want to try to make it sooner. Otherwise, she might pay you a surprise visit here."

Matt didn't talk about his parents much, but based on this conversation, it sounded as if his mom had at least one thing in common with hers. If more than a month passed without a visit from Owen or Faith, Mom started to complain. Thankfully, for Mom's sake, that didn't happen often, especially since Owen and his wife purchased the vacation home in town.

"At least she'll see you next weekend at Adam's wedding. Maybe that will buy you a little more time."

"Mom and Dad won't be there. Adam didn't invite them."

Theo's eyebrows inched toward his hairline. "He didn't invite them?"

Based on Theo's expression, he was just as surprised by Matt's answer as she was. While they hadn't discussed the guest list for his cousin's wedding, she'd assumed his parents would be there since they were Adam's aunt and uncle. If and when she got married, all her aunts and uncles would attend, just like they had attended her brother's and sister's weddings.

"He didn't want to put anyone in an awkward position since Aunt Shannon and Uncle Benjamin won't be there. So they just invited Adam's cousins, a few close friends, and Evie's family."

"Nice try. You almost had me," Theo said.

"I'm not joking. Adam isn't speaking to his parents. You can ask him for the full details, but long story short, they don't want him to marry Evie."

It wasn't any of her business, but she had to know why. "Why not?"

If the woman were a serial killer or a convicted drug dealer, she could understand not wanting your son to marry her. However, disapproving of one's son or daughter's choice of spouse was antiquated.

The fingertips brushing back and forth against her arm stilled. "My aunt and uncle can be...." Matt paused, as if searching for the correct word.

"Snobs," Theo supplied for him when Matt didn't continue.

"That's one way to put it. They have a warped idea of who their children should and shouldn't be with. They expected our cousin Tory to marry the son of a close family friend. They still haven't completely forgiven her for ending that relationship. And Aunt Shannon wants Adam to be with someone more like her."

Liv had never met Matt's aunt, but she had a good idea of what type of woman she found acceptable. She knew without a doubt that Theo's girlfriend fit the bill.

Did Matt's parents share the same view as his aunt and uncle? Matt's uncle and his dad were brothers. They had grown up in the same house. Often, that meant siblings held similar beliefs.

If his parents did have the same view, how would they react when they found out he was dating a caterer who worked as a waitress when needed?

I'm not sure I want to know.

"Adam really didn't invite Aunt Shannon and Uncle Benjamin?" Clearly, Theo was struggling to process the news. "I know Jake didn't invite his parents, but that was different. He wanted to avoid the media attention and the presence of the Secret Service."

"Nope, and according to Adam, Tory's thinking about doing the same when she and Duncan get married. I know Tory isn't getting along with Aunt Shannon and Uncle Benjamin either."

Matt's aunt and uncle sounded like they deserved the "Worst Parents of the Year" award.

"Where are you guys staying for the wedding?" Theo asked.

"I'm staying at the Viking. Unfortunately, Liv's working that weekend."

She was both relieved and disappointed that she couldn't join Matt for the wedding. While she wanted to meet his family, she'd rather meet them one or two at a time, not en masse at a family function like a wedding. Although Matt hadn't complained when she told him she couldn't go, he'd obviously been disappointed.

"That's too bad. What do you do for work?" Theo picked up his wineglass and finished the contents.

"She owns a catering company," Matt answered before she got a word out.

Why did you tell him that?

While she oversaw the day-to-day running of the catering side of things, she didn't own it, at least not yet. Eventually, she planned to take over everything, much like her father had done, but that was still far in the future.

"Is there much need for one in town?"

Liv shot Matt a look, telling him to be quiet. "You'd be surprised. We're the only ones in the area. The next closest one is about forty miles away, so we get business from all over."

"Ocean View is catering the wedding you and Brianna are here for," Matt added, clearly not getting the hint that she wanted him to keep quiet.

It could've been a trick of the light, but it appeared as if Theo cringed at the reminder.

"Not looking forward to the wedding?" Matt asked.

Maybe it hadn't been her imagination.

Stretching his legs out, Theo clasped his hands together. "Some of Brianna's friends can be a bit much, if you know what I mean. Especially her former sorority sisters."

She'd spent little time with Brianna, but if her friends were anything like her, Liv understood why Theo was lacking enthusiasm about tomorrow's event.

"But it's one day. I'll survive."

Next to her, Matt shifted so he could pull out his phone. "I don't know about you two, but I'm starving. What do you feel like having for dinner?"

"Anything is fine with me. If you want, I'll go pick it up, whatever we order," Liv said.

Less than half the restaurants in town delivered. And while DoorDash picked up from almost all of them, she'd noticed Matt tended not to use the service often. Although she hadn't asked him, she assumed it was because he didn't want people to know his exact address. If die-hard fans knew that, she could see them camped out on the street waiting for him to leave or even coming onto his property.

"I vote for pizza. Brianna doesn't eat it, so it's been a long time since I had a decent one."

"Works for me. Do either of you want anything specific?" Matt asked.

When both replied no, he placed an order with Fireside Pizzeria, which was no surprise. The fact that he was having it delivered did surprise her, though.

"Food should be here in about forty-five minutes." Rather than put the phone back in his pocket, he placed it on the table.

"I would've gone and picked it up."

Wrapping his arm around her shoulders, he pulled her in closer and kissed her cheek. "I know, but I don't want you to."

One thing she could say about Matt, unlike her last boyfriend, was that had no issue with public displays of affection. Sebastian hadn't even liked holding hands when they were out together.

"While we wait for the food, how about some pool?" Matt asked.

"I'm up for it. Liv?" Theo replied.

When Matt squeezed her shoulder, she got the hint.

"It's been a while since I played, but sure."

Everyone's definition of a while was different, so she wasn't necessarily lying. She hadn't played since sometime last week.

Thirteen

LIV SAT WATCHING Matt and Theo as they played pool, and although her body was in the same room, her mind remained elsewhere. She'd spent enough time with Theo's girlfriend to know they had nothing in common. That didn't bother her. Even if her and Matt's relationship lasted for the next fifty years and Theo and Brianna stayed together, how much time would she really have to spend with the other woman? And even if they ended up seeing each other once a month, Liv could get along with anyone when she had to.

She was worried about Matt's parents, though. Theo had mentioned he and Brianna had visited them recently, but he hadn't given any indication of what their parents thought of Brianna. While she realized he couldn't do that with Brianna sitting next to him, he'd had plenty of time since she left to share such information.

Was Brianna the only type of woman they'd find acceptable, or were they more open-minded? Unlike Matt and Theo's aunt and uncle, did their parents care more about their children's happiness than about the connections a marriage to the right person might bring to the family?

Then again, they may dislike both Liv and Brianna equally. Perhaps they sought someone with a vastly different personality and background from either of them.

Unfortunately, there were only two ways to find out. She could ask Matt and assume he was being truthful, or she could wait until she met them and see how they treated her.

The wisest move would be to ask Matt. In her book, openness in a relationship was essential, and without it, the relationship would never last. However, it wasn't a conversation she really wanted to have. On the other hand, the waiting was going to drive her crazy. She'd just have to decide which was worse, an uncomfortable conversation or waiting for a meeting that might never happen anyway if their relationship ended soon.

Great options I have.

Across the room, Matt's phone buzzed, alerting him to someone at the door just as he was about to take his turn.

Leaning his pool cue against the table, he pulled out the device. "Food's here. I'll be right back."

Liv stood before he moved from his spot. "I'll get it. You guys are in the middle of a game."

"Thanks. Everything is paid for, including the tip," Matt said as he picked his cue stick up again.

Although she didn't know the delivery driver's name, she recognized her from around town.

"I have four large pizzas, an order of onion rings, and an order of stuffed jalapeño peppers," the twentysomething-year-old brunette said.

How many people does Matt think he's feeding?

"Thank you."

Rather than turn and leave, the woman took a step closer and glanced over Liv's shoulder into the house. "Hey, is this really Matt Sherbrooke's place?"

She didn't know what name he'd given when he placed the order. Should she lie and hope the woman believed her? Usually, she preferred not to lie, but maybe in this case it wouldn't be the end of the world.

"The owner of the home is named Matt Sherbrooke, but he's not the one you're thinking of. I wish he were. I'd love to meet him. Eclipse is my favorite band."

The younger woman took another step closer, and Liv wondered if she planned to walk right in and search the house.

"I don't believe you. My friend Myra said she saw him in Hometown Brews last week."

With her hands full, she couldn't close and lock the door, so using her foot, she started to close it instead. "You can believe whatever you want, but you're wrong. Have a nice night."

Well, she'd tried. Matt should've let her go and pick up their order tonight. If people started camping out in the street, it was his own fault.

"You've been practicing." Theo's voice reached her in the hallway. "I guess there isn't much else to do around here."

Well, that told her what he thought about the town.

"How much longer are you going to be here?" Theo's question brought her to a standstill. "You've already been here for what, a month? You must be getting bored."

"I'm not leaving."

The sound of a ball striking another followed Matt's answer.

"You're not heading back to Florida?"

She could imagine Theo's expression just by the sound of his voice, and if she didn't care so much about Matt's answer, she'd laugh at the mental image.

"No. From now on, this is going to be home."

Excitement rushed through her. Matt had told her he was happiest when he was here and that he planned to stick around, but hearing him tell his brother made it seem more real.

"You can't be serious. You'll go crazy here, especially in the winter. Is there even a place nearby to go skiing? What are you going to do, take up knitting and play bingo at the senior center?"

Even in the winter, there was more to do around town than knit and play bingo, but if she marched in and told him that, Matt and Theo would both know she'd been in the hallway listening.

"Yep, as well as needlepoint."

"I'm serious, Matt."

Theo clearly doubted his brother's words. He knew Matt much better than she did. Should she assume Theo was right?

That, despite Matt's assurance, he would get bored and change his mind about staying in town past the summer.

"So am I. You might go crazy here, but I feel more at home here than anywhere else. And Liv's here."

Her heart skipped a beat at his comment.

"You're going to relocate because a woman you've been seeing for a few weeks lives here? I mean, I like Liv. She seems very nice, but do you know how insane that is?"

Well, at least he likes me.

"You're entitled to your opinion, but that's what I'm doing. And I plan to ask Liv to move in with me."

Somehow, she managed not to drop the food on the floor.

"There must be something in the water around here. You've never asked a woman to move in with you. At least, I don't remember anyone ever living with you."

She'd overheard far more of their conversation than she should've, and the right thing to do would be to let them know she was about to walk into the room so they could change the subject. Unfortunately, Liv's curiosity prevented her from doing the right thing. Later, she'd probably feel guilty about eavesdropping, but not now.

Once again, the sound of a pool ball striking another came from the room, followed by Matt's voice.

"I never have."

Questions swirled in Liv's mind, and her heart rate spiked as the silly organ pounded in her chest. Not only did Matt intend to ask her to move in with him, but it was something he'd never done in past relationships. And while he might want her to move in with him, was that what she wanted?

Sure, they enjoyed spending time together, and she cared about him, but living together was something else entirely.

Oh, who was she kidding? Each day that passed, she lost another piece of her heart to him. Still, that didn't mean they should move in together.

But if he did want that, did it mean he loved her? He'd never said the words. Then again, neither had she.

Now isn't the time to think about it.

If she didn't return soon, he'd come looking for her. After all, it didn't take that long to answer the door and accept a delivery order.

He hasn't asked yet, so worry about it later.

Liv took a deep breath and slowly exhaled before walking into the room. "How many people did you think you were feeding tonight?"

"Theo and I couldn't agree on what to get."

"I need to go back and get some plates and napkins."

After setting his pool cue down, Matt crossed the room and relieved her of the pizza boxes. "No need. I put some paper plates and stuff under the bar so we'd have them whenever we need them."

The word caught her attention. Was he referring to her and him, or was it more of a general *we*—as in whoever happened to be visiting at the time?

Pushing the question from her thoughts, she headed to the bar. "So, who's winning?"

Rather than wait for a plate, Matt opened the top pizza box and pulled out a slice topped with every meat imaginable. "At the moment, Theo is."

Less than ten minutes later, Theo sent the black eight ball into a corner pocket.

"You need to practice more." He leaned his pool cue against the wall and walked over to the table where they'd placed the food. "Are you up for another game?"

"Nah, I want to finish eating first, but Liv might be interested."

Although equally as handsome as Matt, her heart rate didn't spike when Theo turned his full attention her way.

"What do you say? Are you up for a game?"

As he passed by her to return his pool cue to the rack, Matt winked at her. She didn't need any additional hints.

"I might be a little rusty."

"Don't worry about it. You can't play any worse than my brother."

"Trust me, our skill levels are not even close." Somehow, Matt managed not only to keep a straight face, but he also kept any trace of humor from his voice.

"Wow." Genuine surprise appeared on Theo's face. "You're going to let him get away with saying that?"

Biting down on the inside of her cheek, Liv shrugged. "He's not lying."

"It wouldn't matter. If I said something similar about Brianna, she'd still skin me alive."

Theo's comment didn't surprise her. Brianna seemed like the type who disliked being criticized. Of course, in this instance, Matt was doing the exact opposite despite the way he made it seem.

Selecting her personal pool cue from the rack, where she'd been keeping it, she joined Theo near the table. "Do you want to break?"

"Doesn't matter to me," he answered around a mouthful of food.

"Why don't you do it, then. It's my weakest area."

Behind her, Matt coughed, and she glanced over her shoulder in time to catch his grin.

* * *

Theo shook his head as he watched the eight ball glide across the table and into a side pocket. "I can't believe you made that shot."

Matt had spent enough time with Liv to know she made even the most difficult shots look easy.

"I got lucky tonight." Liv kept her face down as she removed the balls from the corner pocket.

"I would've bought that after our first game, but not after this one. No one is that lucky. You lied when you said it had been a while since you played."

As Matt expected, his brother sounded more annoyed than angry.

Liv moved on to the next pocket and removed the solid purple ball. "I didn't lie."

He'd never seen a more innocent-looking expression on someone's face, and he cleared his throat to keep from laughing.

"But I guess my definition of 'a while' is different than yours." A smile tugged at the corner of her lips.

Theo followed Liv's lead and emptied the pocket closest to him. "And when was the last time you played?"

If Matt didn't know better, he'd believe she was actually trying to remember when they last played. Maybe Liv should consider an acting career.

"Probably sometime last week or the week before." She looked at Matt. "Does that sound right?"

"Last Tuesday, I think."

"That explains why my brother played so much better than usual. You've been helping him."

This time, Liv didn't try to suppress her smile. "Guilty as charged."

Theo returned his pool cue to the rack. Rather than sit, he walked toward the bar. "I won't have time tomorrow, but I want a rematch before I leave."

"Tell me when, and I'll be here."

She hadn't said as much, but he'd known Liv had been anxious about meeting Theo and Brianna, although he didn't understand why. It was only his brother. But it sounded like whatever anxiety she had was long gone.

"Can you grab me one too?" Matt asked before Theo closed the refrigerator. "What time is the wedding tomorrow?" If his brother had shared the information, he didn't remember.

Shrugging, Theo handed him a beer. "Sometime in the afternoon. I don't remember the exact time."

"We're serving dinner at five."

"What are we having? Anything good?" Theo asked.

Before she could sit in the chair she'd vacated earlier, Matt grabbed her hand and tugged her onto his lap. "Everything Ocean View makes is delicious."

"Gina has us serving four different dishes. She wanted the guests to have options," Liv explained.

"That's the first I'm hearing about it. Brianna better not have requested a vegetarian meal for me."

His brother's tone told him more than his words did.

"We are serving a vegetarian meal, but I don't remember how many."

"Any chance you can prepare an extra nonvegetarian meal just in case? I don't care what it is as long as I don't have to eat a tofu chicken breast or a soybean filet."

Matt didn't know if soybean filet existed, and he had no desire to find out.

"Don't worry. I'll make sure you don't starve."

"I owe you one. Brianna's been trying to get me to become a vegetarian for weeks. She even tried to convince Dad."

"And how did that go?" Matt asked. Their father liked nothing more than a rare filet paired with his favorite merlot.

"Let's just say Dad told her in the most polite way possible what Brianna could do with her opinion of his diet when she refused to let the matter go."

Matt could easily picture the scene. His father was an expert at telling someone where they could stick their opinions without the other person realizing it. And if Brianna did something similar to him during her stay, he'd be following his father's lead.

"This doesn't leave the room, but I got the impression Mom and Dad didn't care for Brianna."

Matt wasn't surprised by Theo's comment, especially if she'd acted the same way as she had today with them.

Although their parents had never technically disapproved of the women Matt and his brothers dated, they'd clearly liked some more than others. And a good indication of their feelings was how often they invited the two of you over or inquired about the person when they called.

"What about Aiden?"

Unlike their parents, Aiden would share his thoughts about the women they dated with either of them.

"He's not a fan." Theo raised his beer toward his mouth. "But he hasn't spent much time with her."

Matt hadn't expected Brianna and Theo's relationship to last, but if Aiden didn't like her either, it definitely wouldn't.

On his lap, Liv went rigid. Clearly, something they'd said bothered her. While he wanted to ask her what it was, it seemed like a better conversation to have when they were alone.

"Aiden's been traveling a lot for work, and our schedules haven't aligned well. I've only seen him two or three times in the past two months."

While Matt might go months without seeing his brothers, the same wasn't true about Theo and Aiden. Of course, it was much easier for them to hang out with each other since they only lived about twenty minutes apart.

"Is he still with Lilian?" At least, Matt thought that was her name.

"Man, when was the last time you talked to him? Aiden hasn't been with Lilian for at least six months."

He didn't remember the last time he'd had a conversation that lasted longer than three minutes with his brother.

"I called him about two weeks ago, but he was heading out and couldn't talk."

"Unless something changed in the last week, Aiden's single."

When Matt's phone buzzed, he didn't bother to check to see who was at the door because it had to be his brother's girlfriend.

"Brianna's back."

Theo chugged the rest of his drink as he stood. "I'll be back."

Kissing her neck, Matt ran a hand down Liv's back. "What's the matter?"

"Nothing."

"I'm not buying it. You're so tense I could use your back as an ironing board."

"Do you even own an ironing board?"

"I might have one somewhere, but that's not the point. You're upset about something we said."

Liv moved off his lap and into the chair next to him. "Are your parents like your aunt and uncle?"

She needed to be a little more specific. "In what way?"

"You told me your aunt and uncle disapprove of your

cousin's fiancée. Are your parents overly critical of the women you and your brothers date?"

While his parents had some things in common with his Uncle Benjamin and Aunt Shannon, thankfully, that wasn't one of them.

"God, no. They haven't liked all my girlfriends, but they've always been welcoming to them. The same is true of my brothers' girlfriends."

Rather than appear relieved by his answer, Liv's frown deepened.

"You don't believe me?"

"It's not that I don't believe you, but when was the last time you or Theo dated a caterer who waitressed on the side?"

Well, she had him there.

"Your last girlfriend was Jasmine Locke. She's a huge movie star. And Brianna's probably a high-priced lawyer or business executive who graduated from Harvard. Theo met her at a charity event. I'm sure it wasn't the type of event people like me go to."

"Liv—"

"Am I wrong?"

Matt leaned closer. "Brianna's a lawyer, but I don't know what type of charity event it was. However, I know my parents won't care about what you do, and except my Aunt Shannon and Uncle Benjamin, no one in my family will." Cupping her face, he pressed his lips against her forehead. "You've got nothing to worry about. Got it?"

Liv nodded, but the uncertainty remained in her eyes. Unfortunately, he knew nothing he said would completely reassure her. When she met his parents, she'd see he'd been right.

Fourteen

THURSDAY NIGHT, Liv kicked off her flip-flops and claimed her usual spot on Phoebe's sofa. "I think the last time we hung out like this was on St. Patrick's Day."

Between their work schedules and personal lives, every time one of them suggested getting together lately, someone was always busy. And when Liv reached out earlier in the afternoon, she'd assumed one of them would already have plans for tonight. She'd been floored when Phoebe and Emma texted back that they were both free.

After adding a pitcher of sangria and a veggie platter to the already crowded table, Phoebe claimed the other end of the sofa. "No, you both came over when the newest season of *The Fortunate* came out."

"That's right, we did." She didn't know how she could've forgotten that. They'd binge-watched the entire season in one night. After roughly three hours of sleep, she'd catered a baby shower and had fallen asleep in the driver's seat of the delivery van. Thankfully, it had been after the shower ended and the van had been safely parked. Still, it had been embarrassing to be woken up by someone banging on the window.

Emma sank into the oversized armchair she used whenever they gathered, crossing her legs. "Well, it's not my fault. I'm not the one who is always busy."

"Refresh my memory, but who's been going to their boyfriend's lake house in New Hampshire every other weekend for the past two months?" Phoebe asked.

"Definitely not me. I don't remember the last time I left the state." Liv grabbed a carrot stick and dipped it into the home-made hummus Emma brought with her. "And I know it wasn't you, Phoebe. That only leaves one possibility."

Although it meant seeing her less, Liv was happy Emma and Brian's relationship was going well.

"Fine. I'm not around as much as I was in the winter, but I'm free a lot more than either of you lately."

"I'll have more free time in a couple of months." As a profes-sional photographer, late spring through early fall was Phoebe's busy season.

"How many weddings are you working this weekend?" Last weekend, Phoebe had done the photos for two weddings, as well as a young woman's senior pictures.

"Just one on Saturday afternoon. Fingers crossed the bride is easier to work with than Gina was last week. Two of her brides-maids were even worse. You would've thought it was their wedding. Emma, be glad all you had to do was drop off the flowers on Saturday."

While she hadn't been an easy client, Gina hadn't been the most difficult Liv had ever worked with. But it sounded like Phoebe's experience with her had been worse.

"If I'd known Gina was going to be such a pain in the butt, I wouldn't have suggested she call you."

Phoebe waved a hand, dismissing the comment. "A job is a job. You know that. If we only worked for clients we liked, we'd both still be living with our parents or working a second job."

Her friend made an excellent point. "True. And after spending time with one of her bridesmaids, I'm not surprised they were difficult."

"Which one? There were six of them."

Liv had been too busy prepping and serving meals to count how many people made up the wedding party, but she knew there had been more than a few women walking around in the same lavender gown as Theo's girlfriend.

"Brianna."

Rolling her eyes, Phoebe added food to a plate. "Ugh, she was the worst of the bunch. She always needed to have a say in how I positioned her in a photo or where I took the picture. She acted like I was doing a photo shoot for her modeling portfolio. How did you end up spending time with her? Did you lose a bet or something?"

"She's dating Matt's brother Theo."

"That makes sense. I thought the man she was with resembled Matt."

"I forgot Matt's brother visited," Emma said.

Phoebe's phone chimed, and she flipped it over to check the text message. "Aaron says hi," she said as she typed a reply. "Is Theo as unpleasant as his girlfriend?"

Liv shook her head. "He seemed like a nice guy. I got the impression a few times that he wasn't all that happy with Brianna."

"If she acts the same way as she did on Saturday around him, I don't blame him."

"He did say his parents and brother don't like her."

"How many siblings does Matt have?" Emma asked as she refilled her glass with sangria.

"Just two younger brothers. Theo and Aiden are twins."

"It's never a good sign for a relationship when the family doesn't like you." If anyone would know that, it was Phoebe. Her former mother-in-law's constant criticism had played a role in ending her short marriage.

"Theo didn't seem to be worried about it. But I wouldn't be surprised if, when Matt calls me, he tells me they split up."

She'd talked to Matt twice since he left yesterday morning for Virginia, once when he'd arrived at his hotel and then again this morning. Since tonight was the couple's joint bachelor/bachelorette party, she didn't expect to hear from him again until sometime the next day.

"So, I know you only met Matt's brother, but does that mean

things between you are getting serious? Brian and I were together for almost four months before I met his family."

Liv tried not to think about the conversation she'd overheard on Theo's first night in town.

"How long were you and Aaron together before you met his family?" Emma asked Phoebe before Liv could respond to her question.

"Probably about five or six months, but Aaron's parents were in South Carolina for the winter when we met, and his siblings are scattered around the country."

Liv picked her fingernail and tried to mentally prepare herself for her friends' reactions.

"Yeah, I think we've moved out of the casual dating phase. He wanted me to go with him this weekend to the wedding, and he's not going back to Florida. He plans to stay in Orchard Harbor."

Emma smacked the arm of her chair. "Didn't I tell you he might do that! You need to listen to me more."

"When did he tell you that?" If the tables were reversed, she'd be wearing a similar expression to Phoebe's.

"The day we went to Smugglers' Cove."

Phoebe's hand paused over the charcuterie board. "That was like two weeks ago! Why didn't you tell us sooner?"

Shrugging, Liv added some cheese and veggies to her plate. "It seemed like an odd thing to say in a text message, and there never seemed to be a good time for us to get together."

Emma picked up her phone. "Odd, I always thought this device allowed you to call people and have a conversation. Maybe you have to pay extra for that capability now."

"You guys know I don't love talking on the phone." Liv could talk to her friends all day long in person, but she hated long telephone conversations.

"Are there any other exciting details that you haven't shared with us?" Phoebe asked, finally selecting the food she wanted from the spread on the table.

"Well...." Liv raked her teeth across her bottom lip and considered the conversation she'd overheard between Matt and his brother.

"That's a resounding yes."

Phoebe nodded. "I agree with you, Emma. She's holding out on us."

She'd opened her big mouth. Her friends would bug her until she shared, so the sooner she got it out in the open, the faster they'd move on to a different topic. "I overheard Matt telling his brother he plans to ask me to move in with him."

"You do realize you should've started this whole conversation with that, right?" Emma asked.

"He hasn't done it yet. And just because he said that, it doesn't mean it will be soon."

Phoebe exchanged a look with Emma before turning her attention to Liv. "If he told his brother last weekend, then he plans to do it soon. Otherwise, he wouldn't have brought it up now."

"Phoebe's right. When he asks, what are you going to tell him?"

She wished she knew. One second, she planned to say yes, and the next, she intended to tell him she wasn't ready. "I haven't decided."

Other than Phoebe and Sylvie, her college roommate, she'd never lived with anyone except her family. Moving in with someone seemed like a huge step in a relationship.

"That's understandable. You haven't been together long. Aaron didn't move in with me until April."

It was more like Aaron hadn't officially moved in until April. In reality, though, he'd been spending more nights at Phoebe's house than his own for a long time.

"When I decide, I'll let you both know."

"How does Owen feel about you and Matt being together?" Emma asked.

"He's fine with it."

"I'm glad he is. Do you remember how mad my brother got when I dated Ian in high school?"

"Emma, it had nothing to do with Ian and Jarrod being friends. Your brother never trusted anyone you went out with in high school, and he's still overly protective now." While Liv knew

Emma's brother only had his sister's best interest in mind, she'd go crazy if Owen acted in a similar manner.

"Liv's right and you know it," Phoebe said, pointing a carrot stick at her friend.

They'd spent enough time talking about her. She wanted to hear about what was going on in her friends' lives. "Now that you have the 411 on my life, what's new with you guys?"

Phoebe didn't have to be asked twice. "Aaron's going to propose soon." The smile on her face could light up the entire town on a starless night.

"How do you know?"

"Did he tell you that?" Liv asked at the same time.

"No, of course not. I wanted to borrow a pair of his socks, and I found an engagement ring in the drawer. It's gorgeous too. In two weeks, we're going to Cancun. It was his idea, and he planned everything. I think he's going to do it then."

One thing she could say about Aaron was that when it came to Phoebe, there wasn't anything he wouldn't do for her.

"Any chance we can get a sneak peek at it?"

Liv had been about to ask the very same question.

"If I knew for sure when he was going to be home, I'd show you, but I don't. And it would look odd if he came home and found us gathered around his sock drawer. But it's exactly what I would've picked out myself."

* * *

Matt watched the group on the dance floor and shook his head. The song "Y.M.C.A." was as old as dirt, yet everyone seemed to know it, and there always seemed to be one person at events like this who requested it.

"Nice job today," his cousin Jake said as he and his wife, Charlie, sat in the empty seats across from him.

"Thanks, but I had help."

Even before Adam asked him to be his best man, Matt had known that he'd be filling the role when the time came, which meant he'd be responsible for the bachelor party. Unfortunately,

Adam hadn't given him much time to plan. Thankfully, he'd gotten some unexpected help from Evie's maid of honor, because the happy couple wanted a joint bachelor/bachelorette party.

"The brewery tour was Kathryn's idea. I just did the research and booked it."

He'd known, even before they started tossing around ideas, that he wanted to avoid anything that might draw unwanted attention because of him. After all, the day was about Adam and Evie, not him and his fans descending on the group, which could easily ruin it for not just the happy couple but everyone else.

When Kathryn proposed the idea and said she'd heard that some companies offered private tours, he jumped on the internet to see if there were any in his cousin's area. Not only did it sound like something everyone would enjoy, but a private tour would reduce the risk of unwanted party crashers ruining the day.

Matt had found not one but three companies that provided such tours. And when he'd called Kathryn back the following day to discuss the options, he'd shared an idea of his own to prolong the couple's day. Well, maybe it hadn't been 100 percent his own. A sponsored ad for a romantic night of dinner and dancing aboard the *Serenity* as it cruised along the Potomac popped up during his brewery search. And although he hadn't come up with the idea of a dinner cruise, it had been his idea to reserve the entire boat so it was just for their group. Regardless of who deserved the credit, Kathryn had immediately approved of the plan.

In fact, during the entire planning process, they'd only disagreed on one aspect: who should foot the bill. Kathryn insisted she should help, and he'd been just as adamant about paying for everything. It had taken some intervention by Liv before they'd settled on a compromise—one he wasn't honestly comfortable with but had been necessary.

"I should've known. Event planning requires more brain cells than you have," Jake said.

"Hey, I said the brewery tour was Kathryn's idea. I suggested this." Matt gestured around him. "And I wouldn't talk about brain cells, Prince Charming. You'd be lost without your better half."

If looks could kill, Matt would be dead on the floor. His cousin hated it when people used the nickname the media had given him years ago.

"Speaking of better halves, who's the woman you've been photographed with recently? I didn't recognize her."

Before he answered, Theo pulled out a chair for Brianna at the table and raked his fingers through his windblown hair. "Whoever requested this song should be thrown overboard."

"If Sara were here, I'd blame her," Jake said, referring to his younger sister. "She's got a thing for 70s music."

While some of Matt's cousins were there, others weren't arriving until Friday or, in a few cases, Saturday morning, just in time for the wedding. Jake's sister and her husband fell into the second category.

"My money is on Tory. I saw her talking to the DJ, and when the song came on, she jumped out of her seat," Aiden said.

"Maybe I'll bribe the DJ on Saturday night so that if anyone requests it at the reception, he doesn't play it." Theo flagged down a server and ordered a Manhattan.

"Oh, come on. It's a fun song. Everyone loves it. You're just being ornery," Brianna said once everyone placed their drink order and the server walked away.

Matt exchanged a look with Aiden and then Jake, and he knew they were all thinking the same thing. Who used the word "ornery" in everyday conversation?

"Since Brianna likes it, perhaps I'll pay the DJ to play it Saturday night," Matt said.

As he expected, his comment earned him a death stare from Theo.

"Enough about the music. I'm curious too about the woman you've been photographed with. Is she an actress who's just starting out?" Charlie asked.

"In her dreams, maybe." Although Brianna whispered the comment, Matt heard it. Based on everyone's expressions, he wasn't the only one.

He clenched his teeth until he knew he could speak and not tell Brianna what he thought of her.

"No, Liv's not an actress. She owns a catering company in Maine."

"She catered my friend's wedding last weekend. The food is probably the best you'll get, considering the area, but it's nothing special. Gina only hired her because it was the only option. I kept telling her Orchard Harbor was a terrible place to get married, but she wouldn't listen to me."

Why are you joining this conversation?

Matt envisioned himself tying his napkin around Brianna's mouth and then locking her in a storage closet for the rest of the cruise.

"C'mon, Bri. The food at Gina and Blake's wedding was outstanding." Matt hadn't expected Theo to contradict his girlfriend and come to Liv's defense. "And there isn't anything wrong with Orchard Harbor. It's just small and a bit out of the way."

Yes, he had a feeling his brother would be sleeping on the floor tonight.

"You consider what we had at the reception outstanding? What do you consider subpar, then? Dog food?" Without warning, Brianna pushed back her chair and stood. "I need some air."

He'd seen people overreact before, but Matt suspected Brianna was upset about more than Theo disagreeing with her about food.

"Someone's not happy. What did you do?" Jake asked once Brianna was far enough away that she wouldn't hear him.

Theo glanced at the door as it closed behind his girlfriend. "I didn't do anything. She's—"

"Just a bitch and always needs to be the center of attention," Aiden said, interrupting his twin.

"Don't start again, Aiden." Standing, Theo headed toward the door.

"So, um, Liv owns a catering company. How did you meet her?" Charlie asked.

Matt wanted to address Aiden's comment, since it was out of character for his brother to insult someone in that manner. Not to mention, while he'd found Brianna annoying and self-centered, her behavior while she'd stayed at his house hadn't warranted that title. But now wasn't the best time or place to question Aiden about it.

"I've known her brother since college."

He shared a condensed version of how he'd met not just Liv but the Middleton family and recounted everything that had transpired over the past few months.

"Why didn't you bring her with you? Were you worried we'd share all the embarrassing stories we have about you?" Aiden asked.

"I invited her, but she's catering an event."

"Sounds like a convenient excuse to me. Are you buying it, Jake?" Aiden turned to their cousin.

"Nah, he probably thought we'd make sure she got to know the real Matt Sherbrooke and then she'd kiss him goodbye."

"Hey, you're all welcome to visit us anytime you want. We're in Maine, not the other side of the world," Matt said.

"It sounds like you're not going back to Florida." Aiden's comment was followed by the sound of a car horn, and he pulled his phone out.

Who uses a car horn for text notifications? "What, couldn't you find a more annoying sound to use when you get a text?"

"I tried, but this was the best I could do." Aiden responded to the message and then placed the phone on the table. "So, are you staying in Maine?"

Matt nodded as he reached for his drink. "And I'm going to ask Liv to move in with me."

He'd almost done it before he left for Virginia, but he'd decided to wait until maybe next month. While it felt as though they'd been together a long time and he couldn't imagine not having Liv in his life, their relationship was still new. And although he was ready to take the next step, she might need more time.

The annoying car horn came from his brother's phone again.

"Now I've got to meet her," Aiden said as he responded to his newest text.

Pulling out a chair, Adam sat in time to hear Aiden's comment. "Me too. Evie and I plan to visit the second week of August. Why don't you join us?"

Back in May, they'd briefly discussed Adam, Evie, and Reagan visiting, but they'd never finalized things. "When did you plan on telling me?"

Adam slapped him on the shoulder. "I just did."

"Not a bad idea." Aiden opened the calendar app on his phone. "Can't. It looks like I'll be in Dallas for three days that week and then in Phoenix for the rest. However, I don't have anything important scheduled for Monday or Tuesday. I think I'll fly back with Matt on Sunday."

Fifteen

ROLLING OVER for what seemed like the hundredth time Friday night, Liv stared into the darkness. Most nights, she fell asleep the moment her head hit the pillow. But for the third night in a row, sleep refused to come. She wished she could blame it on drinking coffee too late in the day or because she'd taken a nap in the afternoon. She couldn't, though. Her inability to fall asleep was the result of the other side of the bed being empty. Over the past few weeks, she'd gotten too accustomed to falling asleep with Matt's arm around her. If she'd known insomnia would be a withdrawal symptom when he wasn't around, she would've thought long and hard before spending so many nights with him.

Who am I kidding? I wouldn't have changed a thing.

Since sleep seemed impossible, Liv switched on the bedside light and grabbed her phone. Checking out social media wouldn't help her fall asleep, but it would pass the time.

Most people used social media to keep in touch with friends or to see what their favorite celebrities were up to. While she certainly used it for both, she also used it for new recipe ideas.

A quick scroll through her friends' profiles showed most hadn't posted anything since the last time she checked their pages. She was about to switch over to her favorite cooking page when she noticed a new post on Sylvie's profile.

"Now, that's what I call eye candy." Her post was followed by a link and a picture of Matt with his cousin Jake Sherbrooke.

Well, her college roommate wasn't wrong. Both men were gorgeous. Then again, everyone in that family had hit the genetic jackpot.

Nothing about the picture indicated whether it had been taken recently or even where. Curious about what information might accompany the photo, Liv clicked on the link.

Immediately, the *Star Report*'s website popped up. An extremely popular celebrity magazine, it prided itself on getting celebrity news out first. While Liv questioned the accuracy of everything they printed, she did occasionally enjoy reading the magazine or its website.

Tonight, the first story on the website's main page was about Matt.

"Matt Sherbrooke Spotted at Cormac's Brewery," the headline read.

Sources familiar with the event shared that he was attending a bachelor/bachelorette party for his cousin and that following the tasting at Cormac's, the party enjoyed a private dinner cruise. The guest list included several family members, including President Sherbrooke's son, Jake, Senator Brett Sherbrooke, and Juliette Belmont.

Notably missing from the group was the woman seen with Matt numerous times over the past few weeks. Although pretty in a girl-next-door type of way, she can't compete with the beautiful women usually attached to Matt's arm. Was her absence yesterday a clue that Matt is once again single? Or has the new mystery woman photographed with Matt last night already caught his attention? Women around the world, including this reporter, are dying to know.

She had a mirror and perfect eyesight, so she knew the reporter was telling the truth. Still, the sentence insinuating she wasn't attractive enough to be with Matt stung.

She's probably a relative.

Despite the mental reminder, unease settled in Liv's chest as she scrolled down to the photos, the first being the one she'd seen on Sylvie's page. The next one featured Matt chatting with his cousin Juliette. Since the man standing next to her had his arm around her waist, she assumed they were a couple.

When she reached the third photo, she stopped scrolling. In it, Matt had his arm slung over the shoulders of a gorgeous brunette, one she didn't recognize.

That doesn't mean she isn't a relative or family friend.

Four more pictures accompanied the article. While she recognized Matt's brothers, she didn't know anyone else in those photos. Whoever they were, she doubted they catered retirement parties at the local VFW hall or waited tables when their family's restaurant needed help. Although she didn't own one and never would be able to afford one, she recognized the Louis Vuitton purse the blonde in the last picture was holding.

Scrolling up, she studied the first two pictures. When it was just the two of them, it was easy to forget that not only did people around the world know who Matt was, but also what family he belonged to. These photos did an excellent job of reminding her.

How would the people in these pictures react if Matt brought her to an event like the party last night, wearing a dress she'd purchased off the clearance rack at Macy's?

He insisted his parents were nothing like the aunt and uncle who disapproved of his cousin's fiancée. That they would accept her, no questions asked. Maybe that was true. It was also possible he'd just never introduced them to women they didn't like. And even if they didn't object, Matt's parents weren't his only family. At gatherings when his cousins or siblings were talking about their stock portfolios or their vacations to exclusive locations, what would she have to share? She didn't imagine they cared or even thought about how the cost of milk or seafood affected her small catering company's profit margin.

"I should've checked yesterday's baseball scores." Liv dropped the phone on the bed and focused on the ceiling fan.

Yep, if she'd looked to see if the Red Sox won last night's game against the Yankees instead of reading the *Star Report*, she wouldn't be second-guessing her and Matt's relationship.

The sound of her phone vibrating against the bed pulled her

thoughts back to the here and now. She found a text from Matt when she picked up the device.

Matt: Are you still up?

Still up? I never went to sleep.

Liv: Yep.

Matt: Okay if I call you?

No sooner had she replied with a thumbs-up than the device rang.

"What's up?"

"Just got back to the hotel. After the rehearsal dinner, a few of us went back to Adam's house."

She knew Adam was the cousin getting married tomorrow, but she didn't know if he'd appeared in any of the pictures she'd seen.

"I'm not sure why they needed me at the rehearsal. All I need to do is stand there and hand Adam the ring at the appropriate time and then lead the maid of honor down the aisle. It's not exactly rocket science. A trained monkey could do it."

An image of a monkey in a tuxedo materialized, making her smile. "I think it's kind of one of those 'everyone shall suffer' scenarios."

"You're probably right. At least it was quick. We were sitting down for dinner by seven."

In her experience, rehearsals were usually short, but she imagined the wedding Matt was attending tomorrow was more elaborate than any she'd been to.

"Have you finished your speech?" When he'd left on Wednesday, he'd only had the opening lines.

"Yeah, early this morning. I couldn't sleep, so I worked on it. I haven't slept well since I've been here."

Were his sleep problems caused by the same thing as hers? As much as she'd love to know, that was one question she'd never ask.

"What have you been up to today?"

She'd planned to experiment with a new chicken recipe, but her day hadn't gone as she'd hoped. "I ended up working the lunch and dinner shifts at the restaurant. Maggie called in sick.

And before your text, I was checking out the pictures from your cousin's bachelor party. It looks like everyone had fun."

"Damn it. I'd hoped to avoid that. I didn't see anyone outside of our group taking pictures. Where the hell are they posted?"

Was he so upset because he was worried he'd been photographed with another woman?

"I saw them on the *Star Report*'s website. I don't know if they are anywhere else." Until now, she hadn't thought to look. Curious now, she grabbed the tablet she mainly used for reading off the nightstand and typed "Today Magazine" into the browser. She wasn't surprised when a similar headline to the one on the other site appeared.

"How the hell did someone find out about the dinner cruise afterward? What new mystery woman?" It sounded like Matt was on the *Star Report* website. "Liv, that's my cousin's wife. I didn't take anyone with me last night."

A tiny voice wondered if he was telling the truth, but she stifled it. He sounded sincere; not to mention, he'd never given her a reason to not trust him.

"I know you didn't."

Scrolling down the page, she looked for any other pictures of Matt with the woman.

"There's a similar piece on *Today Magazine*'s website. The pictures aren't the same, though."

The website displayed a picture of Matt standing near the woman from the other page, but in this one, he didn't have an arm around her. Instead, it appeared as though Matt, the woman, and a man she didn't recognize were having a conversation. A humorous one at that, judging by their expressions.

While the set on the *Star Report*'s site had all been taken at the brewery, it was clear that a few on the second website were taken somewhere else. Liv assumed it was during the dinner cruise.

The ones at the brewery could've been shared by an employee there. But an employee from Cormac's wouldn't have an opportunity to take pictures at the dinner cruise. "I think a guest at the party sent in at least the ones in *Today Magazine*."

"It had to be."

There was anger in Matt's voice. While she understood it, she found it a little odd that he hadn't realized beforehand that it was a possibility.

* * *

He'd known that none of his family members would share pictures with the tabloids, and he'd assumed the other guests might post photos on their personal social media but not send them to magazines like the *Star Report*. He should've known it was a possibility, though. Those so-called magazines paid well for pictures from events that their own photographers would never have access to, such as the dinner cruise.

"Any idea who might have provided them to the magazines?"

"More like sold." Tossing his shirt onto the floor, he sat. "All I know is it wasn't a family member."

Unfortunately, even with them excluded, that left plenty of other suspects.

"Almost everyone took photos at some point."

"How many guests were there who aren't family?"

He didn't recall the exact breakdown of guests. "Maybe around forty."

"That's a lot of possibilities."

Yep, and even if he discovered who shared the pictures, there wasn't anything he could do about it. They'd already been published.

"Whatever. It's done." Matt opened the soda he'd grabbed from the fridge before calling Liv and took a sip. "Everyone was asking about you. They wanted to know why you weren't with me. I invited them to come and visit whenever they wanted."

"I'm not sure the female population of Orchard Harbor can handle having both you and your cousin, Jake or Trent, in town at the same time."

He smiled for the first time since he'd seen the article and pictures. Although both men were now happily married, those two particular cousins had once been notorious playboys, constantly appearing on sites like the *Star Report* with a different woman.

"I'll make sure they don't leave my house when they come."

"Are you still coming back on Sunday?"

Should he comment on the uncertainty in Liv's voice or just answer the question?

"Yeah, and my brother is coming with me. Why wouldn't I come back then?"

Silence initially met his question.

"You're, um, not far from DC," she said.

He pictured her shrugging and twisting a stand of hair as she tried to come up with a response.

"I thought maybe you'd want to get in some sightseeing. The last time I was in DC, I only made it to the Natural History Museum and the Vietnam Wall. One of these days, I'd like to check out the other museums."

Matt wasn't big into museums, but if she wanted to visit, he'd happily take her to DC. "Let's plan to go in the fall when you're not as busy. I'll arrange for you to get a real tour of the White House, not the one they give tourists." There were perks to being related to the President of the United States.

"Sounds like fun. I'm guessing Aiden's coming back with you, not Theo."

Readjusting his position, he stretched out his legs and took another sip of root beer. "I don't think Brianna would let Theo come back with me even if he wanted to."

He'd spent enough time with Brianna to form an opinion of her, and it wasn't a positive one. Honestly, he couldn't figure out why Theo stayed with her.

"Has she been as unsociable as when she was here?"

Unsociable wasn't the adjective he'd use, especially after the way she stormed off last night during the cruise. On the plane ride back to Maine, he planned to ask Aiden about his comment Thursday night, as well as Theo's response.

"You could put it that way. I don't get what Theo sees in her."

Brianna was pretty and physically fit, the type Theo gravitated to, but she was also a high-maintenance diva based on his interactions with her.

"I'd say maybe she's a great cook, but she seems like the type who struggles to make toast. So maybe he stays with her because the sex is mind-blowing."

Matt choked on the soda he'd just swallowed. "You might be on to something," he said once he stopped coughing and could speak again.

"Is Aiden bringing anyone with him?"

Although alone, he shook his head. "Nope, he's single. Why, do you have someone in mind for my brother?"

"No," Liv answered, drawing the word out. "Most of my friends are in relationships, and the ones who aren't wouldn't be interested in a long-distance one. I was just curious. How long is he staying?"

Aiden hadn't specified a number, and Matt hadn't asked. "Don't know. But I do know that Adam is coming with his family for six days in a couple of weeks."

Ten minutes later, Matt ended the call with Liv and adjusted the temperature in his room. Although he needed his brain to turn off so he could sleep, it immediately returned to the articles and pictures on the two websites—assuming there were only two. There was no shortage of similar sites, and they might have posted pictures as well.

Opening the web browser on his phone, he typed the first site that came to mind. Unlike the other two, there was no mention of him. Instead, a piece about Carter and his wife appeared. Matt hadn't seen or heard from Carter since telling the band he was done until the keyboardist got his shit together or they replaced him. Except for the beard, Carter looked the same as always, including his customary pissed-at-the-world expression. Matt couldn't say the same about McKenna, who was obviously pregnant. He was no expert, but she appeared to be well past the first trimester. Had she forgiven Carter back in March because she'd been pregnant?

Regardless, for both McKenna and the baby's sake, he hoped

Carter got his act together. Whether he did or not, though, it wasn't Matt's problem.

Without reading the short article, he typed in the name of another site known for publishing celebrity news. Much like on the previous one, there was no mention of him. Instead, there was a lengthy article about a charity event held to raise money for a foundation established by a well-known actor several years ago.

Logically, he knew he couldn't change anything even if he discovered who sold the pictures. Still, he wanted to know. Not only had the individual, assuming the same person had given the photos to both sites, shared an event that his cousin might have wanted kept private, but they had also put his and Liv's relationship in jeopardy. Anyone looking at the picture of him with Gianna who didn't know who she was might think they were involved. And the article certainly suggested it. Liv hadn't accused him of anything, but he'd heard the doubt in her voice. He didn't blame her either. If the tables were reversed, he might have concerns too, especially considering how new their relationship was.

Matt pulled up the guest list he and Kathryn created and scanned the names, unsure what he was looking for. While he knew a large chunk of the guests, there were simply too many unknowns. But if someone had sold photos, they might have also posted some on their personal social media. These days, CHAT was the most popular one.

Opening the app, he typed "Matt Sherbrooke" into the search bar. Unsurprisingly, the CHAT accounts for the *Star Report* and *Today Magazine* were the first two results. He skipped them and went on to the next.

"Matt Sherbrooke stopped in Cormac's today," the post read. A selfie taken inside the brewery with him appearing in the background accompanied it. He recognized the employee as one of the three who had served them the previous day.

The next couple of posts were made by people who'd seen him either enter or exit the brewery. There was also one that showed him waiting to board the *Serenity*.

"Brewery tour with my honey. Love ya, Theo." A selfie of his

brother and Brianna followed the post, and much like with the previous selfie, he was in the background.

Unlike the previous ones, though, Brianna's post had a ton of likes and comments. Clearly, she had a large following on the app.

"Is that Matt Sherbrooke from Eclipse?" the first comment read.

Brianna had responded with a photo that appeared similar to the one the *Star Report* shared, which showed him talking to his cousin.

"Who else was there?" another comment read.

Once again, instead of replying with words, she'd posted more photos. Much like the first one, it resembled the ones he'd seen on the magazine sites.

Had Brianna provided the magazines with the pictures?

So he could compare the pictures on CHAT with the ones on the websites, Matt got his laptop and went to the *Star Report*'s website.

He held his phone next to the computer screen. He wasn't surprised that the picture Brianna posted on CHAT of him talking to Jake looked nearly identical to the one on the website. The only difference was that Jake was holding a glass in the photo on CHAT, but in the other one, the glass was on the table.

The following two posts by Brianna didn't match any on the website. But the one of him talking to his cousin Juliette did. In the picture on the computer, Juliette was smiling, while in the one included in Brianna's post, it was clear she was laughing.

Let's see how your pictures compare to Today Magazine, *Brianna.*

He wasn't surprised when the pictures published by the magazine matched one of Brianna's. Like with the others, there were only minor differences.

He'd accept it was just a coincidence if one of Brianna's matched a photo published by a magazine, but not five.

It looked like he had the culprit.

Matt checked his watch. If it weren't so late, he'd call Liv back and let her know he'd solved the mystery.

Or at least part of the mystery. He knew the who but not the why.

Magazines paid well for celebrity pictures, so he understood why some people sold them, even if he disapproved of it. He didn't know much about Brianna, but the fact that she'd met Theo at Clean Water Matters suggested she wasn't hurting for money. The Omega watch she'd worn added to that assumption.

Whatever the reason, tomorrow, before the wedding, he'd have words with Theo. He might not be able to remove what was out there, but he could hopefully prevent Brianna from doing it again. It was Adam and Evie's wedding, not a social event for someone to share on the internet.

Sixteen

AFTER SLIPPING his room key and wallet into his pocket, Matt sent a text message off to Liv and left his room. As part of the wedding party, he needed to be at the beach before the guests for pictures, and he wanted to see Theo before he joined everyone outside.

Theo answered the door dressed in his suit pants and white undershirt, his hair still damp from a shower. "Morning."

"We need to talk."

His brother stepped back and gestured for Matt to enter. "Brianna's in the bedroom getting dressed."

The suite he entered looked identical to his across the hall. The only difference he saw was the art hanging on the walls.

"What's up?"

"You need to make sure Brianna doesn't take any pictures today. Take her phone away if you have to. I don't care. Just make sure she doesn't do it."

"Maybe you tell your girlfriends what to do, but I don't. People take pictures at weddings, Matt. Unless Adam or Evie tells me taking pictures is banned, you're out of luck."

"Do people also sell their photos to the tabloids?" Matt held out his cell phone, which had the *Star Report*'s website already open.

Crossing his arms, he waited as Theo scanned the article and scrolled through the photos. "Anyone could have sold these."

"There are more on the *Today Magazine* website." Taking back the device, he opened the other website.

"Still doesn't prove anything. There were a lot of guests and staff members around," Theo said as he viewed the new page.

"Brianna posted identical ones on CHAT. Check her profile for yourself."

Crossing the room, Theo picked up the phone lying on a table. "Did you look at every guest's CHAT profile or just Brianna's because you don't like her?"

He understood Theo's skepticism, but not his apparent animosity. He'd been friendly when they'd stayed at his house, and on Thursday, he'd spent most of his time with other family members, not so much to be away from Brianna, but because he'd wanted to catch up with his cousins. "Neither. I searched for recent posts with my name in them and went through them."

"The pictures do look similar."

Similar? Maybe his brother needed to visit an eye doctor. "Theo, the differences are minuscule. If it was just one, I'd accept it was a coincidence, but not five."

"It doesn't make sense." Theo looked at him. "People do that kind of shit because they want the money. Brianna doesn't need it. Her great-grandfather started Parker's."

Matt didn't shop there, but he recognized the name. A popular store that sold a wide range of products, including women's clothes, jewelry, and makeup, Parker's was a staple at malls across the country.

"It's just a coincidence that her photos look similar to the others. The most likely culprit is one of Evie's or Adam's friends. Question them."

How could his brother deny what was right in front of him?

"I have a better idea, why don't you go and ask Brianna?" Hell, Matt was tempted to do it himself.

Brianna joined them in time to catch the end of his sentence, dressed in a gown that appeared custom-made for her. "Ask who what?"

Theo looked at Brianna first and then at Matt before rubbing the back of his neck. "Someone sold pictures from the party on Thursday night to some magazines." Theo shot him a dirty look before he continued. "Matt thinks it was you because some are similar to ones you posted on CHAT."

Shaking her head, Brianna touched Theo's shoulder. "I didn't sell them—"

Theo turned back to him. "I told you that you were wrong."

Man, he wanted to wipe the smug smile off his brother's face.

"I gave them to Lily and Naomi to use," she continued.

Theo's head whipped in Brianna's direction. "You gave them to the magazines?"

It wasn't the response Matt had expected, but Theo had heard her correctly.

"Yes, I sent them on Thursday when we got back to the hotel," she said as she examined her perfect manicure.

"Why?"

He heard the confusion in Theo's voice.

Excellent question.

"So they could write articles no one else could. We've been friends forever. Even though her dad owns the *Star Report*, Lily's editor rejects more than half the pieces she submits. I knew the editor wouldn't reject an article about Matt. Naomi has only been at *Today* for a few months and has spent most of her time writing about cosmetics, which she hates. I thought an article, even a short one, about Matt would prove to her editor that she could handle other pieces."

Matt hadn't pegged Brianna as the type to do something to help others.

"Don't do it again." He didn't care if he was out of line. She needed to know her behavior wouldn't be tolerated.

"Oh, please. It's not like the people in those photos haven't been on those websites before."

Matt's phone buzzed, and when he checked the screen, he found a text from Adam.

Adam: Picture time. Where are u?

A glance at his watch told him he was almost five minutes late.

Matt: On my way.

"I have to go. Theo, you need to deal with this."

Tyler, Adam's younger brother, noticed Matt first as he approached the group. "It's about time you got your ass down here. What the hell were you doing?"

"Sorry, I needed to take care of something before the ceremony."

"Is everything okay?" Adam asked, the perpetual smile he'd been wearing for the past three days fading.

He didn't want his cousin worrying about anything today, including whether Brianna behaved herself or not.

"Yeah, just some silly media stuff I needed to deal with. Nothing major. It's all set now."

At least he hoped it was settled. If not, he'd be having words with his brother again, and this time he wouldn't be as polite.

The photographer, whom Adam had been speaking with when Matt arrived, clapped her hands together to get everyone's attention. "Now that we're all here, let's get started."

A hand landed on Matt's shoulder as he scanned the ballroom. About half the guests remained seated while the rest were on the dance floor.

"Great speech. How long did it take you to write it?" Aiden asked as he sat in the empty chair next to him. "Or did you hire someone to do it?"

He didn't know the exact length of time, but it hadn't taken him as long as he'd feared. While he'd struggled to get started, once he did, the rest flowed easily.

"Not too long. The beginning was the hardest part."

Picking up Matt's drink, Aiden took a healthy sip before gesturing toward the bride and groom, who were dancing. "Adam looks happy, but I'm still shocked he didn't invite Uncle Benjamin and Aunt Shannon."

"Order your own." Matt took what was left of the drink back from his brother. "Didn't Theo tell you why Adam didn't invite his parents?"

Aiden shook his head as he gestured for a member of the waitstaff to come over. "The brewery tour was the first time Theo and I had spoken in weeks. But Jake filled me in on the why. Can't say I'm surprised by Aunt Shannon and Uncle Benjamin's behavior, but I'm still surprised Adam excluded them."

Matt tried to digest his brother's statement while Aiden ordered a drink.

Once the waitress took Aiden's order, she looked at him. "Can I bring you anything?"

Thanks to his brother, his drink was almost gone. "I'll have another Manhattan."

"What did you do to piss off Brianna and Theo? I noticed he hasn't spoken to you all day, and she's been sending dirty looks your way since the reception started," Aiden asked once they were alone again.

Matt finished what was left of his drink before filling his brother in on what Brianna had done and his conversation with Theo before the ceremony.

"Brianna does whatever she wants." Aiden paused when the waitress set down their order. "But I'm surprised she was trying to help someone else. She seems too self-centered to do something like that."

He'd had a similar thought that morning. "It's what she said, but it doesn't mean it's the truth."

"She doesn't need the money, so she'd have no reason to sell them. At least on that, I'd believe her. But I also wouldn't trust her not to do it again, regardless of what you said to her this morning or what Theo might have said after you left. She listens to only one person—herself."

Aiden's comment prompted him to scan the room again. Unlike last time, he found Brianna and Theo sitting with a cousin. Judging by Vivian's face, she'd prefer to be in a dentist's chair getting a root canal.

"How well do you know Brianna?"

During his visit, Theo mentioned that their brother hadn't spent much time with Brianna. However, Aiden's comments, both now and during the cruise, gave Matt the impression that he'd spent more than enough time to form an honest opinion.

"Well enough, unfortunately. I don't know why Theo is still with her."

Liv's comment from the other night came to mind. "The sex?" Anyone else, he'd say it was for the money or the connections. People were willing to put up with a lot when money was involved. But Theo didn't need a wealthy girlfriend or the connections.

Aiden's hand paused with his glass halfway to his mouth. "I don't care how incredible the sex was, I still wouldn't stay with her. She's... I don't even know where to start." Before continuing, his brother took a sip from his drink. "You spent some time with her in Maine. What did you think of her?"

"I wasn't a fan either. She fits Theo's usual type in a lot of ways, but there was something about her that I really didn't like."

"Did your girlfriend get along with her?"

Matt considered his question. "I wouldn't say they didn't get along. They didn't argue, but it was obvious Brianna didn't like Liv. Thankfully, Brianna didn't interact with us much. She spent most of her time on the phone."

"Sounds like something she'd do."

Theo and Aiden not getting along was unheard of. Sure, they had their disagreements, especially growing up, but usually within a day, they were back to being the best of friends. For them to have gone weeks without speaking, something significant must have happened between them. Should he butt his nose into the situation or let them deal with it?

He honestly didn't know. "Are you still coming back with me tomorrow?" Matt asked while he considered whether to get involved.

"Yeah, I'm not expected back in the office until Thursday,

and I'm anxious to meet Liv. If you're relocating and asking her to move in, she must be special."

Matt already knew Liv was special. He didn't need his baby brother to tell him.

Aiden nudged Matt's arm with his elbow. "Poor Viv. She looks miserable."

Matt glanced at his cousin, who was still sitting with Theo and Brianna. Although he hadn't thought it possible, she looked even more unhappy now than the last time he'd looked her way. If anyone needed rescuing, it was Viv.

When it came to dancing, he was indifferent. But if he asked Viv to dance, it would give his cousin a reason to leave the table without appearing rude.

Pushing back his chair, he took another sip from his drink and stood.

"Off to the rescue?" Aiden asked with amusement.

"Hey, if you were as unhappy as Viv looks, wouldn't you want someone to rescue you?"

"Hell yeah." Aiden gestured toward Matt's glass. "Do you want me to order you another if someone comes by?"

"Sure."

Although the reception was small by Sherbrooke standards, there were still over one hundred guests there, many of whom were related to him. Tonight, they all seemed to want to talk, and it took him longer than it should've to reach his cousin's table.

"When we get married, I want everything to be outside. I'm leaning toward my parents' home in the Hamptons."

Matt was glad his brother and Brianna had their backs to him so they couldn't see his expression. Not once during their visit had Theo mentioned he was thinking about marrying Brianna. Yet she sounded like it was a done deal.

"But my grandfather's house on Martha's Vineyard is a close second," she continued, still unaware that he stood behind her.

Relief crossed Vivian's face when she spotted him. "Matt, that was a great best man's speech."

"Thanks," he said before turning his attention to Theo. "How's everything going today?" He hoped his brother understood that he was asking if he'd kept an eye on Brianna, as he'd requested.

"Fine," Theo replied, his jaw clenched tight.

Yup, he'd understood the question and hadn't liked it. Not that Matt cared.

"Excellent." With the question answered, Matt turned his full attention to Vivian. "Would you like to dance?"

The words were barely out of his mouth before she was out of her seat.

"I'd love to." Taking his hand, she gave Theo and Brianna the most forced smile he'd ever seen. "If you're not here when I come back, it was great catching up."

Even if they remained sitting there after they danced, Matt knew his cousin wouldn't be returning to the table.

Matt lowered his mouth close to her ear as they walked toward the dance floor. "Don't ever go into acting."

"What are you talking about?"

"You weren't fooling anyone with the smile you gave them."

A slow ballad started the moment they stepped onto the dance floor, and Matt settled his hands on Vivian's waist.

"You're a lifesaver and officially my favorite cousin." Vivian kissed his cheek and then placed her hands on his shoulders. "If I had to hear about all the things that were wrong with the wedding and reception and how she planned to do things when she gets married much longer, I would've stuffed napkins in my ears."

"I'm sorry I intervened when I did. I would've loved to see you sitting there with napkins sticking out of your ears."

She pulled back enough to look him in the eyes. "I take it back. You're not my favorite cousin."

Smiling, Matt kissed her forehead. "Not buying it. I know you love me the most."

They danced in silence for a few seconds before Vivian spoke again. "Are Theo and Brianna engaged?"

"I sure as hell hope not." He couldn't imagine spending the holidays or family gatherings with her.

"Are you sure? It sounded like they are. She kept saying,

'When we get married, I want this.' And she was wearing a ring on her left hand. Not everyone gets a diamond as an engagement ring. If I ever get engaged, I'd rather have a ruby."

Vivian wasn't wrong. A handful of his cousins had proposed with rings that featured something other than a diamond. But he didn't think that was the case. If Theo was engaged, he would've said something to him and Aiden.

The brewery tour was the first time Theo and I had spoken in weeks. Aiden's comment from earlier resurfaced.

No, even if his brothers weren't getting along, Theo wouldn't keep something like that from his twin.

Matt glanced over Vivian's shoulder. Another one of his cousins and his wife had joined his brother, and it appeared as though Brianna was doing all the talking.

"You're not positive, are you?" Vivian asked, pulling him away from his thoughts and back to the dance floor.

Three months ago, the answer would've been easy. But not now. Theo hadn't been himself during his stay in Maine, and the fact that he hadn't spoken to his twin in so long only reinforced the fact that something was off.

"I'm 90 percent certain he's not engaged." But he wouldn't be surprised if Brianna were pressuring his brother for a ring.

"Maybe we should both keep our fingers crossed that you're right. Can you imagine spending Thanksgiving with her across the table? Talk about an absolute nightmare."

"I'd start celebrating alone if she was there."

Vivian patted his shoulder. "Don't worry, you can always come and celebrate with me. Or maybe I should say you and your girlfriend can come. I've seen the pictures. I thought she'd be here with you."

The slow song ended, and one with a much faster tempo took its place.

"Or has that relationship already ended?" Vivian asked as he led them off the dance floor and to the table where Aiden sat.

"Liv couldn't take time off from work. What about you? I noticed you're flying solo this weekend."

It had been eight or nine months since he'd seen Vivian. At

the time, she'd been with someone, but he didn't remember his name.

"Wyatt and I weren't working out. I've been on a few dates since we broke up but haven't met anyone I like enough to go out with a second time."

"I ordered you another drink." Aiden pulled his ringing cell phone out and checked the screen. "It's Dad. I'll call him back later. Does he know Adam got married today?"

"I don't know." Matt's phone rang as he sat next to his cousin. He'd promised to call Liv when he got back to his hotel room and wasn't expecting a call from anyone. For a moment, he considered letting it go to voicemail, but just in case it was Liv, he took out his phone. When he saw the name "Dad" on the screen, a knot formed in his stomach. If their father was calling them, something was wrong.

Pressing Accept, he skipped a proper greeting. "Dad, what's wrong?"

Across the table, Aiden frowned and set his drink back down.

"There's nothing for you to worry about, but I wanted you to know your mom was in a car accident earlier today."

If it had been a simple fender bender, his dad wouldn't be calling him, so how could he say there was nothing to worry about? "How is she?"

"She has a broken leg that's going to require surgery and a broken wrist. Otherwise, she's fine."

He'd broken his leg when he was ten and had been in a cast for weeks. If his mom required surgery, her injury was far more serious than his had been.

"I'm in Virginia right now, but tomorrow I'll fly out there." He hadn't intended to take a trip to California without Liv, but when he explained the situation, she'd understand.

"That's not necessary. I only called so that you'd know what was going on if you had trouble getting a hold of us for the next couple of days."

"I'll—"

Dad interrupted him before he finished. "Your mom wants to talk to you."

He already knew what she planned to say, and it wouldn't change his mind.

"Matt, there's no need for you to come. Your dad's right. I'm fine. Enjoy your time in Virginia."

His mom's speech was slower than usual and slightly slurred, a good indication that the hospital had given her some strong pain meds.

"I'm coming. I planned to leave Virginia tomorrow anyway. When I land, I'll call Dad. And I'll let Aiden and Theo know what's going on."

Matt still held the phone when Aiden asked, "What happened?"

He gave his brother a recap of his conversation as he opened the app for the charter flight company he frequently used.

"Did Dad tell you what hospital she's in or when the surgery will be?"

"No." And he hadn't thought to ask. But it didn't matter. Even if the surgery was done today, he planned to visit tomorrow.

"Do you want to fly back with me or make your own arrangements?"

"With you."

"Can you tell Theo, or do I need to?"

"Hey, you told Dad you would let me and Theo know," Aiden responded as he rubbed his hands together. "Vivian will back me up because she heard you too."

"Actually, I told Mom that." If Aiden didn't even want to talk to Theo to let him know about their mom's accident, their relationship was worse than he'd thought.

"But I'll tell him." Matt finished his drink and then pushed back his chair. The sooner he filled Theo in, the sooner he could once again put distance between himself and Brianna.

* * *

Liv brushed her wet hair enough to get the majority of the tangles out and then put it up in a messy bun. She couldn't remember the last time a shower had felt so good. The manager at the

Crystal Ballroom claimed the air conditioner was on, but it certainly hadn't felt like it. Less than half an hour after arriving to set up, her shirt had been glued to her back. And more than once, she'd ducked into the restroom to apply additional deodorant.

Despite the uncomfortable temperature, the event had been a success. More than one of the Maine Writers' Guild members had asked for a business card, and after the party, Sheila, the guild's president, had pulled her aside and let her know how pleased she'd been with everything, from the food to the staff. Sheila had also promised not only to leave a review but also to pass along the catering company's name to Linda Rose, who always organized a holiday party for her company in December.

Cell phone in hand, Liv switched off the bedroom light and retreated to the living room where she'd left the air conditioner on full blast. While the setting would make the kitchen and living room colder than she'd prefer if she did that and left the bedroom door open, her room would be cool enough to sleep in later tonight.

Since she'd been alone, she'd spent the last few nights rewatching the most recent season of *Starting Point*. She hadn't realized how much she'd either missed or forgotten from when she binge-watched the season with her friends. Liv's plan was to watch three more episodes tonight and the final two tomorrow morning before Matt and his brother got home.

After a slight detour into the kitchen, Liv turned on the television, ready to see Lucinda, her least favorite character in the show, not show up to her wedding. Even before she watched the episode the first time, she'd suspected Lucinda wouldn't go through with the marriage. The character was a gold digger who was always on the hunt for a richer man. Still, Liv hadn't expected her to leave town the day of the wedding when there was a church full of people expecting her.

Despite knowing the events on the screen weren't real, a combination of pity and anger washed over her as she watched first Nick check his watch while standing with his best man and then Lucinda board an airplane. Just as Nick tried calling Lucinda, Liv's phone rang.

Matt hadn't specified a time; instead, he'd promised to call when he got back to his hotel. Unless the wedding had been in the morning, it seemed too early for him to be calling now.

For a moment, she considered letting it go to voicemail since getting through three episodes was already in jeopardy, because while the shower had woken her up a little, she was still exhausted. On the off chance it was someone she wanted to talk to, though she flipped the phone over. When she saw the name "Emma," she pressed Pause on the remote.

"I thought you and Brian were going away this weekend?" she asked.

"We were supposed to, but he woke up with some kind of stomach bug. He can't keep anything down."

She'd gone through something similar earlier in the year. In her case, it had lasted almost two days. Even after the worst had passed, she'd survived on plain dry toast and Pedialyte for a few days.

"That stinks."

"You're telling me. We had tickets to Fenway tonight, and tomorrow we were going on a cruise around Boston Harbor."

Although they were both avid Red Sox fans, neither had ever been to Fenway Park, and it was on both their bucket lists.

"It's only July. There's still time for you guys to go."

Liv didn't know when they stopped the harbor cruises, but baseball season didn't end for a while.

"I know, but we had great seats. Brian has a friend with season tickets. Since he wasn't using them this weekend, he sold them to Brian for half the price they'd usually cost. He might not be willing to do that again."

She'd looked at ticket prices and knew that even the crappy seats were expensive.

"But I didn't call to complain," Emma said. "What are you up to? I know Matt's not back yet."

"Watching television and trying to stay cool."

"Do you want to meet me at Mack's? Back Bay is playing tonight."

She enjoyed listening to Back Bay, a rock band out of Boston that played at clubs and bars around New England. If she weren't so tired, she would head over to Mack's.

"Sorry, I have just enough energy left to get from the sofa to my bed."

Perhaps that was a bit of an exaggeration, but she didn't have it in her to put on real clothes and leave her apartment.

"But if you want to come here and watch TV, you're welcome."

"Hanging out at your place is better anyway, since it means I don't have to change. Do you want me to bring anything?"

"Only if there's something you want."

When she opened the door ten minutes later, she wasn't surprised to see Emma dressed in a T-shirt she'd bought during their trip to Orlando a few years ago and striped sleep shorts.

"I wasn't sure if you had any." Emma held up a container of ice cream.

She hadn't been craving ice cream, but now that it was in front of her, she was glad Emma had brought some with her. "Nope. My kitchen is a little bare. Do you want some now or later?" Liv wasn't quite ready for something sweet, but that didn't mean Emma needed to wait.

"Let's hold off on the ice cream. I ate dinner not long before I called you. But I will have something to drink."

"You know where everything is." Emma and Phoebe knew to treat her apartment as if it were theirs.

"Do you want anything?" Emma asked as she headed into the kitchen.

"I'm all set for now."

"So, what are we watching?"

"*Starting Point*. I've been rewatching season three since Matt left. I have five episodes left. I hoped to get in three tonight and the last two tomorrow morning. But we can watch something else."

Emma snatched a cheese square from Liv's plate before she sat. "Nah, that works for me. I've been wanting to restart the season, and Brian's not a fan of the show."

She'd expected that to be Emma's response.

"What time will Matt be back tomorrow?" Kicking off her sneakers, Emma tucked one foot under her.

If they were going to get through three episodes tonight, they needed to get started, so Liv pressed Play on the remote. "His plane lands in Bangor at ten. His brother is coming too."

"Wasn't his brother just here?"

On the screen, Nick thanked everyone in the church for coming before explaining that Lucinda had left town and there wouldn't be a wedding. If she hadn't known it was fictional, she would've believed Nick truly loved her and was heartbroken. The man's acting was that good.

"Theo was here. Aiden is flying back with him."

Emma helped herself to another piece of cheese as she nodded. "That's right. I forgot you told me he has two brothers. They're twins, right?"

"Identical. I'm not sure how long he's staying."

"Did¾"

The opening chords to "Loving You" interrupted her.

Pausing the television again, she grabbed her phone. "It's Matt."

"I'll get the ice cream while you talk to him."

"Are you back at your hotel already?" she asked after greeting him.

"No, but I wanted to let you know I won't be back tomorrow."

"Oh." A tiny part of her had feared he wouldn't come back despite his reassurances. Still, hearing him say the words was like a slap to the face. "Okay."

Should she ask where he was going and when he'd be back or let it go?

"My dad called a little while ago. My mom was in a car accident earlier today."

Concern instantly replaced the dread his initial comment created. "Oh no. Is she okay?"

"Dad said she's doing okay but needs surgery. He wouldn't lie, but I still want to visit her. Aiden's coming with me."

Liv understood Matt's reasoning, and in his shoes, she'd do the same thing.

"I don't think I'll be gone for too long."

"Don't worry. I get it. Family first. I'd want to see for myself that my mom was okay too."

"Feel free to stay at my house if you want."

Matt had made the same offer before he left for Virginia. And as lovely as it would be to have central air and access to a pool, she'd stay at her apartment because being at his house alone would be too odd.

"Hopefully, I'll have an idea of when I'll be back when I call tomorrow."

Ending the call, Liv picked up the bowl of ice cream Emma had brought in for her.

"Everything okay?" Emma asked, a spoonful almost to her mouth.

"Change in plans. Matt's mom was in an accident, so he's flying to California tomorrow."

"That makes sense. How badly was she injured?"

Scooping up some ice cream, Liv made sure to also get some of the whipped cream too. "She needs surgery, but Matt's dad told him she'll be fine."

"Did he say how long he'll be out there?"

"He wasn't sure. He thinks he'll have a better idea tomorrow."

The peanut butter chocolate chip ice cream melted in her mouth, and she scooped up more before she even swallowed. Peanut butter and chocolate were meant to go together, and she'd argue with anyone who told her differently.

"Look at it this way. Now you have more time to spend with me."

Emma had a point, and Liv would never complain about spending time with her best friend.

Seventeen

WHAT HE THOUGHT of as hospital scent hit Matt as soon as he entered the hospital early Sunday afternoon. How people who worked here every day tolerated it was a mystery to him. Maybe after a while, the scent killed your sense of smell and you no longer noticed it. Whatever the case, every hospital he'd ever been in smelled the same, a combination of industrial cleaner and stale air.

Despite his dad's reassurance, anxiety had plagued him since he got off the phone last night. Now the smell and the surroundings were kicking that anxiety into overdrive.

"Dad wants to know if Theo is with us," Aiden said as he responded to a text message. "Do you know if he plans to visit Mom?"

"He said he would, but he didn't share his travel plans with me." And Matt hadn't cared enough to ask. Theo was a grown man. He didn't need to share his itinerary with him.

The elevator doors opened before either of them could press the button, and two employees dressed in blue scrubs stepped out, deep in conversation.

"Well, if I'm here when he shows up and Brianna is with him, I'll leave and come back later. There's no way I can deal with her today."

Matt shared his brother's sentiment. Hopefully, Theo used his brain and came alone.

"What floor did Dad say Mom is on?" Matt asked.

"Eleventh floor, room 216."

Half a second after jabbing the button, Matt noticed a woman approaching the elevator, carrying a giant floral arrangement with a pink-and-white balloon attached. He pressed the button to hold the door open.

"Thank you." The woman sounded as if she'd sprinted from the parking lot.

"What floor do you need?"

"Tenth, please. I'm going to visit my sister and niece. She was born early this morning."

Since the balloon said "Congrats, It's A Girl," he'd assumed she wasn't there to visit someone who'd had their gallbladder removed.

"She wasn't due until next week, but I guess she didn't get the memo."

He didn't have much experience with pregnancies, but a week early didn't sound unusual.

"I have ten nephews. My older two brothers both have all boys, so this is my first niece."

Based on the excitement in her voice, one would think she'd been the one to have a baby.

"Don't get me wrong. I love my nephews, but everyone hoped my sister would have a girl because even my cousins all have boys."

Maybe it was because he preferred to keep as much of his life private as he could, but he'd never understood why some people felt the need to share personal information with random strangers.

Not responding would make him look rude, but what should he say? He didn't know the woman and didn't care that her sister had given birth to a baby that morning, or that it was the first girl in a long list of boys.

Hoping for some help, he glanced at Aiden across the elevator. The shrug he got in response told Matt his brother was clueless too.

A person couldn't go wrong with congratulating someone, right?

"Congratulations."

The smile on the woman's face somehow grew. "Thank you. They named her Olivia. It's our grandmother's name. I have some pictures."

At the name Olivia, an image of Liv popped into his head. He'd sent her a short text message before boarding the plane, but she still hadn't responded. Usually, she got right back to him within minutes, unless she was at work, and he knew she was supposed to have the day off.

The elevator doors opened just as the woman pulled out her cell phone. "I hope whoever you're visiting feels better soon."

Aiden moved away from the wall once they were alone. "Just a little talkative."

"You think? If we'd been together much longer, she would've started sharing the names and ages of her nephews."

"Hey, at least she wasn't hounding you for an autograph."

"I'd rather she'd done that. I know how to handle people when they do that."

"Ten nephews. Must be chaos at the holidays."

Matt wouldn't label the holidays growing up as chaos, but they'd always been large events. Although not like when he was a kid, even now holiday celebrations tended to be big gatherings.

Floral arrangements, some with balloons attached and cards, covered every visible surface in his mom's hospital room. Clearly, his mom's friends hadn't wasted any time sending flowers. Actually, knowing many of them, they'd probably seen it as a contest of who not only got her flowers first but who sent the largest arrangement.

Flowers weren't the only company his mom had. Unsurprisingly, Matt's dad sat in the uncomfortable standard hospital chair near the window while his cousin Sophie occupied the one closest to the bed.

Considering she'd been in an accident less than twenty-four

hours ago and was in the hospital, he'd expected his mom to look disheveled and tired—or at least as disheveled as his mom could look. He should've known better. Instead, her hair was perfectly arranged, she wore makeup, and there wasn't a hospital johnny in sight. The cast on her leg and wrist were the only signs that something was wrong.

"How are you feeling?" he asked, leaning down to kiss her cheek.

"Much better now that Sophie fixed my hair and did my makeup. I scared all the nurses this morning."

He wouldn't label his mom as vain, but she believed in never leaving the house unless everything from her hair and makeup to her clothes looked perfect.

"She's exaggerating." His dad winked at him. "She only scared two."

Any remaining anxiety disappeared at his dad's comment. If his parents were joking around as usual, his dad had been right when he said there wasn't anything to worry about.

"Do you know when you'll go home?" He'd never spent the night in a hospital as an adult, but he imagined it wasn't the most comfortable place to be.

"We're not sure. How long are you staying?"

"At least until you're home."

"Good. I've missed you. Did your girlfriend come with you? And don't deny you're with someone. Michayla showed me the pictures of the two of you in the *Star Report*."

Michayla Simmins had been the housekeeper for as long as he could remember, and she had an unhealthy obsession with social media. When she found photos or read articles about him or the band, she always shared them with his mom.

"By the way, you look cute together."

Cute? No grown man should be called cute, not even by their mother. Evidently, his mom hadn't gotten the message.

"Liv isn't with me. She had to work this weekend, so she couldn't come to the wedding. But hopefully we can visit in the fall."

At the word "wedding," his mom cringed. "Speaking of

Adam's wedding, avoid visiting your aunt and uncle while you're here. They're livid that Adam went against their wishes. I've never seen them so angry."

Aunt Shannon and Uncle Benjamin had always been his least favorite, and their recent behavior had only solidified their placement at the bottom. "I didn't plan on visiting them."

Other than his parents, he hadn't thought about seeing anyone else while in California.

"How was the wedding? We would've loved to go, but we understood why Adam didn't invite us," his mom asked as a nurse entered holding a tiny cup.

While the nurse administered his mom's medication and checked her vitals, he pulled out his phone to read the text message he'd received. Rather than finding one from Liv, though, he saw a message from his agent.

After replying, he pulled up Liv's number.

Matt: Did you end up working today?

"The wedding was nice. Fairly low key," Aiden answered. "I was surprised you weren't there, Sophie."

"Chase and I already had plans. I wanted to cancel, but I couldn't convince him. He can be stubborn."

More like pigheaded. For the most part, his cousin's husband seemed like a decent guy, but there was no changing his mind about anything.

"Theo just texted me," his dad said, setting his phone down. "They're going to be here in about ten minutes."

His dad's use of the word "they're" meant one thing—Theo wasn't alone.

"Hey, Matt, I'm starving. What do you say we go get something to eat and come back later?" Aiden asked.

He had no desire to stick around and see who was with Theo. "Sounds like a plan. Sophie, do you want to come with us?"

His cousin's eyebrows bunched together, and her gaze moved between Matt and Aiden. "Love to. Chase won't be home until late tonight."

Sophie clearly found it odd that they were leaving without waiting to see Theo first. If the tables were reversed and she was hightailing it out of there when her sister would arrive in a matter of minutes, he'd find it suspicious too. And once they were alone, Matt knew she'd question them about it.

"Do you want us to bring you anything when we come back?" Hospitals weren't known for their delicious meals, and Matt knew his mom was a picky eater.

"Don't worry about it. I'll run out later and get something for us," his dad assured him.

"Well, if you change your mind, call me."

He expected questions from Sophie before they reached the elevator. However, she remained silent until they stepped outside.

"You didn't want to wait for Theo?"

"I haven't eaten a meal since six o'clock Eastern time. I'm starving. We'll see him later."

Technically, Aiden wasn't wrong. They had breakfast at six, but they had sandwiches on the plane.

"It would've taken less than two minutes to say hello. What gives?" she pushed.

"Nothing. I spent the last three days with him, and Matt spent the last week with him. He'll survive without us for one day. If I don't eat soon, I might pass out."

"Whatever. Where do you guys want to eat?" Sophie didn't sound convinced, but at least she was letting the matter go.

Matt opened the passenger door for her. "You pick." Unlike him, Sophie spent a lot of time in the area, so she'd know what places were good.

"Anything specific you feel like?"

"Up for anything. Aiden?" Matt glanced across the roof at his brother.

"As long as it isn't moving, I'm happy," Aiden answered before getting into the back seat.

"There's a sushi restaurant on Lowell that Chase and I love. Let's go there."

While he didn't love sushi, Matt didn't mind it occasionally, and he had told Sophie anything was fine.

"Just tell me which way to go."

* * *

When Liv slipped between the sheets the night before, her plans for today had been simple and downright lazy. Unfortunately, the universe hadn't gotten the memo, so instead of sleeping until her body decided it was time to get up, a deafening clap of thunder woke her at four. The storm then proceeded not only to keep her up with its drum solo and dazzling light show, but also to plunge the street into darkness. Eventually, once Mother Nature grew tired of partying and Liv finished the book she had started—thank goodness her Kindle had a backlight—she fell back asleep. However, the outside world once again decided that she didn't need a lazy day at home. This time, though, the culprit wasn't Mother Nature but rather her ringing cell phone. And even before she picked it up, she'd somehow known it was her dad asking her to help at the restaurant. Sure enough, Francine had called in sick.

Thankfully, though, the lunch rush was winding down, and once she returned the credit card to table ten, she could take a break and eat before they needed to get ready for dinner.

"I had a feeling you were here when you didn't answer my texts."

Removing the credit card from the reader, Liv turned toward Emma.

"Francine was supposed to work until three, but she called in early this morning, and Nancy just called out too, so I'm stuck here until closing. I lost power last night, and my phone was about to die when I got here, so I left it in the back to charge. It's been so busy all day, I haven't had a chance to check it."

Actually, to say it had been busy was an understatement. Starting with when they unlocked the doors until about thirty minutes ago, there hadn't been an empty table in the restaurant. No sooner would one party leave than another would take its place. While great for business, the constant stream of customers made it difficult to even take a bathroom break.

"Well, that answers my question about hanging out again tonight."

"Sorry."

Emma shrugged as she sat at the bar. "No big deal."

"I'm on a break as soon as I return this credit card, if you want to hang around."

"I'll never pass up a free meal."

"What do you want to eat? I'll put our order in before I return this." She already knew what she wanted. She'd heard nothing but rave reviews about the swordfish dish on today's specials list. And if it tasted as good as it looked and smelled, she suspected it would soon be a regular item on the menu.

"Any suggestions?"

Her friend knew the regular menu as well as she did, so it was easy to decipher her question.

"I'm going with the swordfish, but the fried pork chops have been a hit today."

At the words "pork chops," Emma shook her head. "I'll go with the swordfish. The last time I ate pork chops, I also had one too many mojitos, and I spent the rest of the night in the bathroom. Every time I try to eat pork or taste mint, I get sick to my stomach."

"One swordfish special coming up."

"Can you also bring me an iced tea?"

After placing their order and returning the credit card, Liv made a quick pit stop in the office, where she'd left her phone charging. Not surprisingly, she walked in just as her mom sat behind the desk. Like most restaurant owners, the woman rarely stopped working. If she wasn't overseeing things in the dining room, she was checking in on the kitchen staff or doing paperwork in the office.

"Thanks again for working today. I know Matt's coming back today, and I'm sure you'd rather spend time with him."

"Family first."

Her mom's fingers paused over the keyboard. "Family is important, but it doesn't always need to come first, Liv. It's okay to put yourself first."

She appreciated her mom's concerns, but she didn't need a lecture today. "I know, Mom. But Matt's not coming back today anyway. He flew out to California this morning to see his mom. She was in a car accident."

Unplugging her phone, Liv checked the device. Sure enough, she had messages from Emma as well as two from Matt and one from Sebastian. The ones from Matt and Emma made sense, but she hadn't seen or heard from her ex since the day he'd shown up at her apartment out of the blue.

"Oh, dear. I hope she's okay."

"Matt said she's going to be fine."

Before her mom decided to continue her lecture, Liv moved toward the door. "I'm going on my break. Come get me if you need me."

Since Emma sat at the bar waiting for her, Liv deleted the text from her and moved on to Matt's. The ones from him had been sent hours apart, with the most recent coming two hours ago. Usually, she answered messages from everyone soon after receiving them, so Matt asking if she'd been called in after she didn't respond to his first one made sense.

Liv: Sorry. Yeah, working a double today. Did you see your mom?

Unlike many of the restaurants in town, Ocean View Grill brewed its iced tea rather than using a mix. Before rejoining Emma, Liv poured them each a glass and replaced the now-empty container with a new one.

"Any word from Matt on when he's coming back?" Emma asked, squeezing the lemon into her tea and adding sugar as soon as Liv set it down.

"Nothing yet, but I just responded to his messages." Following her friend's lead, she squeezed lemon into her tea and added two packets of sugar before taking a much-needed drink. A new text from Matt appeared on the screen before she put her glass down.

Matt: Saw her earlier. Aiden and I are going to visit her again later.

Liv: How is she?

Three tiny dots appeared, indicating Matt was typing.

"How's Brian feeling?" If Emma had wanted to hang out again tonight, Brian must still not be up for company.

"I talked to him before I came here. He managed to keep down some crackers this morning."

Brian might not be ready to eat the swordfish special, but keeping crackers down was preferable to kneeling before the toilet.

"Did you know Sebastian moved back?" Emma asked "I went to Hometown Brews because my power was still out, and he was there for the same reason. He bought a house on Viking Terrace."

Nodding, Liv read the newest message on her phone.

Matt: Mom's doing okay. I think she'll be home soon.

An invisible weight she hadn't even realized was there disappeared from her shoulders. Although she'd never met Violet Sherbrooke, thanks to all that Matt had shared, she felt as if she knew the woman. Not to mention how devastated Matt would be if his mom's injuries were more serious than he'd been led to believe.

Matt: Call you later. Out right now.

Although not the message she wanted to send, she replied with a simple *Okay* and set the device down.

"Is everything okay?"

"Oh, yeah."

So what if his message was a little dismissive? He said he was out. Sometimes, when she was busy, she sent short, clipped messages too.

"Matt was letting me know his mom is doing well and he thinks she'll be home soon."

William, a college student who'd recently returned from school in New York and started working there again last week, approached with their meals. "Russ asked me to bring these over before I take my break."

"Thanks. Are you working tonight too?"

"Yeah, I need to get in as many hours as I can before I go back to school."

Liv waited until William left before digging into her meal.

After hearing the customers rave about the dish all day, her expectations were high. And her first bite didn't disappoint.

"Swordfish never tastes like this when I cook it."

Emma could whip together beautiful floral arrangements, bring any plant back from death's doorstep, and had a singing voice that left people wondering why she'd never pursued a music career. Her talents in the kitchen, though, were limited.

"Dad's a genius when it comes to seasoning."

"You won't get an argument from me." Emma cut into the carrots that came with the meal. "If Matt's mom is doing well, do you think he'll be back soon?"

Unable to answer because her friend conveniently waited until she had a mouthful of food to ask her a question, Liv shrugged as she chewed.

"He didn't say, but that was his original plan." Liv reached for the freshly baked roll on her plate, but her hand froze as soon as her fingers touched it. "Did you say Sebastian bought a house on Viking Terrace?"

Her grandparents lived on Viking Terrace. Back in the winter, the house across the street had gone on the market. The last time she visited them, she'd noticed that the For Sale sign was gone, but as far as she knew, no one had moved in yet.

"Surprised me too. He hasn't moved in. He's having the inside remodeled."

"Seb mentioned that, but he didn't tell me he bought the house across from my grandparents."

Well, at least now she could tell them they didn't need to worry that whoever purchased the house intended to use it as a vacation home and rent it to tourists to help cover the mortgage. They'd been concerned because a couple who'd purchased a house on their street two years ago was doing just that. Most of the people who rented the house kept to themselves and respected their neighbors. However, there had been a handful of times when the tourists staying there had been anything but respectful. Instead, they'd thrown loud parties in the middle of the week, left the yard littered with trash, or blocked driveways with their vehicles.

"So you've seen him?" Emma asked before eating a forkful of rice.

As if just remembering her intentions, Liv's hand picked up her roll. "He showed up at my apartment one night as Matt and I were leaving. He said he'd just closed on a house in town and was having renovations done before he moved in."

"Now it makes sense why he asked if you were still seeing anyone."

Liv gestured toward her phone. "He sent me a message today."

"I have a feeling I know the answer, but what did he want?"

"Don't know. I haven't read it."

"Well, check." Emma nudged her arm before reaching for her iced tea.

Ignoring the message wouldn't make it disappear.

Sebastian: Love to catch up. Are you free tonight?

He'd mentioned catching up the day she'd seen him too. When he didn't reach out again, she'd assumed he'd either not truly meant it or had changed his mind. The text message on her phone proved both theories wrong.

Next to her, the sound of a transporter from Star Trek came from Emma's phone. Liv didn't need to ask to know the text was from Phoebe. Emma had unique notification tones assigned to everyone in her contact list. She'd assigned her friend that tone because she was such a huge Star Trek fan.

"He wants to get together."

"This is my shocked face." Emma pointed toward herself as she picked up her phone. "What —" Instead of continuing, she replied to the text message.

"Hey, what's up?"

"It's a message from Phoebe."

The transporter sound came from Emma's phone again.

Placing a hand over her heart, Liv did her best shocked look. "Really, wow, I never would've guessed. You stopped midsentence when you read it, though. Is everything okay?"

"Phoebe wanted to know if I was with you and if you'd seen the new photos of Matt trending on CHAT."

She'd barely had time to use the bathroom today, never mind check the social media site. "No, I haven't seen anything."

Sighing, Emma pushed a stray piece of hair over her shoulder. "The first couple are on the *Star Report*'s page. The other ones are posted to an Eclipse fan group page."

Even before Liv took Emma's phone, she knew she wasn't going to like what she was about to see. Still, her heart plummeted when she saw the photo of Matt with his mouth close to a woman's ear. The following picture showed them dancing. Much like in the first, she couldn't see the woman's face, but there was no missing Matt's hands on her waist.

For a second time this week, Eclipse's frontman, Matt Sherbrooke, has been seen in the company of a beautiful woman. Does that mean his summer romance is over, or is he taking a page from fellow bandmate Carter Wheeler's playbook?

"The ones the *Star Report* posted could be from his cousin's wedding. And the woman with him could be a relative."

Emma made a valid argument. While Liv couldn't see the woman's face, her hair was styled in an elaborate updo, and her strapless dress was one you'd wear to a more formal occasion, such as a wedding. Matt was clearly wearing a suit. But according to Matt, the guest list consisted of family and friends. Would a relative or close friend leak photos to the media?

"What fan group page are the photos on?"

"ForeverEclipse."

Something about Emma's tone sent her heart further south, which she hadn't thought possible.

A treasure trove of photos occupied the page. Some were of fans posing with different band members, while some had been taken during various concerts. Others, though, clearly had been taken without the subject's knowledge. The three most recent ones fell into that category. The first one featured Matt and a woman talking near a vehicle. The second showed the woman getting into the car while Matt stood by, waiting to close the door. The final one showed Matt opening the driver's side door.

Liv read the post that accompanied the photos.

"Matt Sherbrooke is in town. Just saw him leaving Omakase. Anyone recognize the woman with him?"

A multitude of comments followed the post, with a few mentioning what she'd already noticed. The woman in the photos had the same hair color and body type as the one from the *Star Report*'s page. They even seemed to be the same height.

If it was the same person and the *Star Report*'s photos had been taken at the wedding, why was she also in California with him?

Eighteen

"HOW MANY GUESTS do you expect at the banquet?" Liv asked as she jotted down the date and location of the high school sports banquet.

"Our fall banquet is our smallest since we only have three sports," Lydia answered.

Liv had assumed as much. Even when she'd attended Harbor Regional, the only sports offered in the fall had been cross-country, soccer, and golf. Although it was a regional school and students from various towns attended, there simply weren't enough students interested in typical fall sports.

"We tried to field a football team but were short on players again."

For as long as she could remember, the school had been trying to expand its athletic program by adding more sports. Sometimes it was football, other years it was field hockey or volleyball. Each time, however, they encountered the same problem: a lack of interest.

"We have forty-four student athletes. Each one is given two tickets, so the maximum would be 132, but we've never had all the athletes show up. Based on past banquets, I estimate there will likely be 120 people there."

Liv's phone vibrated inside her pocket. She'd turned it to silent mode when Lydia walked in because there was nothing professional about her phone alerting her to messages while meeting with a client. Still, she had to fight the urge to pull it out and check who the message was from. Despite telling her he'd call last night, Matt never did. In his defense, he knew she was working a double, so he might have assumed she wouldn't be up for a chat after work. Unfortunately, the lack of a phone call or a text message had kept her awake, leaving her to wonder not only about the photos but also what he was up to.

"Do you want us to prepare enough to serve 120, then?" Liv hated it when customers didn't give her precise numbers, especially since, if there wasn't enough food, people blamed the catering company, not the person who'd planned the event.

"What's the price difference between 130 and 120?"

Her phone vibrated again, and Liv's grip on her pen tightened.

"It would depend on the meal, but it would be less than $200."

Lydia considered the answer for a moment. "Can we go with 130 and adjust once I get the RSVPs back?"

Nodding, she added the figure to the form. "That's what most people do. I'll just need a final number two weeks before the banquet."

Liv flipped open her planner. "So, I would need the final count by Halloween."

With an estimated guest count settled on, Liv moved down the list of required information, and roughly forty-five minutes after sitting down, Lydia was signing the contract and handing over a credit card.

"I'm really looking forward to this year's banquet. I think the student athletes and their families are going to enjoy it so much more than last year's."

When she'd attended the school, there hadn't been an athletic banquet. Instead, at the end of each sport's season, everyone gathered in the auditorium and the athletic director recognized those teams that had performed well or, in the case of her brother, set a new school and state record in the 3200-meter race.

"Where was it held last year?" Liv stapled a receipt to Lydia's copy and handed everything to her.

"The Stage Coach Inn. I won't go back there again."

One of the oldest hotels in Bar Harbor, Liv had attended more than one wedding there.

"The food was awful, and there wasn't enough. Some people ended up with only salad and bread."

She'd heard the kitchen had experienced a lot of turnover since the new owners purchased the hotel.

"The senior class held its prom there in April, and the same thing happened."

"Well, I'll make sure that doesn't happen in November."

Smiling, Lydia patted her hand. "I know you won't."

Sometimes Liv wondered where she might be if she'd taken her love of cooking to a major city, such as Boston or Los Angeles. Instead of living over her family's restaurant and picking up shifts as a waitress, she might be running her own kitchen in a five-star restaurant, or maybe she'd have her own show on a cooking channel.

Lydia's comment, though, told her she was right where she belonged. So what if she didn't have a brand-new car and a house with a yard big enough to grow all the fresh vegetables she wanted? She was not only doing something she loved, but she had also earned a reputation as not only a great chef but also a trustworthy businesswoman.

"If you think of anything you want to change, call or email me."

"I will, and as soon as I have the final count, I'll be in touch."

Liv waited until the door closed behind Lydia before pulling out her phone. Unfortunately, there wasn't a message from the person she wanted to hear from. Instead, there were two reminders: one for an upcoming dentist's appointment and another asking if she wanted a quote on new windows.

Deleting both, she checked the time. It was almost nine in California. More than likely, Matt was awake. Should she call him or wait and see if he reached out?

And if she did call him, what should she say? She didn't want to accuse him of cheating yet. Despite repeatedly telling herself not to jump to that conclusion, last night she'd been unable to think about anything else every time she thought about the pictures.

Wait a little longer. He might be on his way to see his mom.

While she waited, she'd tackle the next item on her to-do list—this month's invoices. After selecting a playlist from her phone, she opened her accounting program and got to work.

"Knock, knock."

At the sound of a male voice, Liv's heart rate shot through the roof, and she spun in her chair. Usually, she heard the door chimes when someone walked inside. Whether it was because of the music or the fact that she was so focused, she hadn't heard them.

It took her brain a second to recognize that Sebastian and not some crazy serial killer stood opposite her desk.

"Sebastian, it's only you." Closing her eyes, she placed a hand over her heart and took a deep breath. "Man, you scared me."

"Sorry about that."

Her brain recognized she wasn't in danger, but her body still hadn't received the message, and Liv took another slow, deep breath. "It's not your fault. I shouldn't have the music on so loud."

A mistake she wouldn't make again.

"I'm sorry I didn't get back to you yesterday." Maybe if she'd answered his text, he wouldn't be standing across from her desk now. She'd been exhausted by the time she got home last night. "I worked a double at the restaurant. How are you?"

And what are you doing here?

"Don't worry about it. I'm good. I started moving my stuff into my new house this weekend. The kitchen was finished on Friday, and the painter should be done on Tuesday."

"Sounds like you had a lot of work done."

Without asking, Sebastian sat in the chair in front of her desk. "Yeah, the house hadn't been touched since it was built. I had the bathrooms and the kitchen remodeled and new hardwood floors put down."

Sounded like an expensive endeavor.

"I wouldn't have been able to have it all done at once, but Paul gave me a huge discount."

She'd forgotten Seb's brother-in-law owned his own business.

"You must be glad it's done."

"I've been sleeping on a twin-size air mattress with pink ballerina sheets in Regina's living room for the past week. Glad doesn't begin to describe how I feel."

Liv couldn't contain her laughter at the thought of Sebastian, who'd wrestled in college, sleeping on a twin mattress while covered with ballerina sheets.

"It beats sleeping outside with no mattress."

"Not by much." Leaning forward, Seb rested his arms on the desk. "Once I'm all moved in, I'm having a housewarming party."

Would it be asking too much if he'd come in because he wanted Ocean View to provide the food for this party?

"Well, if you need the name of a great caterer, I might know of one."

"I might take you up on that offer," Seb replied with a smile.

Although the smile transformed him from the average-looking guy down the street to someone cute, it didn't have the same effect on her as Matt's smile.

"But I didn't stop in to talk about my house. I wanted to see if you had any plans for tonight."

Yesterday, Emma mentioned that he'd inquired about her relationship status. Until now, though, Liv didn't realize she'd never asked Emma what she told him.

She always felt bad when she turned down a man's invitation to go out—well, unless the man asking was the Worm. Now wasn't any different.

Liv bit down on her lip while thinking of the nicest way to turn Seb down. Although their relationship had ended, she truly didn't have any hard feelings toward him.

"Sorry, I have plans with Emma. And I also have a boyfriend."

"So what? Since when does being in a relationship stop a person from going out with a friend?"

"Well, it doesn't."

"So what's the problem?"

I don't believe you're asking because you see me as a friend.

"Is it safe to assume you're still seeing Matt Sherbrooke? I knew he looked familiar that day outside your apartment, but I didn't know that's who he was until Regina showed me the pictures of you and him playing mini golf."

Unsure of the point Seb intended to make, Liv nodded.

"How long do you really think things between you will last?" Despite his compassionate tone, the question stung. "Someone like him isn't going to be happy here year-round, and we both know you'll never move." Seb's fingers curled around her hand. "And let's be honest, celebrities aren't known for lasting relationships."

Why did he have to bring up all the arguments she'd managed to bury?

"Have dinner with me as just a friend, nothing more, while he's gone."

"How—"

"It was hard to miss the pictures of him on the *Star Report* while I waited for my espresso. It said it was taken on a harbor cruise in Virginia."

She hadn't seen the magazine cover, but she assumed it featured the same pictures as the website. In those photos, he'd been with a pretty brunette whom he claimed was his cousin's wife. Liv had accepted his explanation. Now, though, she wondered if he'd lied.

"He appeared to be spending time with a friend."

Based on the way Seb said "friend," he suspected Matt and the brunette were more than that.

"So why can't you?"

Liv slipped her hand out from under his. "I appreciate the offer, but Emma and I have plans."

He knows I'm lying.

"If your plans with her fall through, you have my number. And when things with Sherbrooke don't work out, you know where to find me."

She hated how confident he sounded, but she couldn't deny that he might very well be right.

Rather than wait for a response, Seb stood and left.

Ten minutes later, Liv remained seated, staring off into space as Seb's comments and the pictures of Matt with other women bounced around her mind.

She didn't believe he'd lied about his mom so he could put off coming back and spend time with someone else. But that didn't mean he wasn't seeking out companionship while away—not that he'd have to do much seeking. For him, it would be more like choosing from the line of females his smile alone would summon.

Before Liv could stop it, an image of Matt looking over a long line of gorgeous women formed. Somehow, each one was more beautiful than the one before her. When he reached the last woman, one who looked like the individual he'd helped into a car, he kissed her.

The vibrating cell phone jolted Liv from her ugly daydream. Unlike earlier, she found a message from Matt when she picked it up.

Matt: Do you have time to talk?

Pinching the bridge of her nose, she considered her answer. Thanks to the photos from last night and Seb's visit, she was in a crappy mood. It might be better if she waited until her mood improved. At the same time, though, she wasn't sure that would happen anytime soon, especially now that Seb had brought all her concerns to the surface again.

And if they spoke now, maybe he'd explain the newest photos and put her concerns to rest.

Liv: Sure.

No sooner had she sent the message than the opening of "Loving You" came from her phone.

"Sorry I didn't call last night. By the time we got home, it was almost three o'clock where you are," Matt said after greeting her.

"I was definitely asleep then. Are you staying with your brother?"

"More like the other way around. Aiden lives almost four hours from the hospital, so he's staying with me."

Liv hadn't known Matt had a home in California, but it made sense. It seemed like every other celebrity owned a home there, and he certainly had the means. Hell, he could afford to own as many houses as he wanted.

"How's your mom doing?"

"Okay. The surgery on her leg went well, according to her doctors, but she'll be in a cast for a while, and she'll need physical therapy eventually. She has a broken wrist too."

"Any idea of when she might go home?"

And you'll be back?

"The doctor didn't give an exact day, but it should be before the end of the week."

"That's good. Are you heading back to the hospital soon?"

"Some of my mom's friends are visiting her this morning. Dad's going to call when they leave. Aiden and I might just hang around here until then. What are you up to?"

"I have another client coming in soon. Until then, I'm working on the bills. And tonight I'm finishing the laundry I started yesterday."

"Laundry. You really know how to have fun when I'm not around."

"What can I say? I go wild and crazy when you're away."

What kind of fun kept you out so late last night?

While he'd given her no reason to not trust him, she couldn't seem to help it.

"Besides seeing your mom, what have you been up to?"

She sounded suspicious to her own ears, but if Matt noticed, he didn't comment.

"Aiden and I went to our cousin's house last night. Sophie was at the hospital visiting when we got there, and I hadn't seen her in a while."

If Matt and Aiden visited a cousin last night, how did he explain the photos she'd seen? Aiden hadn't been present in any of them. And what about the similarity between the woman seen getting into his car and the one he'd danced with at the wedding?

"You have more cousins than anyone I know."

"Don't remind me. No matter where I go, I run into them."

"Sophie didn't go to the wedding?"

Okay, so she was a chicken and afraid to ask the questions she wanted answers to.

"No, she and her husband had plans already, and he wasn't willing to change them. Chase can be inflexible."

"Were there a lot of guests at the wedding?"

"About a hundred, I'd say. For a Sherbrooke wedding, that's tiny."

Over the past six years or so, members of the Sherbrooke family had been getting married left and right. Photos of many had graced magazine pages and been splashed all over the internet, so she had an idea of their typical size as well as the well-known guests usually in attendance. She didn't know anything about the bride and groom but assumed their guest list had been similar.

"Everyone wondered why you weren't with me, including my mom when I saw her yesterday."

The second part of Matt's comment caught Liv's attention. "You told your parents about me?"

Maybe she was letting her insecurities get the better of her. If he'd told his mom and dad about her, perhaps he really did see their relationship lasting.

"I didn't have to. Mom saw the pictures of us together. Michayla has worked for my parents for years and makes sure to share every headline or article she finds with my mom."

There goes that optimistic theory.

"She wants to meet you. I told her we'll hopefully visit in the fall. When I get back, let's pick a date that works for you."

Right now, she wasn't convinced he'd remember her name by the fall.

"Uh, yeah. We, um, can probably do that."

* * *

She'd sounded off since she answered the phone. Liv's answer just now, though, convinced Matt he wasn't imagining things. Something was wrong.

"Are you not ready to meet my parents?"

Liv hadn't blinked an eye when he'd proposed the idea before he left. But it sounded like she was having second thoughts now.

"Of course I am."

"Then what's the problem?"

"There isn't one."

Bullshit.

"Your answer when I mentioned picking a date says otherwise, Liv."

He never should've told her about his aunt and uncle's treatment of Adam's wife. Liv probably worried his parents would be the same way toward her.

"My parents are going to love you."

Liv cleared her throat, a time-honored stall tactic by people when they needed to fabricate an answer. "The fall might, um, be too busy. Already we have something booked for every Saturday in September, and the weekends in October are starting to fill up."

"We can wait until winter. Or I can invite Mom and Dad to visit us."

Now that he thought about it, she might be more comfortable meeting them in familiar surroundings.

"They've never visited me in Maine."

"That, uh, sounds like a better idea."

She still sounded uncertain about the meeting, but for now, he'd let the matter go.

"Who's the client you're meeting with this afternoon?"

"Someone who attended the retirement party we did in May. She doesn't live in town, so I've never met her. She wants us to cater her company's holiday party. Hopefully, it all works out."

"If she contacted you because they attended the other party, they've already decided they want you to do the event."

"We haven't talked numbers yet."

Not only was Ocean View Catering the only catering company in the area, but they also had a website. He'd checked it out. More than likely, the potential client had as well, and it listed approximate costs for events. If she wanted to worry, there was nothing he could say to change that.

"I'm sure it will work out."

"So, I know you'll visit your mom today, but do you have any plans tonight?"

Stepping outside, Matt sat and propped his bare feet up on the railing. "Not sure yet. Aiden wants to check out Covert. It opened in April, and neither of us has gone, but I'm hoping to find a way to change his mind."

Matt watched a sailboat glide across the ocean. He preferred boats with an engine to those with sails, but an evening out on even a sailboat sounded better than one spent at Covert. But he didn't get many opportunities to spend time with his brother, so if Aiden really wanted to go, he'd join him.

"I've never heard of it. Is it a restaurant?"

"No, it's a nightclub."

"I've never been to one."

"You're not missing much." If he never stepped inside another, he'd be okay.

"Since one won't be opening in Orchard Harbor anytime soon, I'll take your word for it."

In his opinion, Orchard Harbor didn't need one.

"When I get back, we can go to Boston for the weekend. There are plenty of options there that we can check out if you'd like. We can even take the boat down."

Matt would rather take her to Newport or Sanborn Island, but he'd go wherever she wanted.

"Nah, I don't think I'd enjoy one."

"Then let's plan to visit Sanborn Island or Martha's Vineyard before the summer ends. If we take the boat to Martha's Vineyard, we can stop in Newport too."

"I'm not sure when I'll have a full weekend off."

"Then we can go during the week."

Since they'd been together, she was busiest on the weekends.

"Yeah, that might work."

Behind him, the glass door opened, and Aiden stepped outside with a coffee in one hand and his phone in the other.

"I need to go. My appointment is approaching the door. But I'll check my calendar later and see when I have some days off so we can go somewhere."

Was her tone the same as when he'd mentioned meeting his parents, or was he imagining it?

"I'll call you later," Matt said before ending the call.

Sitting in the other chair, Aiden stretched his legs out and crossed his ankles. "You look as if you're contemplating how to achieve world peace."

"Just trying to figure Liv out."

"Figuring out how to achieve world peace would be easier than figuring out a woman."

Aiden's comment brought some much-needed humor to his morning. "You're probably right about that."

"Hold on. Did you just say I'm right? I should make a note of this."

Matt raised his coffee toward his mouth but paused to offer a reply. "Don't let it go to your head. You got lucky."

"I'm guessing you were just talking to Liv and not Dad."

He nodded. "I didn't get a chance to call her last night, so I wanted to do it before we head to the hospital."

"Is that the problem? She's upset because you didn't call?"

He'd anticipated her being a little annoyed because of that, but she hadn't been.

"Women can be weird about that. Shelly used to tear into me if I promised to call and didn't."

He would've preferred that to Liv's tone when they discussed meeting his parents or going on a short vacation.

"She didn't give me a hard time about not calling."

"Then what's the problem?"

Aiden wasn't a relationship guru, but he was better than nothing, and he was the only one there at the moment.

"She seemed uncertain or maybe reluctant to meet Mom and Dad."

"Dude, you've been together less than four months. Maybe she's just not ready."

Had it really been less than four months? It felt much longer.

"That's fair. But she was also reluctant when I suggested we go away when I get back."

"Hey, I'd be reluctant to go on vacation with you too."

Usually, he appreciated his brother's sense of humor. Not so much right now.

Matt threw his brother a dirty look. "You're not helping."

"Maybe you imagined it."

Aiden could be right, but his gut told him otherwise.

"Or maybe she's having a bad day and what you heard was related to that and not you. If you're that worried, call her back and ask her."

"She has a meeting with a client. That's why she had to go."

"Since you can't do anything about it now, don't stress about it. And when you talk to her later, ask her."

Not that he'd tell him, but Aiden was right again.

"Mrs. Lawson and Mrs. Reed will probably spend all morning with Mom. Are you up for a round of golf?" Aiden asked.

Matt would never find himself on the PGA Tour, but he was a better-than-average player.

"Don't want to admit I'm right, do you?" Aiden asked.

Some questions didn't deserve an answer.

"Hey, if you're afraid you'll lose, we can skip it."

"You beat me? That's funny," Aiden scoffed.

"If that's a yes, I'll call the club and reserve a tee time." Despite not being around much, Matt maintained his membership at Skyview.

Aiden nodded. "And after you lose to me, you can admit that I was right not once but twice this morning."

He'd played golf with Aiden enough to know their skill level was the same. "Sure, but if I win, we skip Covert and go indoor rock climbing."

"You should pick out what you're going to wear now so you don't have to waste time tonight," Aiden said as he stood.

Rather than respond, Matt picked up his phone and followed his brother back into the house. Before he could find the country club in his contacts, though, the device rang and his agent's name appeared on the screen. He had left Matt a voice-mail the night of the harbor cruise. Between Adam's wedding and his mom's accident, he hadn't gotten around to calling him back.

"What's up, Ryan?"

"Did you lose my number? I called you four days ago."

To an outsider, Ryan's question would seem inappropriate, considering he worked for Matt, not the other way around. However, while Ryan was indeed his agent, he was also a close friend.

"I know you were in Virginia for a wedding. I saw the pictures. But you're not there now. How long are you here for?"

He hoped Ryan was referring to the pictures from the dinner cruise, because if he'd seen some of him at the wedding, it would mean Theo had ignored the conversation they'd had before the ceremony.

The last part of Ryan's comment registered before Matt got a syllable out. Ryan represented some of his friends, but he hadn't seen any since he'd arrived.

"How do you know I'm in California?"

"Don't you ever check CHAT?" Matt could hear the guy shaking his head as he spoke. "There were some pictures of you and a woman I didn't recognize getting into a car. The person who posted it said they'd just seen you leaving Omakase. Anyway, are you sticking around for long or heading back to Florida soon?"

They hadn't spoken since May, so Ryan didn't know of his plan to make Orchard Harbor his full-time home.

"I'll be here a few more days at the most. As soon as my mom is discharged from the hospital, I'm heading back to Maine."

"Oh, man. What happened? Is she okay?"

Matt added his coffee mug to the dishwasher and then leaned against the counter. "She was injured in a car accident Saturday, but she's going to be okay."

"That sucks. Before you leave, we should meet. Nathan Barkley reached out to me. He wants you for *Coldblooded*. He's already gotten CJ, Anderson, and Trish on board. He wrote the role for you. I also think now is a good time to seriously talk about a solo career."

Trish Robinson was a phenomenal actress, but supposedly she was a diva and a royal pain in the ass. He had no desire to find out for himself if that was true. But CJ and Anderson were not only equally talented but also friends.

"How about tomorrow?"

"I'm busy all day. Wednesday afternoon, I'm free from three o'clock on."

"I'll see you at three." With a bit of luck, Mom would go home tomorrow or Wednesday, and he could fly back to Maine Thursday morning.

Nineteen

"**WHOEVER CAME** up with the idea for this place must've been on drugs," Aiden said from across the table.

If he didn't know Anderson didn't touch anything stronger than ibuprofen, he'd agree. He'd expected Covert to be similar to Sapphire, another nightclub co-owned by Anderson and his younger brother. The only similarities between the two were the clientele. Actually, Covert was unlike any nightclub he'd been to. Instead of the hottest dance music or this month's Top 40 hits, the speakers pumped out 80s classics. The décor, however, looked more like a 1920s speakeasy. The combination shouldn't work, yet somehow it did.

Sipping his drink, Matt scanned the room. While he knew a fair number of the people dancing to an old Whitney Houston song and enjoying drinks, he'd yet to see anyone he'd consider a friend.

"It's probably hot right now because it's so different," he said.

"Maybe you and I should open a place and combine music from today with an interior from — the 50s."

"Don't see it working."

"How about if it resembles a disco?" Aiden asked.

Matt shook his head. "It's your crazy idea. You do what you want. I have no desire to own a nightclub." He gestured toward

Anderson, who was walking toward their table. "Pitch your idea to him. Maybe he'll bite."

"Hey, I thought you were in Maine," Anderson said as he sat.

"I'm only here for a few days."

Other people would've asked why he was in town. Not Anderson. Having spent almost twenty years in the spotlight, he valued his own privacy and respected that of others.

Anderson turned to Aiden. "What's the idea you should pitch to me?"

"I suggested we open a club that resembles a 70s disco but plays the latest music."

"Every club is playing the current stuff, but a disco theme might work. We could pair it with music from the 90s." Anderson rested his forearms on the table and wrapped his hands around his drink, scanning the room as if imagining it.

"Yeah, I think that could work. If you're free next week, let's get together and flesh out the details. I'll talk to Paul and see if he wants in." He glanced across the table. "Are you in, Matt?"

"That's a hard no."

Shrugging, Anderson turned his attention back to Aiden. "Is there a day that works for you?"

"Monday afternoon?"

"Works for me," Anderson replied. "So, has Ryan talked to you yet?"

"Briefly. I'm meeting with him on Wednesday."

With CJ and Anderson in the film, it was guaranteed to be a success. Plus, with them around, filming would be a lot of fun. Still, he was reluctant to agree to anything right now.

"You can't turn it down. Barkley wrote the role for you."

"Ryan said the same thing. I need more details before¼ shit."

The day was going downhill fast. First, he got his ass handed to him by his brother on the green; now his ex was here.

"What's wrong?" Aiden asked.

"Jasmine is here."

"Maybe she won't see you."

He couldn't be that lucky. "She's headed this way."

Aiden started to turn but stopped when Matt kicked his shin. "Is Ellie with her?" he asked.

Ellie Baker had found fame before her tenth birthday, and her career had been going strong ever since. His brother, like a lot of other guys, had grown up with a thing for her.

"You're the last person I expected to see here tonight. Do you mind if we join you? There aren't many empty places to sit," Jasmine said.

Across the table, Anderson shrugged, while Aiden shot him a "don't you dare turn them away" glare.

"Of course not."

Jasmine was seated and plastered against Matt's side before he finished his response.

"It seems like forever since I saw you." She finished her drink and placed the glass on the table.

Matt adjusted his position so Jasmine was no longer touching him. "It's been a while." He knew exactly how long it had been.

"I don't think I've seen you since that party at Jordan's."

The night before Eclipse headed out on their last tour, Jordan had thrown a party. It had been the last event they'd attended together. Things between them officially ended two months later, although their relationship had been headed in that direction for a long time.

"Sounds right."

"Well, it's been way too long." Jasmine shimmied closer until her body was once again touching his, setting off warning bells.

Across from him, Anderson gestured toward the waitress. "I'm going to order another drink. If anyone wants anything, it's on me."

What Matt wanted was to leave, but there was no way he was getting Aiden to go as long as Ellie sat next to him.

"I could use another," Aiden said, his expression easy to read. Matt risked his life if he tried to get them to leave now.

Considering the clientele that frequented Covert, Matt wasn't surprised when the waitress remained professional when she took their order.

"How long are you going to be around?" Jasmine's hand settled on his forearm. "We need to catch up."

Although she hadn't done it when their relationship ended, he knew Jasmine talked trash and spread lies about her exes. He'd prefer to not piss her off tonight for that very reason. So rather than simply pulling his arm away, he reached for his drink, dislodging her hand at the same time.

"I'm only here another day or two." At least he hoped that was the case, because ever since he'd landed, the restlessness he experienced whenever he was away from Orchard Harbor had plagued him.

"How about tomorrow?" Jasmine's fingertips slowly worked their way down his chest as her other hand settled on his shoulder. "Or tonight. We can head back to my place now." Her lips brushed against his ear as she spoke. "Or yours."

Matt grabbed her wrist to stop her trek south. "Jasmine —"

Her mouth covered his, silencing him.

Pulling away, Matt put as much space between them as he could without landing on the floor. "I'm seeing someone."

The waitress who'd taken their order returned, halting their conversation. Her eyes glanced from Matt to Jasmine as she set the drinks down. "If you need anything else, let me know."

Jasmine pouted as she traced his ear. "So? She's not here. What she doesn't know won't hurt her." She closed the distance between them again. "I've missed you. We were so good together."

Jerking his head away, he grabbed her wrist before she touched him again. "I'd know."

Not to mention, I'm not interested.

"We're better off as friends. You know that."

The phone in his pocket vibrated, alerting him to a text, and Matt pulled it out.

Liv: Sorry, I missed you earlier. Is now a good time to call?

After they left the hospital, he'd called Liv to give her an update. Unfortunately, he'd gotten her voicemail.

Covert wasn't the optimal place to talk, but by the time he

got home, it would be too late. He'd have to find a quiet place, or at least a relatively quiet one, to talk.

Matt: I'll call you in a few.

Standing, he looked at his brother. "I need to call Liv. Be back in a bit."

Aiden looked over at him long enough to nod before he turned his full attention back to Ellie.

Yeah, he wasn't getting Aiden out of here anytime soon.

He'd frequented enough nightclubs to know the quietest area would be near the restrooms.

"How's my girl?" Matt asked after Liv answered.

"Tired. I ended up covering the last half of Brenda's lunch shift. Her daughter went into labor, and she wanted to be there. Then Phoebe and I went to the movies. I got home ten minutes ago."

"See anything good?" He didn't even know what was out right now.

"*A Flower for Every Day*. It came out last week."

If he'd heard about it, he didn't remember.

"It sounds like you didn't talk Aiden out of going to the club."

"I tried. I made a bet with him. If he won our golf game, we'd go to Covert. If I won, we'd go indoor rock climbing. He won. He failed to tell me he's been taking private lessons." One of these days, Matt would get even with him for that.

"How's your mom?"

Matt backed farther into the corner and leaned against the wall. "She's going home tomorrow."

"That's great. She must be happy."

It was a toss-up as to who was happier, his mom or dad. "I'd say that's an understatement. Did you check your calendar to see when we can go away?"

Now wasn't the best time for a prolonged conversation, but although they'd been apart for less than a week, it felt much longer, and he wasn't ready to let her go.

"Right now, the first week of October looks good."

He'd hoped for something sooner, but he'd take what he could get. "We can start planning when I get back."

Their destination didn't matter to him, and Matt wanted their vacation to be a place she'd enjoy.

"Sounds good. Since your mom is going home tomorrow, does that mean you'll be back soon?"

"Not as soon as I'd like. My agent called and wants to go over a few things. Since I'm out here, I figured I'd get it over with. I'm meeting with him on Wednesday afternoon. My plan is to fly back first thing Thursday morning."

Silence followed his response. Matt was about to ask if she was still there when Liv spoke.

"Oh, yeah, that makes sense. Do you know what time you'll be back?"

He hadn't called the charter company yet, but he planned to be back in time for dinner.

"Not yet, but don't make any plans for Thursday night. I want you all to myself."

"That can be arranged. But I'm going to let you go. My bed is calling my name."

Ending his call, Matt made his way back to the table. Unlike earlier, he bumped into several people he knew. Each conversation intensified his desire to leave.

"Shit," Matt said when he had eyes on his table, the pulsing music drowning out his voice. His brother and Ellie were gone, but Jasmine remained with Anderson. He considered his options before taking a seat in Aiden's empty chair, the spot across from Jasmine rather than next to her.

"Wow, you were gone for a long time. I was starting to worry you'd left," she said.

Something told him he should've. After all, Aiden was a big boy. He could find his own way home.

"Where did my brother go?" If Jasmine said he'd left with Ellie, he was heading for the exit.

"He's over there somewhere with Ellie." She gestured toward the dance floor.

Trying to find Aiden was pointless, yet he glanced that way.

In one sip, Jasmine finished her drink, stood, and came around the table. Before his brain could register her intentions, she dropped onto his lap and wrapped her arms around his neck.

"Let's go someplace private and catch up. Ellie can give your brother a ride home."

Jasmine's lips covered his before he could argue.

Aiden could find his own way home, because he'd had enough. Matt resisted the urge to push her off his lap and onto the floor. He didn't want to hurt her.

"Damn it. We're not doing this." Grabbing both wrists, he pulled her arms away. "I'm with someone. Unless you want to be sitting on the floor, get off my lap."

"Don't be like that. I know you want me. Why are you fighting it?"

He'd never realized Jasmine had rocks for brains. Despite his warning, he'd never dump a woman onto the floor. Slipping one arm under her legs and another around her waist, he stood.

"Tell my brother I went home," he said, depositing her in the seat she'd vacated.

"You won't get another chance with me."

I'll live.

"Good night, Jasmine."

* * *

Afraid of who she'd find there, Liv turned toward the door when she heard the chime. Relief washed over her at the sight of Emma standing there. Although she hadn't seen or heard from Seb since his unexpected visit, she suspected it was only a matter of time before she saw him again.

"Good, it's only you."

"Only me? I don't know if I should be offended or not." Emma crossed to Liv's desk with a large floral arrangement in each hand.

"You know I didn't mean it like that. Are these both for me?"

"No, I was afraid the flowers would get scared if I left them

231

alone." Emma pointed to the vase on her left as she sat. "Of course they're both for you."

Okay, it was a silly question, but why would Matt send her two arrangements?

"Who are they from?"

Emma shrugged. "Mom processed the orders."

"And you didn't peek at the cards?" Liv plucked the card out of the vase filled with red and pink roses.

"Of course not. I'd never do that."

"It's against store policy, isn't it?"

"Yeah, and Mom was in all day."

Liv could read between the lines. If Emma's mom hadn't been there, she would've read the cards before delivering the flowers.

"Come on. Open the envelope, I bet they're from Matt."

One, sure, but why send two?

Miss you. Can't wait to see you on Thursday. Love Matt.

"From Matt, right?" Emma snatched the card out of her hand before Liv could put it back. "Is his mom out of the hospital?"

"She's going home today."

"Why isn't he coming back today?"

"He has a meeting with his agent tomorrow."

At least, that was what he'd told her. A tiny part of her wondered if he was putting off coming back because he had access to a way of life that didn't exist here.

"Why do you sound as if you don't believe him?"

"Of course I do." Rather than meet Emma's eyes, Liv turned her attention to the second vase, which was a mix of sunflowers and roses, and grabbed the card.

"Your voice says otherwise."

The downside of being friends with someone for so long was that they picked up even subtle differences in your tone.

"Do you think these are from Matt too?" Liv asked, changing the subject.

Unlike the first card, this one didn't contain any hearts. Instead, a row of flowers ran across the top.

I thought these would look nice on your desk. Thinking of you, Seb.

"Are you going to tell me who they're from, or is it a secret?"

Liv stuffed the card back into the envelope. "Sebastian."

"Your ex is sending you flowers? Have you seen him?"

"He came in yesterday."

"And?"

"And I told him I'm with someone."

Emma gestured toward the flowers. "Either he didn't believe you or he thinks you'll pick him over Matt."

"Oh, he believed me. But he's convinced we won't last. He said I'd know where to find him when Matt splits."

"What a jerk."

"It was a crappy thing to say, but he wasn't wrong. Celebrities aren't known for their long-term relationships."

"There are plenty who are. Should I make you a list?" Plucking the card out of her hand, Emma dropped it on the desk.

"C'mon, do you really think Matt is going to be happy living here?" She'd thought it many times, but until now she'd kept it to herself.

"Yeah." Emma removed the card from Matt and held it up. "What does this say?"

"'Love Matt.' But¾"

"But nothing. He's not given you any reason to doubt his feelings or that he'll get tired of living here, so don't make problems that don't exist. He wants you to meet his parents. If that doesn't say serious, I don't know what does."

Why had she told Emma that? "You're right."

"I know I am. Now, since you're free tonight, why don't you come by? The newest season of *Under Fire* starts tonight. Phoebe is coming."

She'd planned to watch it already, but it would be more fun with Emma and Phoebe. "Count me in."

"Good. Come over as soon as you're done here." Emma handed back the card and picked up her keys. "I'm heading to the grocery store for snacks, and then I'm going home."

"I'll be over around five." That gave her time to finish here and stop by her apartment to change.

A little over an hour later, the scent of garlic greeted Liv when she walked into Emma's house.

"It's about time you got here." Emma looked up briefly before going back to cutting a pan of brownies.

"I said around five, not at five." She didn't ask before snatching a garlic knot off the baking sheet. "It's only ten minutes after."

Phoebe entered the room and, like Liv, grabbed a garlic knot. "I want it known that I beat you here today."

While one of Liv's pet peeves was being late, Phoebe seemed to have the opposite problem. The only time you could count on her being on time was when she was working.

"Is the world going to end tomorrow?" Liv asked.

"If it does, you'll both save money because you won't have to buy bridesmaid dresses." Phoebe held up her hand and wiggled her fingers.

"When did Aaron ask?" Emma practically jumped over the table to give Phoebe a hug.

"Why didn't you tell us?" Liv asked at the same time.

"Saturday. It was our three-year anniversary."

Only three years? It seemed like they'd been a couple forever.

"This calls for champagne," Emma exclaimed.

"Do you always keep champagne in your fridge, or did Aaron tell you?"

Emma set the bottle and three glasses on the table. "I always have a bottle. You never know when you're going to have something to celebrate."

And she thought she knew everything about Emma.

"Have you guys set a date?" Liv asked as she filled the glasses.

"Not an exact date, but we're thinking sometime in the summer."

"If you need a caterer, I have the name of a great one."

"Don't worry, you'll be the first I call. Now let's start the show. Otherwise, we'll only have time for one episode."

"First, we need a toast." Emma picked up her glass and waited for everyone to follow her lead. "Congrats, Phoebe! Liv and I can't wait to see you walk down the aisle carrying flowers from Exquisite Flowers before eating a meal prepared by Ocean View."

"Real subtle." Rolling her eyes, Phoebe touched her glass against Emma's. "So, do you think Mya and Steve will get together this season?" she asked, referring to two of the characters in the show.

"Not if they stay true to the books. Mya stays with Daniel throughout most of the second one."

Of the three of them, Emma was the only one who'd read the popular book series the television show was based on.

"I don't know if I can stand another season watching Daniel sleep with every woman who crosses his path and then going home like nothing happened." Liv popped a cheese-covered nacho into her mouth as the sound of an oven timer alerted her to a text.

"Oh, don't worry. He'll get what's coming to him." Emma pressed Play, and a recap from last season started. "Let me guess, it's Matt."

Since she was with Emma and Phoebe, it was a logical guess.

Sebastian: Hey, Liv.

"No, it's Sebastian."

"He probably wants to know if you liked the flowers."

"Seb sent you flowers?" Phoebe asked.

Nodding, she considered whether she should respond or ignore him.

"Matt did too," Emma added.

No, she'd ignore him. Maybe if she did, he'd get the message that she wasn't interested.

Liv was about to put the phone down when another message appeared.

Sebastian: Regina found this on CHAT. Wasn't sure if you saw it.

A third message came through. This one contained a photo of Matt and Jasmine Locke, as well as a link to the *Star Insider*.

"It's not about the flowers."

Before her brain had a chance to realize what her hand was doing, she opened the link that Seb had sent. Immediately, the homepage of the *Star Insider* filled the screen, featuring a large photo of Matt with Jasmine glued to his side, her hand on his chest, sending ice through Liv's veins.

"Rekindling their romance?" the headline read.

Matt Sherbrooke and Jasmine Locke were hot and heavy at Covert this week. Last year, friends and family were shocked when they broke up. According to those closest to the couple, Matt had been about to propose when Jasmine ended their relationship because she was tired of Matt's rigorous tour schedule. It seems as though the two have overcome their differences and are ready to give their relationship another try.

Several smaller pictures accompanied the article. In one, she could see his brother and Ellie Baker. He'd told her they'd ended up at the nightclub because he'd lost a bet. Had that been a lie? Had he planned to see Jasmine all along? What about the other pictures? Were those women really who he'd said they were?

"Liv, what's wrong?"

She barely heard Emma's voice over the blood pounding in her ears.

Had he lied about his mom too?

Grabbing her shoulders, Emma spoke again. "Hey, what happened?"

Liv swallowed, but the giant knot in her throat remained. "I think Matt's cheating on me."

"Why do you think that?" Phoebe paused the television and changed seats so she was closer.

"Seb sent me a link to the *Star Insider*. There's an article and pictures about Matt. See for yourself." She handed Emma her phone.

Emma briefly looked at the pictures before handing the device to Phoebe. "It might not be what it looks like. She might have been drunk and come on to him. I remember reading she did that to CJ Ferguson while his wife was sitting right there."

"Emma's right. I read about that too. That photo is a single moment. He might have pushed her away or moved the second after it was taken."

"Did you read the article?" Liv asked.

"And the *Star Insider* is known for its journalistic integrity. C'mon, Liv, we all know the magazine writes whatever will sell."

Phoebe wasn't wrong. The *Star Insider* had printed stories that were later proven to be incorrect. But they did sometimes print ones that were 100 percent accurate. Not to mention, the photos provided compelling evidence.

"Don't jump to a conclusion because of this," Emma said.

"What about the other pictures?"

"He was at his cousin's wedding. It makes sense there would be photos of him with female relatives or family friends."

"Ask him about this before you do anything," Phoebe said.

Taking back her phone, Liv turned it off. "I don't want to talk about this right now. Please put the show back on."

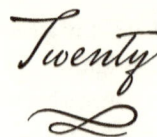

Twenty

MATT: *Can you talk?*

Liv started a reply and then deleted it. Yesterday, she'd avoided talking to Matt by lying and telling him she was working at the restaurant. If she sent a similar response now, he'd believe her. But avoiding him wouldn't solve anything.

Liv: Sure.

"Loving You" filled the room. Yeah, she needed to change her ringtone. Perhaps she'd return the device to its default tone. The last thing she needed was a reminder of Matt every time someone called her.

"Sorry I didn't call earlier."

Two weeks ago, she would've smiled at the sound of Matt's voice. Today, it had the opposite effect.

"I was with my parents until after lunch, and I just left my meeting with Ryan."

Maybe he had been with his parents and then in a meeting. Liv didn't know if she believed him anymore.

"How's your mom?"

"Glad to be home and already sick of the casts, especially the one on her leg."

"I bet. I broke my ankle when I was fourteen. The cast made everything ten times harder."

"I talked to them about visiting. They're going to come as soon as the casts come off."

"That's great. Hopefully, they come in time to see the fall foliage. How did your meeting go?"

She was stalling, and she knew it. Last night she'd scripted out everything she intended to say. If she were smart, she'd tell him and get it over with.

"More or less, he's pushing for me to release a solo album. He wasn't happy when I told him I wasn't ready. But since I agreed to accept the role in *Coldblooded*, he forgave me."

Yep, she never should've ignored her conscience. Matt never planned to stay in Orchard Harbor.

"I'm looking forward to working with Anderson and CJ again."

Just tell him.

"With the three of you in the movie, it'll be a huge hit."

When had she become such a chicken?

"I'll tell you all about it tomorrow. I land in Bangor at four. I should be home around five. Do you want to meet me there or for me to stop by and pick you up?"

I can't put it off any longer.

"Neither. You actually don't need to come back. At least not to see me."

She'd rather he never set foot in town again, but since he owned not only a home but the building she lived in, he was bound to visit occasionally.

"Is this the opening to a joke? Because if it is, it's not funny."

The confusion she heard left her wishing she'd sent him a text message ending things instead.

"It's not a joke, Matt."

Silence followed her answer, and she wondered if he'd hung up.

"What's going on? We were making plans to go away yesterday, and now you don't want to see me."

"Nothing. I just don't want to see you again."

"Something happened, and I deserve to know what."

She'd debated telling him she knew about the other women.

Ultimately, the voice that kept telling her Phoebe and Emma might be right convinced her to just end things without accusing him of cheating. The anger coming from him now had her reconsidering her decision. After all, she wasn't the one who'd been photographed with other people.

"Fine. I saw the pictures, Matt. So maybe you're the one who owes me an explanation."

"Liv, I already told you that was my cousin's wife."

"And I'm sure the woman you danced with and the one you were seen with on Sunday were also married to your cousins. And I must have missed the announcement. Which one of your cousins married Jasmine Locke?"

"I don't know what pictures you saw, but I can explain."

So he intended to play dumb.

"Even if you can, there's no point. You would've eventually gotten bored here with me. I'm just saving us some time."

"Damn it, will you listen to me? I haven't been with anyone else. And yeah, I saw Jasmine the other night, but she just sat down. I didn't ask her to join me."

That photo is a single moment. Phoebe's words repeated in her head. But so what if it was. Ending this now was better than waiting for him to do it in a few months.

"Goodbye, Matt."

The dam holding back her tears broke as she put the phone down.

I did the right thing.

Maybe if she told herself that a few hundred times, she'd believe it.

* * *

Matt snagged the first empty spot he saw and once again wondered why he'd listened to his brother last night. If he'd changed his departure time and left last night as soon as a crew could get to the airport, he would've gotten here hours ago, before Liv even had her first coffee. But no, he'd listened to Aiden, who insisted it was better to wait so he wasn't angry when he confronted Liv. He'd also pointed out that if he waited, he could use the time to figure out what pictures Liv was talking about and find a way to prove they weren't what she thought.

It hadn't taken them long to solve that mystery. Unfortunately, waiting hadn't lessened his anger. If anything, it was worse, only now it wasn't all directed at Liv. The photos on Eclipse's CHAT fan page and the *Star Insider* website looked bad. He couldn't deny that, but he deserved a chance to tell her the truth.

More than one person walking by looked his way as he stood there deciding where to try first. At almost five o'clock, she could be anywhere, including the restaurant. If she was covering a shift there, he'd have to wait until she finished.

A few raindrops hit him as he passed Fireside Pizzeria, and by the time he reached Ocean View Catering, what was supposed to be a gentle shower had turned into a downpour. As if that wasn't bad enough, the door to the catering company was locked and all the lights inside were off.

Why did I listen to you, Aiden?

With the dinner rush starting, it was pointless to check the restaurant, so Matt walked around to the back, to the entrance to the apartments upstairs. If Liv wasn't home, he'd wait for her.

Even though her car was in its usual spot, he wouldn't have been surprised if she wasn't home. However, he wasn't prepared to see a man standing outside her door. Although he couldn't see his face, the man's height and hair color ruled out Liv's brother.

The floor creaked under Matt's foot, and Liv's visitor looked his way just as he knocked. While he didn't remember the guy's name, he recognized him from earlier in the summer.

"Get lost," Liv's ex said.

"Excuse me?"

Liv's door opened before either spoke again. Bloodshot eyes looked from her ex to him. "Seb, Matt. What are you doing here?"

Now he knew the dude's name, but it didn't explain what he was doing there.

"We need to talk," Matt answered first.

"Does she look like she wants to talk?"

She looked like she either wanted to cry or hit him. Maybe both.

"Get lost. You've done enough damage." Seb said.

"Not happening." Under different circumstances, Matt would walk away rather than provoke the man. Tonight, he wasn't going to let an ex-boyfriend get in his way.

Seb stepped closer, one hand clenched. "If you don't leave, I'll help you."

"Knock it off." Liv grabbed Seb's arm and Matt's shoulder. "Seb, I don't know why you're here, but I'm not in the mood for visitors."

"I wanted to —"

"Go home." Liv turned her attention to Matt. "And you shouldn't have come. We said everything there was to say yesterday."

"You might have said everything you wanted, but I didn't. You hung up on me before I could."

This wasn't going how he'd hoped.

"Liv, you —" the ex tried again.

"Seb, go home. I don't need or want your help."

Seb's jaw twitched, and Matt knew the guy wanted nothing more than to punch him. "Call me if you need anything. It doesn't matter what time it is."

They both watched Seb walk down the hall. Once he started down the stairs, Matt focused on Liv.

"Can I come in?"

Her eyes searched his face before she sighed and took a step back into her apartment. "I guess, but not for long."

He'd told Aiden he knew what he was going to say. He'd lied.

"Are you going to speak or stand there looking at me?" Liv asked, breaking the uncomfortable silence.

"I've never cheated on anyone, including you." Matt pulled out his phone and opened the photo app. "The woman I danced with is my cousin Vivian. This is a picture of us last Christmas." He turned the phone so she could see the group picture.

"And the woman you saw me helping into a car was my

242

cousin Sophie. She's Vivian's sister." He swiped down to the next photo in the folder he'd created while on the plane. "I don't remember when this picture was taken, but that's her husband standing with us."

Again, he turned the phone so she could see the picture of him with Sophie, her husband, Aiden, and Theo.

"I already told you the woman I was standing next to on the harbor cruise is my cousin's wife. This photo was taken at their wedding." He showed her the last picture.

"None of that explains you and Jasmine."

He'd seen the photos, and they looked bad. Unfortunately, he didn't have concrete evidence to hand her.

"Nothing happened. I didn't know she would be there. When she asked if they could join us, it didn't seem like a big deal. When she suggested we get back together, I made it clear I was with you."

"She looks unconvinced in those photos."

"I know how it looks." Matt raked his hand through his hair. "But I went home alone. Aiden will tell you the same thing. Do you want me to call him? Anderson will too."

Liv frowned and shook her head as she sat. "I don't want you to call anyone. If you say nothing happened, then fine, I believe you."

If she believed him, why was she frowning?

"But it doesn't change anything. You're still going to get bored with me and Orchard Harbor and leave. Maybe you'll stay until you start filming the new movie. Once you leave, you won't come back. At least not for anything more than short vacations."

"The only reason I agreed to do the film is because it's being filmed in New England."

"Oh, that still —"

He already knew what she planned to say. "Doesn't change anything, right? That's what you were about to say."

Nodding, Liv looked down at her hands.

"What can I do to convince you I'm not going anywhere?"

Until tonight, he hadn't realized how stubborn Liv was.

"You can't change the facts. You're used to traveling around the world and going to exclusive clubs. You're happy here with me now because it's a novelty. When that goes away, you'll be looking for a change. Please just accept my decision and go home. I didn't get much sleep last night, and I'm tired."

Matt recognized a stalemate when he saw one. She'd made up her mind, and at the moment, nothing he said would change it. And she did look as exhausted as he felt.

"I'll go, but this isn't over." Somehow, he'd convince her she was wrong.

The downpour ended before he left the center of town. Then, as if mocking him, a rainbow appeared over his house.

Once inside, he made a pit stop in the kitchen for a can of Coke and then went in search of his brother. Since he'd left Aiden playing pool earlier, he started with the game room.

"How did it go?" Aiden asked when Matt walked in.

What a stupid question.

"I'm here with you. How do you think it went?"

"Sorry. Is there anything I can do?" Aiden asked as he sent the last ball on the table into the corner pocket.

"Not unless you've got magical abilities that can change a person's mind."

"Skipped that lesson at school." Aiden nodded toward the table. "Are you up for a game?"

Matt removed a pool cue from the wall. A game would help pass the time. "We're not making any bets this time." Maybe if he hadn't made that bet with Aiden, he wouldn't be in this mess.

"Do you want me to call her? Maybe she'll listen to me."

He appreciated his brother's offer but knew it wouldn't help. "There's no point. She's got it in her head that I'm going to get bored and leave. I need to prove her wrong."

244

Twenty-One

"WE WANT to go with package B," Vera Blackwell, the president of the PTA, said. "There are a few staff members who'll need special meals. Here's the list of what we'll need."

Liv reviewed the list before adding it to the folder for the staff appreciation lunch, for which the PTA was hiring Ocean View Catering to provide the food.

"That won't be a problem. Let me get our menu, and we can finalize your order."

Behind her, the door opened, and Liv knew she'd see Emma when she turned around.

"Wow, those are beautiful," Vera said, confirming Liv's suspicion. "I wish someone would send me flowers. Whoever sent them must really care about you."

Emma placed yet another vase full of flowers on the table. "I keep telling her that. Every few days for almost a month, he's sent her flowers."

"That's so sweet. But don't expect it to last. Simon used to send me flowers all the time when we started dating. Now I only get them on my birthday and our anniversary," Vera said.

Liv had expected the first bouquet to be a one-time occurrence, a single attempt to change her mind, and when she didn't rush back to him, he'd give up. Today's roses were the twelfth bunch. Flowers weren't the only thing he sent either. Every afternoon at two, a latte and a snack from Hometown Brews arrived. While the snack varied, a note was always included with it.

"Thanks for delivering them. I'll talk to you later." Liv didn't want another lecture from Emma, period. But she certainly didn't want one in front of Vera. The woman loved to gossip, and Liv didn't want to be the next topic discussed in the produce section.

"Here are the options available for package B." Liv handed Vera the binder as she sat.

"Aren't you going to open the card?" Vera asked.

She didn't need to. The previous ones had all said the same thing. Today wouldn't be any different.

"I'll do it later. If you look at page 3, we have the vegetarian options listed."

Fifteen minutes later, her afternoon latte arrived as Vera headed out. On Friday, she'd found an oversized chocolate chip cookie in the bag; today, she pulled out a cinnamon bun and, of course, a note.

Thinking of you. Hope you're having a good day. Love Matt.

Liv couldn't figure him out. When he left her apartment, he'd told her this wasn't over. She'd assumed that meant he'd return in a couple of days and try to change her mind. When he couldn't, he'd drop the issue and return to Florida or wherever he planned to spend the rest of the summer. When the weekend came and went and she didn't even get a text from him, she'd decided he'd rethought everything and realized she was right.

Then on Monday, Emma showed up with a dozen roses. Liv's first thought had been that Seb sent them. She'd been speechless when she opened the card and saw Matt's name. Later in the day, when the latte and scone showed up with a note, she'd chalked the deliveries up to Matt's single attempt to change her mind. And for the rest of the day, she'd waited for him to call or stop by. Neither happened.

Although he hadn't come to her apartment or visited her at work, she'd seen him. The day after he had given her the first dozen roses, he came into the restaurant with his brother while she was working. He'd come in again last week too. On neither occasion had he brought up their relationship. Instead, he'd eaten his meal and left like any other customer.

Unable to resist, she retrieved the card with the flowers. *Thinking of you. Love Matt.*

What's your game plan?

Emma came through the door as Liv put the card back down. "So, what does today's card say?"

"Please, like you don't already know."

"I didn't work this morning. I had a doctor's appointment, so Mom took the order."

Liv checked the card again. Emma had a distinct way of writing the letter *T*, and it was absent on the card. "Read it yourself."

"Has he called?" Emma accepted the card without hesitation.

Liv stacked up the binders on the table. "Nope."

"You should call him. At least to thank him for the flowers and daily lattes."

She'd already had that argument with herself. Each time, she convinced herself it was better not to. "I'll think about it."

"It's weird."

"What's weird?" Removing the cover, Liv sipped the latte and then offered Emma half of the cinnamon roll.

"He sends flowers and lattes, so he's clearly thinking about you, but he doesn't call or visit. Why?"

"He's bored."

"Maybe he wants you to make the first move, or maybe this is his way of reminding you he's still here and not leaving."

"That's the dumbest thing I've ever heard."

"It makes more sense than he's bored."

"How about we agree to disagree." Liv didn't want to argue with Emma, especially not about Matt's motives.

"Okay, I need to go anyway. Brian and I are going to the fair tonight. You'll be there, right?" Emma helped herself to the half of the cinnamon roll she'd turned down moments ago.

Every year in mid-September, Orchard Harbor held a fair, which started on Friday night with an antique car show and ended on Sunday night with fireworks. Since today was Saturday, the festivities had kicked off with a 5K road race and a parade. Tonight would be the usual concert in the park. Throughout the three days, vendors sold a wide range of items, from jewelry to homemade soaps. Food trucks were always on hand, and the local dance school always performed. As far as Liv could recall, she'd never missed the event.

"I don't know. I think I might skip."

"Wrong answer. Besides, where else can you get a deep-fried Snickers?"

She did love the unusual treat, but that didn't mean she felt like dealing with the crowds tonight.

"I'm not really in the mood to go."

"Liv, we've been going together forever. This year isn't going to be any different. Either you meet me and Brian there, or we'll come to your apartment and drag you there."

Emma wasn't wrong. Plus, she wasn't joking about coming to her apartment. If she didn't agree to go, Emma and Brian would show up and refuse to leave until she left with them.

"Fine. I'll go. Where do you want to meet?"

Liv intentionally arrived at the fair early so she could get in a little shopping before she met up with Emma and her boyfriend. And since the only place she'd ever found licorice-scented candles was at the fair, she made that vendor her first stop. After making several more purchases, including a pair of handmade earrings, Liv made her way toward the food area—a task made difficult because everyone she knew seemed to be between her and her final destination, the food truck selling gyros.

"I never looked at the newsletter. Do you know who's performing tonight?" the woman in line behind her asked her companion.

Every year, the town sent out a newsletter that listed all the information about the fair. Since Liv came regardless of what was scheduled, she hadn't opened it.

"Back Bay."

The committee had tried to book Back Bay last year, but

they'd already committed to an event, so Ultimate Survivor performed. While a good band, she much preferred Back Bay. Many people, including her, believed it was just a matter of time before the band made it big.

Food in hand, Liv headed toward the old library where she had agreed to meet Emma and Brian for the concert. Every other step she took, though, someone seemed to stop her. Some just wanted to say hello and catch up. Others, like Linda McCarthy, wanted the 411 on Liv and Matt's relationship. Linda, like so many others, had seen the pictures earlier in the summer. While other people in Orchard Harbor might also be curious, most minded their own business. Not Linda. Tonight, to avoid answering, she'd claimed to be running late and unable to stand around and chitchat. Liv didn't know if Linda believed her, but if she heard a rumor circulating tomorrow, she'd have her first suspect. Somehow, despite the crowd that was growing by the minute and the constant interruptions, she made it to the library before her friends.

"OMG. Jared just asked me to the homecoming dance," a blonde, who Liv guessed was sixteen or seventeen, said to her friend with pink hair. The two of them sat in front of the former library, eating french fries.

"The goalie from the soccer team?

"Yes. What should I say?"

Liv remembered similar conversations with her friends. Clearly, the people changed, but the events remained the same.

"Are you really asking me that?"

Yup, some things never changed.

"Sorry we're late. The line for barbecue moved super slowly, and then we ran into Isabella. You know what that's like." Emma said.

Oh yes, she knew.

"I think I saw Matt when we got here."

"It's a free world. He's allowed to come." Liv would never admit she'd scanned the crowd a few times since she got here, looking for him.

"You should go see him. I know deep down you want to."

"Not now. I just want to enjoy the concert."

Emma opened her mouth as if to speak but snapped it shut after Brian nudged her.

A crackling came from the speakers positioned behind them. Darlene Weber's voice came from the device a moment later.

"Good evening. I hope everyone is enjoying this year's fair. While I have everyone's attention, I want to thank the planning committee. Your hard work and dedication make this event possible. And now it's time for my favorite part of the weekend. Please help me welcome Back Bay to the stage."

Applause erupted from the crowd as the band took the stage.

The band's front man, Lance, accepted the microphone and faced the crowd. Liv had seen them perform several times, and they always kicked off a performance with two rock songs and then a slower ballad. Then they'd thank everyone for coming before launching back into their show. Today, the instruments remained silent as he gestured for the crowd to quiet down.

"We're going to do things a little differently tonight," Lance said. "About a week ago, a resident, someone many of you know, contacted us asking for our help. After he explained the situation, we couldn't say no." The musician gestured toward the stairs leading onto the temporary stage. "Everyone, please welcome Matt Sherbrooke."

Liv's iced tea slipped from her fingers as a deafening cheer erupted from the crowd as Matt joined Back Bay onstage. For the past few weeks, she'd struggled to block out thoughts and memories of him. With Matt standing mere feet away, they bombarded her. Urged her to wait for him to come off the stage and tell him she'd changed her mind. That she'd made a mistake.

"Thanks, Lance," Matt said, accepting the microphone and then turning to face the crowd. "How are you doing, Orchard Harbor?"

The question elicited another cheer from the crowd.

"Tonight, I'm performing a new song I wrote for someone very special to me. Someone I want to spend the rest of my life with here in Orchard Harbor. Liv, if you're here tonight, this song is for you."

Stunned, she stood there, her heart racing a thousand miles a minute as Matt's voice filled the air, accompanied by Back Bay. A gentle nudge pulled her back to reality.

"Did you know about this?" Liv asked.

Emma nodded. "He asked me to make sure you were here tonight."

Now her insistence that Liv come tonight made sense.

"Go up there," Emma urged her.

She'd rather run down Main Street naked. "No way."

"At least move close enough so he sees you." Emma gently pushed her when she remained frozen in place.

"Now I know what love is." Matt's voice washed over her, and she swallowed, hoping to dislodge the golf-ball-sized lump that had taken up residence in her throat.

She's right. I should move closer.

Liv weaved through the crowd far easier than she would've imagined. Soon she found herself almost close enough to touch the stage, and when Matt spotted her, he gestured for her to join him, drawing the attention of many concertgoers her way. As if someone had waved a magic wand, the crowd created an opening for her.

Everyone fell silent; the only sounds were Matt's voice and the band. As if in a dream, she climbed the steps. Heat filled her face and spread down her neck, and she didn't need a mirror to know she resembled a tomato when Matt took her hand and led her to the center of the stage.

She could handle performing karaoke at the Northside Tavern during the offseason when the restaurant resembled a ghost town. But this was about as different as you could get from that.

Matt's eyes never left hers as he finished the song. Even as the final note rang out through the air, the crowd remained silent, their attention fixed on the stage, wondering what he had planned next.

"For a long time, I've felt as if someone was missing from my life. I didn't know until this summer you were the one I needed, Liv. I know you have doubts, but I love you and want nothing more than to spend the rest of my life with you here in Orchard Harbor, the only place that truly feels like home."

Wiping away the tears slipping down her cheeks, Liv struggled to hold back a full onslaught of emotion.

After pulling something from his pocket, Matt dropped to one knee. "Olivia Middleton, will you marry me and let me spend my life showing you how much I love you?"

Words deserted her. She'd accused him of cheating, ignored him for weeks, and yet now he was on one knee asking her to marry him. She'd imagined this summer ending many different ways, but she'd never allowed herself to think a marriage proposal from Matt was in her future.

"Say yes," someone in the crowd shouted.

The comment was quickly met by another. Soon, everyone was urging her to accept.

* * *

Matt couldn't decide which was louder, the crowd or his heart pounding in his chest. When Liv told him things between them were over, all he knew was that somehow he had to change her mind. He started sending her flowers and daily lattes—not to sway her, but because it was a way to let her know she was on his mind. It had also made him feel as if he was doing something while he formulated a proper plan. He'd known it needed to be something from the heart. Liv wasn't the type won over by expensive jewelry or exotic vacations.

The idea to write a song for Liv only came to him after Aiden suggested he focus on what he did best. Once he sat down with his guitar, the song flowed in a way that hadn't happened in a long time. Writing it had solved part of his problem while creating another. How would he get Liv to listen?

Fortunately, the town newsletter about the fair provided a solution. After Back Bay agreed, he sent them the music, and then he traveled to Wellesley so they could practice it together. And Emma had helped with the last possible hurdle.

With his plan executed, all he could do now was wait and hope he got the answer he wanted.

Nodding, Liv wiped fresh tears from her cheeks as the band joined the crowd's chant of "Say yes."

Before he could ask her to say the words, Liv threw her arms around him. Only quick reflexes kept him from landing on his ass. Cheers erupted from the crowd, and Matt barely heard Liv say, "Yes," before kissing him. Although he never would've thought it possible, the cheering intensified as soon as her lips touched his.

Far sooner than he would've liked, Matt pulled his mouth away from hers. "I promised I'd perform a few songs with the band, but afterward, I'm all yours."

Performing with them wasn't the only thing he'd offered the band. He'd also lined up a meeting with his agent for them, because once his performance with them went viral, which he knew it would, Back Bay was going to need a good agent to negotiate a record deal.

Liv squeezed his hand before kissing his cheek. "I'll wait with Emma and Brian."

He'd prefer to keep her close, but he recognized not only how impractical it would be but also how uncomfortable she'd feel if she remained onstage.

Three songs later, Matt fought his way through the crowd. He'd managed to avoid the attention when he arrived since no one expected him there. Now that fans knew he was at the fair, they repeatedly stopped him to get a photo or an autograph. A few even stopped him to offer their congratulations on his engagement. Clearly, he should've prepared an escape route before taking the stage tonight.

Somehow, he reached Liv while Back Bay continued the concert. Without asking if she was ready, Matt grabbed her hand and kept walking.

"Thanks again, Emma," he said. If she replied, he didn't hear her.

"You owe me a deep-fried Snickers," Liv said.

He could still hear the band playing, but they were far

enough away now that they could have a conversation without shouting.

"What?"

"I was going to buy a deep-fried Snickers after the concert. We left before I could, so you owe me one."

He hadn't misheard her. "We can go back."

"Maybe tomorrow. I'd rather get away from the crowd."

Matt couldn't agree more.

A cool breeze washed over him when he stepped back outside. When they'd returned home, they'd gone to the rooftop patio. Now that the sun was long gone, the temperature had dropped, and he'd gone inside to get them each a sweatshirt and something hot to drink. Liv had offered, but he figured if he went, it would give her a chance to answer some text messages. Her phone started exploding on the ride home, and it hadn't stopped. He'd received his fair share too, which he'd expected, considering he'd asked Liv to marry him in front of hundreds of people.

"People I haven't heard from in ages are texting me and sending me messages on CHAT." Liv looked away from her phone as she spoke.

Earlier in the summer, she had a small taste of the media intruding on her life, but it was nothing compared to what it was going to be like for the foreseeable future.

"I knew word would spread around town quickly, but I didn't think friends in Pennsylvania and Florida would know already too. Even Phoebe's mom messaged me, and she's on vacation in Hawaii."

Matt handed her the sweatshirt and placed both mugs on the table.

"Videos of you proposing and performing with Back Bay are being shared all over social media. I think you made their career."

"I had a feeling it might, so I arranged a meeting for them with my agent."

"Talented and smart. How did I get so lucky?" Liv asked as she pulled the sweatshirt over her head.

"Actually, I think I'm the lucky one. If I hadn't roomed with Owen in college, I never would've met you or found my home."

Liv pulled her braid free from the sweatshirt as a serious expression settled on her face. "When you said Orchard Harbor is the only place that truly feels like home, did you mean it?"

"I told you that before. It's why I always came back as much as I could."

"And I thought it was for the exciting nightlife."

"Well, there is that too, but when I'm not here, I feel restless —that's the best way I can describe it. Like I need to be somewhere else. When I'm here, I don't want to leave."

"You've never spent a winter here; you might have second thoughts then."

"As long as you're here to keep me warm, the temperature can drop below zero and the snow can be over my head, and this will still be home to me." He brushed his lips across hers.

"Don't worry, I'll keep you warm."

Although she sat next to him, he needed her closer. Slipping one arm under her legs and another around her waist, he moved her onto his lap. "Promise?"

She nodded as she lowered her lips toward his. "Promise. Always and forever."

Other Books By Christina

Loving The Billionaire, a novella
The Teacher's Billionaire
The Billionaire Playboy
The Billionaire Princess
The Billionaire's Best Friend
Redeeming The Billionaire
More Than A Billionaire
Protecting The Billionaire
Bidding On The Billionaire
Falling For The Billionaire
The Billionaire Next Door
The Billionaire's Homecoming
The Billionaire's Heart
Tempting The Billionaire
The Billionaire's Kiss
A Billionaire's Love, a novella
The Irresistible Billionaire

The Courage To Love
Hometown Love
The Playboy Next Door
In His Kiss
A Promise To Keep
When Love Strikes
Her Forever Love

Born To Protect

His To Protect

Love And Protect

One Of A Kind Love

Unexpectedly In Love

It Was Always You

Just One Kiss

About the Author

USA Today Best Selling author, Christina Tetreault started writing at the age of 10 on her grandmother's manual typewriter and never stopped. Born and raised in Lincoln, Rhode Island, she has lived in four of the six New England states since getting married in 2001. Today, she lives in New Hampshire with her husband, three daughters and two dogs. Currently, she has four series out, The Sherbrookes of Newport, Love on The North Shore, Elite Force Security and The Sherbrookes. You can visit her website or follow her on Facebook to learn more about her characters and to track her progress on current writing projects.